"Reading a book by Karen Hawkins is a guaranteed good time."
— *The Romance Dish*

# KAREN HAWKINS

*New York Times* and *USA Today* bestselling author

*How to Entice an Enchantress*

The
Duchess
Diaries

Don't miss any of

## The Duchess Diaries

by *New York Times* bestselling auth

## KAREN HAWKINS

And look for this special Duchess Diaries eNo
available only from Pocket Star Books

## Scandal in Scotland

"An entertaining romantic battle of wits."

—*Chicago Tribune*

"A humorous, fast-paced dramatic story that's filled with sensual tension. Hawkins's passionate, intelligent characters make it impossible to put down."

—*RT Book Reviews* (4½ stars, Top Pick)

"Rollicking good fun from beginning to end! Pure, vintage Hawkins!"

—*Romance and More*

"Humor aplenty, as well as tenderness and steamy love scenes."

—*The Romance Dish*

## One Night in Scotland

"Perfect pacing, humorous dialogue, and sizzling sensual romance."

—*RT Book Reviews* (4½ stars, Top Pick)

"Filled with intrigue, humor, and plenty of passion."

—*The Romance Dish*

"A lively romp."

—*Booklist*

"Charming and witty."

—*Publishers Weekly*

"Filled with laughter, passion, and emotion . . . mystery, threats, and plenty of sexual tension."

—*Single Titles*

## Also by Karen Hawkins

### The Duchess Diaries Series
*How to Capture a Countess*
*How to Pursue a Princess*

### The Hurst Amulet Series
*One Night in Scotland*
*Scandal in Scotland*
*A Most Dangerous Profession*
*The Taming of a Scottish Princess*

### The MacLean Curse Series
*How to Abduct a Highland Lord*
*To Scotland, With Love*
*To Catch a Highlander*
*Sleepless in Scotland*
*The Laird Who Loved Me*

### Contemporary Romance
*Talk of the Town*
*Lois Lane Tells All*

### Other
*Much Ado About Marriage*
*Princess in Disguise*

**Available from Pocket Books**

# KAREN HAWKINS

## How to Entice an Enchantress

Pocket Books

New York  London  Toronto  Sydney  New Delhi

Pocket Books
A Division of Simon & Schuster, Inc.
1230 Avenue of the Americas
New York, NY 10020

This book is a work of fiction. Any references to historical events, real people, or real places are used fictitiously. Other names, characters, places, and events are products of the author's imagination, and any resemblance to actual events or places or persons, living or dead, is entirely coincidental.

First Pocket Books paperback edition October 2013

POCKET and colophon are registered trademarks of Simon & Schuster, Inc.

For information about special discounts for bulk purchases, please contact Simon & Schuster Special Sales at 1-866-506-1949 or business@simonandschuster.com.

The Simon & Schuster Speakers Bureau can bring authors to your live event. For more information or to book an event, contact the Simon & Schuster Speakers Bureau at 1-866-248-3049 or visit our website at www.simonspeakers.com.

Manufactured in the United States of America

10 9 8 7 6 5 4 3 2 1

ISBN 978-1-4516-8522-0
ISBN 978-1-4516-8525-1 (ebook)

To my husband, Hot Cop, who spent an entire weekend looking up the rules and history of battledore in exchange for an icy six-pack of Newcastle.

You're not only the perfect Writer's Husband, but you're cheap office help, too.

# Acknowledgments

Thank you to my fabulous web team for Hawkins Manor at www.karenhawkins.com, where readers can explore Scottish and English recipes, ooh and aah over Princess Charlotte's silver wedding gown, learn about famous women of the Regency, view the castles associated with each book, and more!

*One*

**From the Diary of the Duchess of Roxburghe**

Ah, the burdens of fame! I am now known throughout the breadth of Scotland (and indeed, most reaches of the kingdom) as the most talented of matchmakers, a veritable Queen of Hearts. It is a burden that goes against every principle of my character, for intruding upon the private lives of others is anathema to me. Yet because of my vastly successful entertainments and my uncanny ability to spot potential matches between the most unlikely people, I'm credited with assisting a number of unmarried men and women to make brilliant matches.

And so now, whenever I so much as mention having a house party or a dance, I am positively *inundated* with hints, suggestions, and—yes, pleas for invitations.

Those who know me realize the truth, of course, which is that I never get involved in the affairs of others. Still, once in a great, great while, I am moved to reach past my natural reserve and, with the most delicate of touches, assist nature. But only with very, very few, and very, very special cases. In fact, one such case—the most challenging I've ever faced—is even now awaiting me in the Blue Salon . . .

The Duchess of Roxburghe sailed down the stairs, her red wig firmly pinned upon her head. Her morning gown of pale blue silk swished as her pugs bounded after her, two of them trying to catch the fluttering ribbons of the tie at her waist.

There were six pugs in all—Feenie, Meenie, Teenie, Weenie, Beenie, and Randolph. Randolph was the oldest by several years. Graying and usually dignified, of late he'd refused to scramble down the steps after the younger dogs, but stood at the top step, looking so forlorn that her grace had assigned a footman to carry the pudgy pug.

Her butler, MacDougal, thought the measure extreme. Seeing the relative ease with which Randolph could bound up and down stairs when tempted with a tidbit, MacDougal thought her grace was being played a fool. Not that he dared suggest such a thing aloud. He'd been with the duchess far too long not to know that, while it was perfectly fine to allude to her grace's pugs as stubborn, unmannerly, and unruly, they were never to be accused of trickery or sloth.

Her grace reached the bottom step and the footman, Angus, stooped to place Randolph with the other pugs panting at her feet. "That's a good boy," cooed her grace.

A proud expression bloomed on Angus's freckled face. "Thank ye."

MacDougal locked a stern gaze on the young footman. "Her grace was talkin' to the dog, ye blatherin' fool."

Angus flushed. "Och, I'm sorry, yer grace."

"I was getting to you next," she said graciously. "You did a fine job carrying Randolph."

Angus couldn't have looked more pleased. "Thank ye, yer grace!" He hazarded a superior look at the butler.

MacDougal scowled back so fiercely that the footman's smug expression instantly disappeared. Satisfied he had quelled the upstart, MacDougal turned to the duchess and offered a pleasant smile. "Yer grace, yer guest is in the Blue Salon, as ye requested, but we dinna ken where Lady Charlotte might be."

"Perhaps she fell asleep in a corner somewhere. She's gotten very bad about that since she's taken to reading novels at all hours of the night."

MacDougal nodded thoughtfully. "Verrah good, yer grace. I'll send someone to look upon every settee in the castle." He cast his eye toward the hapless Angus. "Off wit' ye, and dinna miss a single settee until ye find Lady Charlotte."

"Aye, sir!" Angus hurried off.

Her grace glanced at the doors leading to the Blue Salon. "I hope you made our guest comfortable."

"Aye, yer grace, we did wha' we could, but—" The

butler sighed. "'Tis no' me place to say aught aboot yer visitors, but this one is a bit—" He scrunched his nose, obviously searching for a word. Finally, his brow cleared. "—*abrupt*."

"You mean rude," she said in a dry tone.

"I would ne'er say such a thing aboot one o' yer guests, yer grace."

"I would. 'Tis well known that Lord Alasdair Kirk growls at everyone in sight. The man has beastly manners."

"Tha' might be understandable, considerin'—" The butler glanced about the empty hallway before he tapped his cheek.

"Because of his scar."

"Jus' so, yer grace. 'Tis a horrid sight. He's a handsome man except fer tha', which makes it all the worse. He limps, too, and seems to be in a bit o' pain when he walks. 'Tis only fair to say tha' if I had a horrid scar upon me face and a mighty limp, I might be rude meself."

"Pah!" the duchess said impatiently. "There's no excuse for bad manners."

MacDougal wasn't so certain of that, but he nodded sagely. "Verrah true, yer grace. I dinna suppose he's here fer yer help in findin' a match? Tha' might be a tall order."

"Of course that's why he's here. Lord Kirk is my godson. But never fear, for Lady Charlotte and I are quite aware of the challenge he presents." The duchess looked at the closed door and added in a wistful tone, "His mother, God rest her soul, died when he was quite young, a year after his father."

"Tha' is verrah sad, yer grace."

"That's not all of it. He was then placed in the care of an uncle who, busy with his own family, left Lord Kirk to be raised by the servants. Overcome with sympathy, they spoiled their charge atrociously. Kirk then compounded his misfortune by marrying a lady who, though lovely, was sadly lacking in backbone."

"There's a Lady Kirk?"

"No. She died in the same accident that injured Lord Kirk. After her death, he locked himself away and has rarely graced society with his presence since."

"Och, the puir mon. He'll be a difficult case, yer grace."

"More than you know. But his mother was a dear, dear friend, so I can't turn away from his request for assistance, no matter how trying he may be." The duchess looked at the doors, visibly straightening her shoulders. "I suppose it won't help to put this off any longer. Please send Charlotte as soon as you find her." Much like a general marching into battle, the duchess crossed to the Blue Salon, the pugs waddling after her.

Once inside, Margaret closed the door behind her and looked across the room at her guest. Tall and broad shouldered, Alasdair Dunbar, Viscount Kirk, stood by the wide windows that overlooked the front lawn. The bright morning sunlight bathed his skin with gold. His dark brown hair was longer than fashion dictated, curling over his collar, a streak of gray at his temple. In profile he was starkly beautiful but bold, a statue of a Greek god.

She took a deep breath and crossed the room. At the rustle of her skirts, Lord Kirk's expression tightened and he turned.

Though she knew what to expect, she had to fight the urge to exclaim in dismay. One side of his face was scarred, a thick, horrid slash that bisected his eyebrow, skipped over one eye, and then slashed down his cheek, touching the corner of his mouth and ending on his chin. It had been a clean cut, but whoever had stitched it together had done so with such crudeness that it made her heart ache.

Had he been in the hands of an accomplished surgeon, Margaret had little doubt that his scar, though still long, would not be so puckered or drawn. But Lord Kirk had been at sea when he'd obtained his injury and thus had been left to whatever "doctor" was available aboard ship.

His lordship inclined his head, barely bowing, the stiffness of his gesture emphasized by the thick, gold-handled cane he held in one hand.

Margaret realized with an inward grimace that she'd been staring far longer than was polite and she silently castigated herself even as she swept forward, her hand outstretched, the pugs dancing about her skirts. "Lord Kirk, how do you do?"

He took her hand and bowed over it, sending her a sardonic look through his lashes as he straightened.

"I'm as well as one can be while bearing a scar that causes even society's most stalwart hostess to gasp in horror."

"Pray don't exaggerate. I might have stared, but I didn't gasp. To be honest, I cannot see your scar without wishing I could have put my own physician on to it. His stitching is superb."

Kirk's smile was more of a sneer. "I assure you I am quite used to being stared at."

"Nonsense. It was rude of me and few people have cause to call me such, so please accept my apologies." She gestured to the chairs before the fireplace. "Shall we?"

He shrugged and turned toward the seating, leaving her to follow or not, as she deemed best.

Margaret bit back a sigh. A gentleman would have offered his arm or bowed and allowed her to lead. Kirk, however, continued, completely unaware of his gaffe.

The pugs, who'd been following her, scampered along. Elderly Randolph hurried to Lord Kirk and gave the man's shoes a friendly sniff. Kirk threw the dog a frosty glance, brushing by with a hint of impatience.

Margaret discovered that her hands had curled into fists. Poor Randolph had done nothing to deserve such a sneer. The man was beyond rude. *What have I gotten myself into?*

Kirk limped to the chair closest to the fire, leaning heavily upon his cane, as if one leg would not bend properly. She watched as he dropped into the seat, not waiting for her to sit first.

She sighed in exasperation as she took the chair across from his. "I see you are in something of a mood. Your leg must pain you in this cold weather."

He threw her a sour look, the lines upon his face even more pronounced. "A brilliant assumption. Will you next note that my eyes are brown, and that I favor my left hand?"

That did it. She fixed her iciest gaze upon him. "Alasdair, stop being such a beetle-headed boor!"

His eyes widened. After a short silence, he burst into a deep laugh that surprised her. "I haven't heard that name or tone since my mother died."

When he laughed, he looked so much like the young, handsome boy of her memory that Margaret's heart softened. "Which name? Alasdair or beetle-headed boor?"

"Both."

She had to smile. "Your mother would never have stood for you behaving in such a manner."

"No, she wouldn't have." He eyed Margaret with something akin to respect. "I'm sorry I brought my poor temper with me."

"And I'm sorry our meeting began in such a poor fashion." She leaned back in her chair. "Now, come. What brings you?"

"You know exactly why I'm here; I've come because I am now ready to marry. Or remarry, I should say."

He said it so matter-of-factly that she couldn't help

feeling a small flair of hope. "Then you have secured the affections of a certain young lady? One you've mentioned before?"

His brows snapped down. "I thought that was your strength, to make a match between unlikely candidates."

"Ah. So the match is now unlikely."

"It's never been anything but, which is why I've come." Kirk leaned his cane to one side. "As you've noticed, I'm not very good at the niceties. Since my wife died—"

"Six years ago, I believe?"

"Seven. I married Elspeth when I was barely eighteen, and our union, though only three years in duration, was happy."

That was promising, and it made her wonder what he'd been like in those days. He couldn't have been the surly, ill-comported man he was today.

Kirk shifted in his seat and then winced and gripped his knee, his mouth white.

Margaret wisely didn't say a word and after a moment, he relaxed back in his seat. "I'm sorry. My knee sometimes—" He grimaced and waved his hand impatiently. "As I was saying, since Elspeth's death, I've lived alone and I rarely mingle with society."

"Why is that, pray tell?"

His expression grew bleak. "I tired of the way people recoiled when I walked into a room."

"Ah," she said. "So you hid from those reactions."

"Hid? Nay. I just refused to care. I was happy

enough among my books and music. Or I was until—"
Something flashed in his brown eyes, but he looked
down at his hand where it gripped his knee, his thick
lashes shadowing his thoughts. "As much as I dislike
it, it has become obvious that my isolation has ruined
what few graces I once possessed."

"So I've noticed. I can only be glad that your
mother is not alive to witness your fall. She would
have had you by the ear for letting all of her hard work
disappear."

His eyes gleamed with humor. "So she would
have." His voice, a deep rich baritone, warmed. "She
wasn't afraid to let her opinion be known."

"Far from it. I always admired her for her ability to
speak her mind."

"She admired you, too, which is why she named
you my godmother." The humor left his face. "When
I came to you some months ago, we spoke of a—"

The door flew open and Lady Charlotte flew into
the room, a book tucked under one arm and one hand
on her askew mobcap, the lace edge flapping over her
ear.

The pugs barked hysterically, running toward the
door.

"Hush," Charlotte scolded as she hurried through
the small pack.

The pugs lowered their barking to an occasional
woof and wagged their tails, falling in behind her.
"Lud, Margaret, I had just reached the part where
Rosaline finally kisses Lord Kestrel and—"

"Rosaline? Lord Kestrel?" Margaret frowned. "Who on earth are—"

Margaret held up her book.

"Ah."

"You should read it. It's vastly entertaining. Anyway, as I was saying, Rosaline was just getting ready to kiss Lord Kestrel when a footman rudely interrupted my reading and practically dragged me into the foyer—which was horrible, for I am quite certain that Lord Kestrel is not the nice man that poor, dear Rosaline thinks him, despite his protestations of holding her in the deepest affection, and— Oh!" Margaret came to an abrupt halt. "Lord Kirk!" She curtsied. "I'm sorry, but I didn't see you there."

Kirk inclined his head, but made no move to stand and welcome Lady Charlotte.

Margaret had to fight the urge to reach out one of her slippered feet and kick him for his lack of manners. She had to make do with saying in a sharp voice, "Lord Kirk, you remember Lady Charlotte?"

"Of course."

"How do you do?" Charlotte came forward, her hand outstretched in greeting.

He looked past her hand, his jaw tight. "I'm sorry, but I was in the middle of a private discussion with her grace."

Charlotte's smile never faltered, even as she dropped her hand to her side. "Of course," she said in a soothing tone. "It must seem impertinent I'm even here." Smiling sweetly, her soft blue-gray eyes gentle, she ignored Kirk's outraged look and instead crossed to the chair nearest Margaret and sank into it.

"Apparently I didn't make myself plain enough. I've private business to discuss with her grace."

"Yes, but I already know your personal matters. *All* of them."

Kirk stiffened and Margaret hastily added, "Lady Charlotte is my confidante. Very little happens at Floors Castle without her knowledge."

Kirk's mouth thinned. "I do not like being a topic of discussion."

"Oh, none of us do," Charlotte assured him, her smile sunny. "But how am I to assist her grace if I don't know what's what? Consider it 'gossip by necessity.' Perhaps that will take some of the sting out of it."

"I doubt it."

"A pity." Unfazed by Kirk's chilliness, Charlotte placed her book on a side table and held a slippered foot toward the fire. "If it helps, you'll be glad to know that it wasn't a very long conversation and, to be honest, not particularly interesting, either."

For a moment, Margaret thought they might be subjected to an outburst, but instead, a glint of humor warmed his lordship's fine brown eyes and he gave Charlotte a very reluctant look of approval. "You're honest, I'll give you that. Painfully so."

"I dislike people who butter their words until they're too slippery to hold."

"That's understandable." He leaned back in his chair, seeming a bit more at ease. "I don't suppose it makes any difference who knows what, so long as it stays inside this room."

He turned his gaze back to Margaret. "I shall make this short. Several months ago you offered to assist me in fixing my interest with the lady I've an interest in."

"Miss Dahlia Balfour, if I remember correctly."

"Yes. You offered your help in exchange for a favor, which I found most curious."

"Curious, but necessary."

"What I did not know was that the task you requested turned out to be much more distasteful than I'd imagined."

"Come. I only asked you to request that your neighbor, Sir Balfour, repay a loan you'd so generously made him months before. You did so, and your actions returned very positive results."

"For whom?" he asked, looking none too pleased.

"Why, for Dahlia's sister. It sent Lily flying to me, her godmother, looking for assistance. And with very happy results."

"*Very* happy," Lady Charlotte said. "The happiest of all." In case Kirk didn't understand, she leaned forward and whispered, "Marriage."

An impatient look crossed his face. "You are saying that because I pressed for repayment of that loan, Lily Balfour attempted to contract an eligible marriage?"

"She didn't 'attempt' to contract an eligible marriage; she did so. In fact, she's blissful."

"And wealthy," Charlotte added. "Why, she's now a princess!"

Kirk's lips thinned. "While the outcome might have been happy for Miss Lily, it was less so for me."

Margaret arched a brow. "Oh? Sir Balfour hasn't repaid you?"

"Yes, he has. But my issue is not with the funds, which I never needed, but with Miss Dahlia's opinion of me, which was already shaky at best. Because I pressed her father for the payment of that loan, she now thinks I'm the lowest, vilest, most reprehensible man to walk the earth."

Margaret tried to look surprised, but must have failed, for Kirk's brows lowered to the bridge of his nose. "You knew she'd be angry with me."

"I didn't *know*. I merely *suspected*."

"And yet you *still* asked me to pursue that course, even though you knew my feelings for Miss Dahlia."

"Oh!" Lady Charlotte clapped her hands together. "You are in love with Dahlia Balfour! How delightful!"

"Nonsense," Kirk returned sharply. "I hold Dahlia in the highest regard, which is just as it should be."

Charlotte couldn't have appeared more disappointed. "Just regard? Nothing more?"

"A *sincere* regard."

"But what about love?"

He waved his hand impatiently. "Love is a messy, chaotic state suitable for the youthful and silly. Now that I'm older, I've no need to bother with it again. I will be more happy—as will Miss Dahlia—if we instead seek compatibility."

Charlotte looked astounded. "I beg your pardon,

but did you say you've no need to 'bother' with love again?"

"I've been married before. I've tasted the grand passion, as some call it, and I'm done with that chaos. Now, I want peace, quiet, and the enjoyment of a quality companion."

Margaret had hoped that Lord Kirk's feelings might have progressed over the last few months. She now realized that hope had been sadly misplaced. "Lord Kirk, you may see yourself as no longer youthful— which I question—but Miss Dahlia *is* young. Very young, in fact, and she may feel differently."

"I'm sure she does. If there is one failing in Miss Dahlia's character, it's an inclination to over-romanticize life."

Charlotte blinked. "So you— While she— Oh dear."

Margaret shook her head. "Lord Kirk, before we continue, have you ascertained how Miss Balfour feels about you as a suitor?"

"Oh, I know quite well. She sees me as an older, decrepit neighbor who harshly pressed her father for the repayment of a loan, forcing her sister to sell herself in marriage."

"You sound very certain about that."

"I am; she told me so in those exact words."

*Oh dear. This is going to be much more difficult than I imagined.* Margaret sighed. "That's not good news." She hadn't expected Dahlia to harbor a grudge once her sister was happily wed. "Surely you've seen some softening in her demeanor since her sister's wedding?"

"You don't know Dahlia if you think she will soften her feelings toward anyone she believes has insulted her family. She's very protective of them. Ridiculously so."

"Surely she knows that Sir Balfour was at fault for asking for such a loan to begin with?"

Charlotte nodded. "*And* for pretending he wanted the funds for his daughters, as he told you when he first borrowed the sum?"

"Which was a lie," Margaret continued. "For he spent it on expanding his greenhouses and buying more roses."

"It doesn't matter what he did with the funds, or if he lied," Kirk said firmly. "Dahlia's protective of her family, right or wrong. Now she won't speak to me, won't answer my letters, won't even look in my direction when we meet. It's as if I'm dead to her."

Charlotte bit her lip and looked at Margaret. "Oh dear."

Margaret thought the same thing, but she wasn't about to give up before she'd even begun. She absently patted the pug closest to her foot, a thought striking her as she straightened. "Lord Kirk, perhaps I can rectify whatever ill Miss Dahlia thinks by simply telling her the truth—that you pressed for the loan at my request."

"You can't tell her a damn thing."

"And why not?"

"Because then she'd want to know why I agreed in the first place—and you cannot tell her it was because I wished your help in securing her affections. If her guard is high now, imagine what it would be if she knew that?"

He was right, blast it all.

He added, "We are stuck, your grace. We cannot admit the truth."

Margaret tried not to let her dismay show. "It's a minor problem. I shall think of something to smooth this over, never fear. Meanwhile, there are other issues to be addressed."

"What other issues?" Kirk rubbed his knee and Margaret noticed how long and beautiful his hands were, like those of an artist or a violinist.

"If you wish to attend my house party, then you need to brush up on your society manners."

"On my— No. That's not necessary."

"Oh yes. I promised you a way to win Miss Balfour, and that is part of it; you will learn to be a gentleman."

His jaw firmed. "You are making this unnecessarily complicated. What I want is simple: marriage to Miss Dahlia Balfour."

"And to get that, you'll have to relearn all that you've forgotten in the way of manners."

His mouth was white with fury. "I cannot countenance this."

"You'll have to."

"May I remind you that I was married once before? Elspeth never noticed my manners."

"Elspeth was not Dahlia Balfour, whom you've already said is a romantic."

Charlotte leaned forward, her eyes bright with curiosity. "Pardon me, but you're a widower?"

"My wife died on our return from India seven years ago," he said shortly.

Charlotte clicked her tongue in sympathy. "Did she die from a spider bite? There are over twenty types of spiders in India."

Margaret looked at Charlotte. "How would you know about spiders in India?"

"There was an article about that very thing in *The Morning Post* last week."

"There was no spider." Kirk's voice crackled with impatience. "My wife and I were sailing back from India when a fire broke out on the ship. We didn't realize it, but in addition to our luggage, the ship was carrying kegs of gunpowder."

"How dangerous."

"And illegal. I found out later that the captain had hidden the kegs on board to make additional money and didn't wish to pay the port tax. Thus they were not declared on his manifest, damn his greedy black heart."

Margaret's heart tightened at the bleakness in Kirk's voice. "It should never have happened."

"It is history," he said shortly. And yet he looked furious, as if he'd like to kick history right in the shin. "I'm fine with my life now."

"You mean you were until you met Miss Balfour," Margaret said.

He started to disagree, but after meeting her gaze for a long moment, he added, "It's odd, I'll admit it. I'd met her many times before, you know. She's my neighbor and we must have ridden past one another a hundred times without really paying each other the slightest heed. But this time—" He shook his head, a faint hint of wonder in his dark eyes.

Charlotte clasped her hands before her. "Yes?" she encouraged. "This time?"

"The Balfours have been my neighbors since before I wed at the age of eighteen, but I'd never had much contact with them. The girls were much younger than I, and once I married, I rarely saw them. And after the accident—" He shrugged.

"You didn't see anyone after that," Margaret guessed.

"Not intentionally. One day my butler was ill, so I took the carriage to pick up some books I'd ordered. As I was coming out of the postal office, I ran into Dahlia. Literally. I was so piled with parcels that I couldn't see over them, and . . . well. There she was."

Margaret and Charlotte exchanged glances. There was a deepening to his lordship's voice that couldn't be denied.

He rubbed his knee absently. "I'd seen her before, of course, but we'd never done more than nod at one another. But when she saw the books in my hands, her eyes lit up like—" He lifted his hands. "I can't describe it."

"That sounds promising."

"It sounds *romantic*," Charlotte said.

"It was indeed promising, but it was *not* romantic. All that moment did was show me that here was a person—a woman—who shared my passion for reading. I'd never had that, you know. Elspeth never read." He shrugged. "Anyway, we started talking about books we liked, and which authors we enjoyed. Odd as it sounds, we stood there in the street for two hours, quoting poetry and discussing stories we'd both read." He turned a bemused look to Margaret. "It was as if, in opening a book together, we discovered ourselves between the pages."

Margaret nodded. *Goodness, he is head over heels. And yet he doesn't realize it.*

"Oh my," Charlotte said in a breathless voice. "That sounds just like one of my novels."

Kirk frowned. "Pray don't make this into something it's not. Dahlia and I have a lot in common. We both like to read, we love poetry, and we enjoy the same music, as well. I invited her to borrow whatever books she might wish from my library. I have an extensive collection since books were my only companions for those empty years."

"So you share a few common interests. That's a beginning, I suppose," Margaret said cautiously. When Charlotte sent her a surprised look, Margaret flashed her a warning look.

Kirk didn't seem to notice. "Dahlia was in raptures when she saw my library and she couldn't stay away. She began to visit weekly and we'd talk about whatever book she'd read. Once, while she was there, I convinced her to play the pianoforte I'd brought from France as a wedding present for Elspeth. Dahlia's amazingly talented."

"She sounds perfect."

"She'll do. She is pleasant to look upon, loves books, dislikes random conversation, and can sit for hours not uttering a word whilst reading." He nodded, almost to himself. "She will make a suitable bride."

"Suitable?" Charlotte almost stuttered over the word. "Is that all you can say?"

Kirk boldly met her gaze, though his face was slightly flushed. "It's enough."

There was a stubborn note to his voice that said far more than he was able or willing.

Before Charlotte could answer, Margaret said, "I see." She rather thought she did, too.

He raised a brow. "So you'll assist me as you'd promised when I agreed to press Lord Balfour for that cursed loan?"

"Of course, but I must be plain. While I will do what I can to assist you in making a case for Miss Dahlia, you must make an effort, as well."

"An effort? To do what?"

"Whatever I say." She tapped her chin with a finger, her gaze never wavering. "Fortunately, you have an amazing amount of potential."

Charlotte tilted her head to one side, regarding Kirk from head to toe. "*Unrealized* potential."

Margaret followed Charlotte's expert gaze. While

Kirk didn't adhere to fashion in any way—his brown coat and trousers were at least a decade old in style— he was very neatly dressed, his neckcloth knotted about his throat, the ends tucked into his brown waistcoat, his boots firmly placed upon the ground. There was a solidness about him that a woman could appreciate. *An older woman, yes—but perhaps not a younger one. No, if he wishes to woo Dahlia Balfour, he will have to gain some polish.* "We must get him a tailor," she told Charlotte.

"New clothes, definitely," Charlotte murmured. "And some proper boots."

"And someone to teach him to tie a neckcloth."

"Oh yes." Charlotte reached down and picked up a pug, then plopped him in her lap, though her gaze never left Lord Kirk. "Can you dance?"

"With this?" He gestured toward his knee. "No, damn it."

Charlotte tsked. "Such language."

"He'll have to work on that, too," Margaret said thoughtfully, her mind racing as she made a mental list. "And his address, for he's rude as a—"

"That's enough." Kirk grasped his cane and struggled to his feet, his face set. "I did not come here to be insulted."

"No, you came to be transformed into a man worthy of a beautiful woman—one you believe is clearly out of your reach." Margaret waited until her words had sunk in. "She's lovely."

"Yes."

"And lively, as well, if she's anything like her sisters."

"Very much so."

"And intelligent—"

"She's everything, damn it!"

"Then you will have to be everything to her."

His fingers were white where they gripped the handle of his cane. "What the hell was I thinking, to come here? I should have admitted the truth, that she's not for me, and just be done with it. But oh no. I *hoped*." He laughed bitterly, and then walked toward the door. "I'm a fool."

Charlotte exchanged a surprised glance with Margaret.

"Lord Kirk," Margaret called. "Please. Just one question, and then you may go." When he didn't pause, she added, "For your mother's sake."

He stiffened, but stopped. After a moment, he turned back to face them. "Yes?"

"I know this may seem rude, but how old are you?"

"What's that—" At her raised brows, he grimaced. "I turned twenty-eight a week ago."

"That's all?" Charlotte exclaimed. "I would have thought—" She caught his dark gaze and flushed. "I mean, twenty-eight is a *lovely* age."

"No, it's not a lovely age." Margaret stood and walked toward him. "It's the age of a man who should be settled and married."

His eyes blazed with anger. "I'm finished with this conversation. I'm sorry I wasted your time." His scowl grew blacker with each word, the scar menacing. He started to turn back to the door.

"Since you don't wish to win Miss Balfour's regard, then you won't mind if I turn her attention elsewhere."

He froze in place as if suddenly nailed there. When he slowly turned, his face was a mask of frozen fury. "*You* will turn her attention elsewhere?"

He really had the most amazingly beautiful eyes, sherry brown and thickly fringed. Looking at them made her think of his mother, and the memory stiffened Margaret's resolve. "We'll need two months of your time."

"Two months? For what?"

"To teach you the basics of seduction, of course. Or courtship, if you prefer to call it that."

"It will also take that long to order your new wardrobe," Charlotte added. "That coat—" She wrinkled her nose.

Kirk looked down at his coat. "What's wrong with it?"

"It's out of fashion and ill fits you," Charlotte answered without pause. "Worsted is a horrid material for a coat, and your cravat is a mere knot, rather than a properly tied arrangement. But even more distressing than your clothing are your manners." Charlotte smiled kindly. "They could use a little polish. Actually, they could use a lot."

"I'm surprised you allowed me in your presence."

"You're a friend of her grace's. I had no choice," Lady Charlotte pointed out fairly.

Lord Kirk's lips thinned. "Is there anything else I must change?"

Margaret looked him over. "Your hair."

He looked exasperated. "What's wrong with my hair?"

"It's far too long for current fashion. It's a bit aging."

"I am my age, madam. I cannot change that."

"You look thirty and seven, perhaps even forty."

He started to turn back to the door and Margaret called out, "Leave if you wish, but know this: Miss Balfour has already accepted an invitation to my Christmas Ball. She will attend my house party for the three weeks beforehand, and she will not leave unattached."

"You don't know that."

"But I do. I shall see to it that she receives at least one offer for her hand in marriage, if not more."

"You would work against me?"

"While I genuinely wish you to succeed in your endeavors, Miss Dahlia is also one of my godchildren, and I wish to see her happily and well settled. She knows that I invited her to my house party for the express purpose of assisting her in making a fortuitous match."

He fixed an incredulous gaze on Margaret. "She specifically stated that was the reason she's coming here? To make a match?"

"Lord Kirk, she's twenty years of age; if she waits much longer, she'll be upon the shelf. When I invited her and assured her that she would receive at least one palatable offer, I thought you were serious about wishing to win her. Believing in your steadfastness, I committed myself to that end. So you can see that I cannot rescind my offer merely because you are getting cold feet and refuse to make an effort to win her attention, much less her hand in marriage."

"I'm not getting cold feet. I am merely questioning the intelligence of this idea. I cannot transform into something I'm not."

"Something you're not? And what is that? A gentleman? Your mother would weep to hear such an admission."

His jaw tightened. "As much as I loved her, my mother is no longer with us."

"Which only means that now *you* are responsible for living up to your potential. The invitation has been issued; Dahlia Balfour will leave this house attached to someone. Whether that is you or not is entirely your—and her—decision."

The white lines beside his mouth told Margaret how furious her words had made him, but he didn't leave. Indeed, he stood rooted to the floor as if every word had set him even more firmly in place. *Ah yes. That's promising.*

Margaret turned away, leaving him to collect himself. "We are understood, Lord Kirk. You will put yourself in my hands, and you will be a willing and enthusiastic pupil. By the time Miss Balfour arrives two months from now, you will be ready to meet her, a new—and vastly improved—man. One capable of competing with the other gentlemen who will be present, men bound to notice her and her beauty."

There was a long silence and then he gave a sigh so deep that it seemed to come from his toes. "Damn you! I will admit I need some polish, but you are right, this is my last chance to secure Miss Dahlia's interest." He raked a hand through his hair, his expression bleak. "I'll return home and make arrangements to spend two months here. But take note: I will not be turned into a fop."

Charlotte blinked. "We could never hope for that in two months. The best you can expect is that you'll become a gentleman of some address and possess a much better wardrobe. Becoming a fop would take another three, perhaps four months, and we haven't that much time."

Kirk started to argue, but one look at Charlotte's wide, sweet gaze and he closed his mouth. He turned stiffly and then limped out the door.

The door closed behind him with a loud thump and Margaret dropped into her seat, her gown fluttering about her. "Good God, that was ridiculously difficult!"

Charlotte nodded. "He looked as if he would breathe fire upon us."

"He's furious, there's no doubt, but he asked for my help and now he will take it." Margaret stretched her feet out and plopped them on a small footstool. Feenie rose and jumped into her lap.

"Do you think Kirk can learn what he must in such a short time?"

"He has to, or the fairy tale will be quite offset."

"I hate an offset fairy tale."

"Don't we all? Fortunately, we have a secret weapon."

Charlotte's eyes brightened. "We do?" She waited. When the silence merely grew, she sighed. "You're not going to tell me what it is."

"In due time, Charlotte. I can't express what I only suspect, but do not know."

"I suppose not. Very well. I shall be patient." Charlotte found her book and began to search for her place. "But whatever your weapon might be, I can only hope it will tame our Beast before our Beauty arrives."

"So do I, Charlotte. So do I."

*Two*

**From the Diary of the Duchess of Roxburghe**

It took two entire months, but Lord Alasdair Kirk has completed what Charlotte and I privately called "beast taming" but in public called "gentleman training." I shall not sully the pages of this diary with the title bequeathed upon this time by Lord Kirk.

Be that as it may, both Charlotte and I are pleased by his improvements, which are many and noticeable. While not perfect, his overall appearance and manner have enthused us both. My secret weapon was a most worthy valet named MacCreedy, who was once in the employ of the Duke of Wellington himself, and thus used to dealing with rough and ready men possessing an irascible manner.

MacCreedy did his work much better than even I had hoped. Our Beast, if not tamed, is at least better mannered and far better dressed.

Now to see if Beauty notices . . .

Coaches lined the ancient cobbled courtyard of Floors Castle as the guests arrived for the duchess's house party. Amidst the mass confusion, Angus the footman waited for the Roxburghe coach to appear with Miss Balfour inside. After what seemed an interminable wait, during which the duchess leaned out the salon window no less than four times to ask if the coach had yet arrived, the blasted thing finally lumbered into the courtyard.

Angus gave a sigh of relief and grabbed the heavy wooden steps he'd been sitting upon and hurried to meet the coach. The famed Roxburghe crest, a bold unicorn flanked by a muscular arm holding a scimitar in a very audacious manner, was emblazoned upon a side panel, making the coach hard to miss even in the busy courtyard. Angus wished his family had a crest, something equally intimidating. Perhaps a golden dragon carrying arrows or a large snake eating a baby, something to give his neighbors pause when they thought about fishing from his da's pond.

Reaching the coach, he nodded a greeting to the coachman before placing the carpeted steps upon the cobblestones. Then, just as MacDougal had taught him, he smoothed his hair and made certain his uniform was in place before he opened the door and stood at attention.

Nothing happened.

He remained still, straining his ears.

Still no guest stirred within the coach.

Angus frowned, wishing Miss Balfour would

hurry, as the chill November wind was seeping through his woolen breeches. But the interior of the coach remained shrouded in silence.

Other coaches pulled away, their occupants already walking toward the front door, their trunks being carried to the back entrance. Frowning, Angus shifted from one foot to the other, wondering what he should do. MacDougal's instructions hadn't covered this.

The thought of her grace's impatience made Angus sweat despite the chilly air. What if Miss Balfour hadn't come? Surely the coachman would have said something . . . wouldn't he?

Finally, unable to stand the silence a moment more, he stole a quick glance inside the coach.

It was not empty. The duchess's guest was stretched out upon one cushioned seat, her head propped upon a bunched-up cloak, an open book under one hand, a carriage blanket on the floor where it had been across her legs. Her arm was thrown across her face as the softest of snores drifted from her lips.

Angus rubbed his jaw. What was he to do now? He couldn't just leave her sleeping in the coach. Nor could he stand here holding the door for hours on end. He would have to wake her—but what was the proper way to awaken a snoozing lady guest?

Well, something *had* to be done. Angus glanced around the courtyard and, seeing no one within earshot, he leaned forward and cleared his throat as loudly as he could.

Miss Balfour stirred, but didn't awaken.

Angus frowned. Nothing. Not a bloomin' thing. He peered around again, and then rapped hard upon the door before stiffening to attention, his hands back at his sides.

The young lady stirred more, and the book slipped off her lap. Instantly, as if yanked from her sleep by an invisible connection to the book, Miss Balfour lunged for it, catching it by the cover just before it hit the floor.

Angus, who had jumped at her sudden movement, stared. The young lady was bent at the waist, her sudden movement leaving her hair partially undone and falling in odd loops about her face. Angus gulped as the young lady stared at him, her gray-blue eyes wide.

Angus managed a smile. "Miss Balfour?"

She blinked, her long lashes shadowing her eyes. "Yes?"

"Pardon me fer wakin' ye, but I'm to help ye fra' the coach."

"Coach?" She blinked again, sleep still heavy in her eyes, and looked about as if she'd never seen a coach before.

"Aye, miss. Ye were travelin'," he added helpfully. "Ye're comin' to visit her grace, the Duchess of Roxburghe."

"Oh. Oh yes." Miss Balfour slowly straightened. "For the Christmas Ball."

"Aye, miss! Ye were sleepin'. Ye were on yer way here, to Floors Castle, but ye've arrived and, ah . . ." He kindly pointed to the steps.

"Of course." She surprised him with a sleepy smile

that warmed him despite the wind. "I cannot believe I fell asleep—during the best scene in this book, too. There was a fight between the hero and the villain, and it was most thrilling. But apparently not thrilling enough to keep me awake."

She shook her head as if to clear the cobwebs and then tried to smooth her riotous brown curls. As she patted them, she glanced around the coach floor. "Oh dear. I'm missing some pins. I'm *always* missing some pins."

Angus wisely kept quiet, though secretly he thought she looked rather nice, friendly even.

She flashed a rueful smile. "I suppose I shall just put my bonnet over the whole mess and refuse to take it off until I've reached the safety of my bedchamber."

"Tha' should work, miss."

"I hope so, although what shall I do if someone asks for my bonnet?"

"MacDougal—he's the butler—he will ask ye fer it, but jus' tell him no and he'll leave off. He dinna tease the guests as he does the footmen."

Miss Balfour sent Angus an amused glance that made his stomach do an odd flip. Though she was every bit as encased in lace and silks and other what-not as the other ladies who graced Floors Castle like so many butterflies, Angus couldn't remember a one who'd spoken to him directly, except to give him an order. Certainly none had sent him that laughing look through what he was now realizing were amazingly pretty gray-blue eyes.

Miss Balfour finished tying her bonnet, making a large bow under one dainty ear before she pulled a pair of gloves from her pelisse pocket and donned them. She then retrieved a large reticule from the tangled blanket on the floor of the coach, and tucked her book inside. "There. I'm ready. I daresay you thought you'd never hear me utter those words." She tilted her head to one side. "I know I've kept you waiting and— I'm sorry, but did you tell me your name?"

"No, miss. It's Angus."

"Very well, Angus, I'm *finally* ready." Miss Balfour then climbed down from the coach, graciously taking Angus's gloved hand to steady herself.

She was short, barely reaching his shoulder, and he was far from a tall man. She was generously fashioned, too, unlike so many other ladies, some of whom were precariously close to having sticklike figures. Miss Balfour was rounded and pleasingly plump, rather like a certain rosy-cheeked milkmaid he'd once been enamored of.

Miss Balfour stepped away from the carriage, tightening her pelisse about her throat. "Goodness, it's cold here!"

"Aye, miss. We've ha' odd weather this year, warm one day and chilled the next. I ne'er know whether to wear me wool coat or the lighter one!"

Dahlia decided she liked the freckled-faced footman. "I faced the same dilemma while packing—do I bring warm clothes or cooler ones? I finally just brought them all, which is why I have so much luggage."

"I'll see tha' it is unloaded and taken to yer bed-chamber." Angus motioned to some groomsmen who hurried over, and together they set about taking down Dahlia's rather battered trunks and her precious band-boxes.

Dahlia looked up at the castle she'd be staying in for the next three weeks, and her breath caught in her throat. *I've stepped from a coach and into a fairy tale!* She tried to absorb it all but couldn't. Though she'd been here once before on the occasion of her oldest sister's wedding, Dahlia couldn't stop staring at the grand castle her godmother, the renowned Duchess of Roxburghe, deigned to call "home."

"Home," Dahlia whispered to herself. Floors Castle was beyond beautiful. Large mullioned windows shone silver, reflecting the late-afternoon sun, as proud banners of the Roxburghe blue and gold flapped gently from the ramparts, while puffy ivory clouds lazed overhead in a crystal blue sky.

This was it, what she'd dreamed about since the duchess's invitation had arrived six long months ago. Both of her sisters had attended one of the duchess's much-acclaimed house parties and balls, and both had fallen in love while under this very roof. Dahlia was ready for her chance at that precious thing she'd thus far only read about—true love.

Her heart thudded with excitement. This was what she'd been waiting for her entire life, the culmination of all of her dreams, the—

"Miss?"

She turned to find Angus nearby. "Yes?"

He offered a tentative smile. "Shall I escort ye to the door, miss?"

"Not now, thank you. I wish to look about before I go inside. I'm still half-asleep and I need to wake up before I meet the duchess."

"As ye wish, miss. Jus' be careful ye dinna walk in front of a coach." He glanced about him and then leaned forward to say in a low voice, "Some of the grooms, they do like their drink."

"Ah. I shall be cautious, then. Thank you for your assistance, Angus. You've been most kind."

He beamed. "Och, 'twas naught. Good day, miss." He gave her an obviously much-practiced bow. "Ha' a lovely stay, miss, and if ye e'er need anythin', jus' say the word."

"Thank you, Angus. I shall."

He hurried off, pausing to pick up the carpeted steps as he went.

As a coach started up and rolled past, Dahlia moved out of the way, glancing about the bustling courtyard. She didn't know any of the dozens of guests who were walking toward the huge oak doors held open by liveried footmen. Not that she'd expected to know any of them, for with the sole exception of her oldest sister's wedding, which had occurred in the gardens behind this very castle, she'd rarely had reason to leave the villages around her home, Caith Manor, which was deep in the Scottish countryside near Aberdeenshire.

A peal of laughter caught Dahlia's attention and

she saw a young lady surrounded by a bevy of handsome gentlemen, all vying for her attention. The lady
was about the same age as Dahlia, and dressed in a
pelisse of green velvet trimmed with brown braid.
Though she was no more fashionably dressed than
Dahlia, somehow she managed to look . . . better.
More fashionable. *Prettier.*

Dahlia bit her lip. Was it the woman's perfectly
coiffed blond hair? Dahlia liked her own hair, though
it was far from fashionably cut. Instead of being neatly
trimmed so it required few pins to attain the latest
styles, her hair was long, thick, and curly, rather in the
manner of the heroines in the novels she loved. She
wasn't as fond of the color, which was a mundane light
brown, but fortunately, due to her long walks through
the fields around Caith Manor, the sun had streaked
the brown with honey gold.

So perhaps it wasn't the woman's hair, but her
creamy complexion. Sadly for Dahlia, the sun had
been just as encouraging to her freckles, which now
dotted her nose. She'd powdered her face before leaving the house, but the powder would be gone by now.

Her sister Lily used to warn her about the effects of
the sun, but a walk was so much less enjoyable when
one had to pin on a bothersome hat and wear ridiculously long-sleeved gowns as if preparing for a snow-
storm.

But now, watching the pretty lady disappear
through the castle doors with her admirers, Dahlia
wished she'd heeded her sister's advice a bit more.

Well, there was nothing to be done about it now. Freckled, tanned, and curly mopped she might be, but she was also the duchess's goddaughter. And her grace had promised to assist her in meeting the most eligible men society had to offer. Surely that would be enough. Dahlia wanted to find true love, the kind that wasn't frightened away by a few freckles. *The kind of love my sisters have found.*

She headed toward the marble steps leading to the massive castle doors. As sad as it was, she'd never been in love. Once, when she'd been much younger, she'd thought she might be, but that had turned out to be a mere infatuation. The man had proven to be most unworthy of her burgeoning affections, for he had no manners and no true heart, either—he'd ridiculed anything romantic, mocked anything tenderhearted, and eschewed anything that smacked of "silly feelings."

She almost scowled at the thought, but there was no point in thinking about that now. With the encouragement of her family, her short infatuation had ended. Now, if someone wished to woo her, she wanted it to be done correctly, passionately, with soft words and whispered compliments, flowers and soulful glances, romantic notes and—oh, this time she wanted it *all*!

So here she was: walking into a real castle, ready to begin her own fairy tale, ready to be blessed by a godmother who, better than a mythical fairy godmother, was a wealthy duchess who threw fabulous balls and was known for her matchmaking skills. *Such good fortune!*

Hurrying her steps, she walked into the castle behind two young ladies who'd arrived in separate coaches. They'd fallen upon one another like lifelong friends and were excitedly chattering about a variety of people Dahlia had never heard of.

The second she stepped into the foyer, all thoughts fled. Though she'd seen the room once before, she couldn't help but stare yet again. Her amazed gaze followed walls covered in blue Chinese silk painted with gilt and green flowers, to the high ceiling that featured a mural of a flowered paradise with plump angels and a benevolently smiling God. She noted that, though it was partially hidden by a large tree decked in silver and red ornaments, even the parquet floor had not been spared adornment, as the center had been fashioned into a trompe l'oeil pattern.

Added to the normal decoration was a flurry of glittering seasonal candelabras and garlands of greenery and holly, until Dahlia scarcely knew where to look next. Her dazed attempt to absorb all of these beauties at once stole her breath. It was an ostentatious display, yet it was so artistically done that the words "garish" or "vulgar" could never apply. It was simply beautiful beyond—

A giggle made Dahlia turn and she realized she'd been slowly spinning in a circle, her head tilted back to take in as much of the foyer as possible, one hand plopped upon her bonnet and holding it firmly in place. Her face heated, and she lowered her gaze and released her bonnet.

The two women continued to smirk, and Dahlia didn't suppose she could blame them. She tried for a friendly smile. "Hello. I daresay I look the bumpkin, staring in such a way, but—" She waved at the ceiling. "It's simply beautiful."

They glanced indifferently at the mural. The taller of them said loftily, "I daresay you haven't yet seen the pavilion in Brighton. It's far more opulent. Ah, Mac-Dougal. There you are."

The duchess's very proper butler appeared as if from nowhere. MacDougal bowed and spoke in a deep tone that was surprisingly thick with a brogue. "Lady Mary, so ye've returned. How's yer father, Earl Buchan?"

"He's well, thank you. He'll be joining us before the ball."

"Tha' will please her grace. I'll make certain his favorite bedchamber is readied."

"Thank you." Lady Mary threw a hand toward her companion. "I'm sure you remember Miss Alayne Stewart. The Stewarts are neighbors of ours. She was a guest here last year, too."

"O' course I know Miss Stewart." The butler bowed. "If'n ye're ready to be escorted to yer bedchambers, I'll take yer pelisses and bonnets and ha' them brushed and returned to ye."

Lady Mary inclined her head and removed her pelisse and bonnet, revealing a beautiful traveling gown of blue with gold trim. The color set off her deep auburn hair to perfection.

Dahlia had to admit that Lady Mary was attractive, although her blond-haired companion was less so. Miss Stewart's face was longer, her nose pointed and her teeth protruding the slightest bit, so that she looked like an annoyed rabbit. Despite this unfortunate tendency, her traveling gown of pale pink adorned with green satin bows proclaimed her a woman of fashion.

Lady Mary peeled off her gloves. "MacDougal, where is her grace? I'd like to say good afternoon before I retire to rest before dinner."

"She's welcomin' other guests at the moment, but will be glad to hear tha' ye asked fer her."

Lady Mary didn't look too happy about the butler's answer, but he didn't seem to notice, turning away to assign a footman to escort her and Miss Stewart upstairs. As the two walked toward the grand staircase, he mentioned that—if the two ladies were so inclined—a light repast had been laid out in the dining room along with ratafia and sherry. That seemed to go a long way toward soothing Lady Mary's ruffled feelings.

When the other women had disappeared, the butler turned to Dahlia and his visage softened. "Och, Miss Balfour, how pleasant to see ye again. How are yer sisters?"

"Both still upon the Continent, enjoying themselves."

He smiled gently. "They be true ladies, the both of them."

"Indeed, they are." She hesitated and then confided, "I miss them very much."

"I canno' wonder at tha', fer we miss them here and we hardly had them wit' us fer a month. We've been lookin' forward to yer visit fer quite a while now."

Dahlia smiled. "Thank you."

"'Tis naught but the truth, miss. Shall I take yer coat and bonnet?"

"I believe I'll wear my bonnet up to my room. My hair—" She curled her nose. "It's not fit for human eyes."

He chuckled. "As ye wish, miss."

She'd just handed her pelisse and gloves to him when a feminine voice tinged with the faintest hint of a Scottish accent rang across the hallway. "MacDougal, has she come yet?"

Dahlia turned to see the duchess hurrying across the foyer, a herd of pugs panting behind her. The duchess wore a beautiful morning gown of yellow silk more suited to a much younger woman. Beautifully made, the gown swished as she walked and was the perfect foil for the red wig perched upon her head. One could instantly see the intelligence in the bright blue eyes that peered over a beaked nose at the butler.

"MacDougal, you must tell me the second she arrives! I've been waiting in the salon for— Ah!" The duchess stopped in front of Dahlia. "Why, you are already here! My dear Miss Balfour, finally, you have come!"

MacDougal, beaming fondly, announced in an impressively deep voice, "Miss Balfour jus' now arrived, she did."

Aware of the bright blue eyes now examining her from head to toe, Dahlia sank into a quick curtsy. As she did so, one of the pugs ran up to sniff her skirt. Dahlia chuckled when it sneezed so hard that it jumped back several inches.

"Feenie, stop snuffing Miss Balfour's skirt!" The duchess frowned at the dog. "I'm sorry, but they are sadly unruly. I keep a firm hand on them all, but the servants spoil them wretchedly."

Dahlia thought she detected a flash of disbelief on MacDougal's face, although the butler quickly hid it. To hide her smile, she bent to pat some of the less bouncy pugs. One of the dogs seemed to be considerably older, his eyes milky, his tail wagging calmly. She smiled at him and rubbed his ear before straightening. "What delightful dogs. I've always wished to have one, but my father does not believe they belong in the house."

"I'll remind you of that when they steal one of your good ribbons and run madly through the hallways, streaming it after them like a comet." The duchess's eyes gleamed with humor. "Come, Lady Charlotte has been impatiently awaiting your arrival, too, and— Oh. You still have on your bonnet."

"I can't remove it, as my hair was sadly mussed on

the way here. No two strands are pointing in the same direction. I fear that I slept upon it and only a damp brush will set it to rights."

The duchess nodded in understanding. "Then by all means, keep your bonnet. My hair used to give me such fits, too, but I've since tamed it."

Dahlia glanced at the duchess's wig. Was that how the duchess had tamed her unruly hair, or were there other secrets underneath?

Her grace slipped an arm through Dahlia's and, as inexorable as the ocean, led her toward the salon. "I'm so glad you've arrived! We've such delights planned. It seemed to take the coach forever to bring you to us; Charlotte was certain you'd forgotten."

"Forgotten? To come here? I've been holding my breath for weeks, thinking the day would never come. To be honest, it feels as if I've been looking forward to this event for most of my life."

The duchess looked pleased. "We feel the same, I assure you. I think you'll enjoy our Christmas Ball. It's much larger than our annual Winter Ball, which was our most festive occasion until Charlotte and I decided to expand our social calendar. It's so expanded now that Roxburghe swears he cannot come home without finding the house full of people. He's right; we've fairly packed the months with house parties and balls. But then, what's a castle for, if not to entertain?"

"All year long? That must be taxing."

"Charlotte and I find it quite worthwhile. All of our

balls have been huge successes—well, all except our Butterfly Ball, which we held last year but will not be doing again."

"Why not? Lily said it was lovely."

They reached the huge double doors and the duchess led the way through. "Your sister was being kind. For reasons I dare not explain for fear of making you shudder, Lady Charlotte and I've decided to never again— Ah! Charlotte, look who I found in the foyer."

A kindly looking woman came forward. Her fashionable gown of dove gray accented with heavy cream lace rustled as she walked, while the lace-trimmed mobcap perched upon her curls bounced with each step. Short and plump and beaming, she looked like a small, good-natured fairy. "Miss Balfour, what a pleasure!"

"Lady Charlotte." Dahlia dipped a curtsy. Just as she was rising, she caught sight of a tall figure behind Lady Charlotte, near the fireplace. The man stirred the fire with a brass-knobbed poker but, to her faint surprise, didn't look around at her arrival. His lack of interest piqued hers.

He was fashionably dressed, his broad shoulders and narrow waist well displayed by his fitted coat and breeches. Why was he here, waiting in the room the duchess had practically dragged her to? Could her grace think this gentleman could be a good suitor? Dahlia's pulse quickened.

Her grace's gaze followed Dahlia's to the stranger. The duchess frowned and, obviously impatient with the gentleman's lack of attention, she cleared her throat.

The man finished banking the fire, apparently not in a hurry to heed the duchess's hints. As she watched him, Dahlia had the oddest impression that he was hesitant to turn around. *Perhaps he doesn't wish to be presented as a suitor. Has the duchess forced him into this meeting?*

Her uncertainty grew until, just as he bent to replace the poker, she caught a glimpse of his profile. Her heart gave an odd leap. Before he turned to face her, she already knew what she'd see—the red slash of a jagged scar, marring a face of such masculine beauty that it was worthy of the best Greek tragedies.

She was prepared for the scar. But what she wasn't prepared for was the fashionably cut hair that made him look younger. Much younger. It made him seem like a new man, one she didn't know at all.

But know him she did, although she was astonished to see him here, dressed and pressed into a man of fashion.

Before she could stop herself, she blurted out, "Lord Kirk, who invited *you?*"

*Three*

**From the Diary of the Duchess of Roxburghe**
Lord Kirk has much to explain. *Much*. After hearing a few hard, cold facts from Miss Balfour, I've half a mind to refuse to assist him further. Fortunately for him, I enjoy a challenge, and this will be the biggest I've ever faced. I only wish he'd told us all to begin with . . .

As soon as the words left Dahlia's lips, her face heated and she sent a hurried glance at the duchess. "I'm sorry. I didn't mean to be rude, but I never expected—" She gestured toward Lord Kirk, her onetime friend, longtime neighbor, and now, sworn enemy.

"I daresay you are surprised," Lady Charlotte offered kindly.

"Very."

Kirk took up his cane from where it had been resting unnoticed by the fireplace and limped forward.

Dahlia watched him with a narrowed eyes, her gaze

flickering from his perfectly tied cravat to his pressed breeches and shined Hessians.

He stopped before her and bowed.

She blinked. A *bow*? From *him*?

And yet he did it with amazing grace, glinting a smile at her as he did so. "Miss Balfour, what a pleasure to see you here."

In all of the times they'd met, he'd never offered such a pleasantry. His greetings were always so informal as to border on the impolite. She'd never questioned it, for it was simply his way and he treated everyone the same. But this greeting, combined with the perfect bow, was different—a nice mixture of formality and warmth, like that of someone used to polite society.

She didn't know what to say. *By Zeus, what's happened?* The Lord Kirk she knew was unfashionable, abrupt, and reclusive, while this one seemed everything opposite.

And she couldn't stop admiring his clothing. His snowy white neckcloth was starched to perfection, a wonder of twists and clever knots. His blue coat fit his broad shoulders well, so well that she couldn't help but be aware that he was actually quite handsomely built, with broad shoulders and a narrow waist, his legs powerful and well defined in his buff knit trousers, his thighs astonishingly muscular and—

"Miss Balfour?" he gently teased.

Heat flooded her face as she dragged her gaze up from his thighs. "I'm sorry. I didn't mean to stare. I was just— I mean, you're so— And before you weren't at all—" She pressed her hands to her hot cheeks.

He inclined his head. "I'm honored to be an object of your curiosity."

He was smiling at her. Smiling as if he weren't the somber, reticent man she used to know. *What had happened to change him?*

But it didn't matter. No matter what—or who— had changed him, she would *not* return his smile. She didn't care that he was properly dressed and could now greet her with the utmost politeness, for he was the same man who'd insulted her family, and then—not content with that—had taken advantage of her poor father, who was as innocent and lacking in guile as a newborn lamb. History couldn't be erased by a mere spate of good manners, no matter how surprising.

The memory of the distress he'd caused her father flooded her with irritation and, aware the duchess and Lady Charlotte were watching, Dahlia offered him a chilly, barely there curtsy. "I must say, I'm surprised to see you so far away from Fordyce Castle. I thought you'd sworn to never leave."

Kirk's smile dimmed at her frosty tone, his gaze flickering to the duchess and then back.

The duchess said cautiously, "Miss Balfour, I see that you already know Lord Kirk."

"We know each other well. *Too* well," Dahlia said tightly. "We were—are—neighbors."

"Neighbors?" Charlotte tilted her head to one side,

her bright gaze never leaving Dahlia's. "So you must have spent some time in one another's company?"

"No. Not recently, anyway. We once— I mean, there was a time when we spoke more frequently, but of late we scarcely see one another." She didn't add "which is for the best," although she thought it so loudly that she was certain he'd heard it. "I thought you had an aversion to balls and house parties, Lord Kirk. Or so you said, for what that's worth."

His smile had long since faded and his expression was now wary. "I made an exception for the duchess. We are old friends and I couldn't refuse her kind invitation."

"Had I known you would be here, I would have rearranged my plans."

"Oh dear," Lady Charlotte said, looking from Dahlia to Kirk, and then back.

The duchess sighed and bent to pick up a pug that had been looking up at her with a longing gaze. "You two seem to have some ill history between you."

Ill history? Dahlia almost laughed. Not only had this man duped her father into signing a most unfavorable loan, but he'd also managed to insult her in the worst possible way. When she thought of his words, her chest ached with anger.

"I do hope you will be civil to one another." The duchess looked at them with a faintly stern expression.

Dahlia forced herself to unclench her hands, moving her heavy reticule on her wrist so that the bands weren't so tight. There was no need to recall that embarrassing time. "You need have no fear, your grace. With so many guests here, I'm certain that Lord Kirk and I will scarcely have the opportunity to speak. And if we do, we'll both be civil." She looked at Kirk. "Won't we?"

He seemed to be struggling with the need to argue, but after a long moment, he gave a curt nod. "Of course."

"Excellent!" The duchess scratched the pug's ear. "I have no idea what Lord Kirk has said in the past about his proclivities for society, but he was certainly eager to attend our Christmas Ball, weren't you, Lord Kirk?"

Lord Kirk bowed stiffly, his expression now grim. "I thought it would be most enjoyable." His dark gaze flickered over Dahlia. "I hope it may still be so."

Her grace nodded. "Miss Balfour, you may be unaware of this fact, but Lord Kirk is my godson, just as you are my goddaughter. I knew his mother well."

"I had no idea."

"Yes, I have so many godchildren that I have trouble keeping up myself. I hope to invite all of them to visit me at some time or another."

"Not all at the same time, of course," Lady Charlotte offered helpfully. "That would be far too many."

The duchess smiled and, in what seemed to be a determined effort to start some common small talk, said, "Miss Balfour, Lord Kirk just returned from Edinburgh."

That was unusual. Kirk rarely left the grand, rambling castle that made Caith Manor look like a gatehouse. As far as she knew, he only left his home to travel the short distance to Aberdeenshire to fetch purchases, so it was indeed a surprise to find that he'd been elsewhere.

Despite wishing to appear uninterested, Dahlia asked, "What took you to Edinburgh?"

"I was—" His gaze flickered to the duchess, a plea in it.

The duchess hurried to say, "Lord Kirk was rusticating."

She frowned. "Rusticating? In a *city*?"

A dull color crept into his face. "Yes, for I did not attend any amusements. I had business to attend to."

"Ah, business." The word burned on her tongue as her temper took flame once more. "I daresay that now you've used up all of your prospects near Aberdeenshire, after tricking my father into an impossible-to-repay loan, that you must go afield to find more victims for your schemes."

"Miss Balfour!" The duchess looked far from happy. "I specifically invited Lord Kirk because I knew he was a neighbor of yours. I thought a familiar face would serve as a reassurance, but I can see now that I was wrong."

"I'm sorry, your grace, but I am not on speaking terms with Lord Kirk."

His dark gaze locked on her. "You once were."

His voice, deep and rich, made her chest tighten. "That was long, *long* ago."

The duchess looked from one to the other before

she gave a huge sigh and placed the pug back on the floor. "Miss Balfour, I know about the loan Lord Kirk made to your father." Lord Kirk slashed the duchess a dark look, but she continued as if she hadn't noticed. "I'm certain he meant no harm."

Lady Charlotte nodded enthusiastically. "Lord Kirk would never harm your father. Why, he was actually trying to *help* him."

"By offering terms that could never be repaid?" Dahlia remembered how wan and frightened her father had been as he'd struggled to deal with the loan, and her heart hardened. "I cannot believe it."

The scar near Kirk's mouth grew white. "You know I'd never intentionally hurt your father or anyone else."

"All I know is what you did to my father, who, in a moment of weakness, asked you for a loan he had no right to request."

"I didn't know he couldn't repay it," Kirk growled. "And even if I had, I didn't really care if he repaid it or not."

"Then why did you demand that he do so, and so quickly that he was put into a horrid state of terror? He thought he'd lose his house to you!"

Lady Charlotte tsked. "Her grace and I can explain that. The reason Lord Kirk—"

"Pardon me, but I can speak for myself." Lord Kirk's abruptness and glare reminded Dahlia of the Kirk she knew.

Oddly reassured, she lifted her chin. "Had you been a gentleman, you would have made certain my father could repay such a loan, and refused him when you determined he could not."

"It was precisely because I *was* a gentleman that I didn't ask him if he *could* repay it, but assumed he would when—and if—he chose to do so. As I've said, I didn't care if he ever repaid that damned loan. I had no need of those funds."

Dahlia fisted her hands at her side. "But then you pressed him to do so, and pressed him so harshly that my sister felt impelled to ask for her grace's assistance in marrying a wealthy man in order to offset the ultimate cost to our family, that of losing Caith Manor."

He flushed. "There are things you don't understand. You'll have to trust that I would never have done so had I known your sister would act in such an impetuous fashion."

"*Impetuous—oh!* You are so *arrogant!*"

"And you are so determined to believe I was out to harm your family, for no good reason whatsoever!"

"You, sir, are a—"

"Stop it, both of you," the duchess demanded.

Lady Charlotte leaned toward the duchess. "Oh, no! Margaret, you do not understand! In but a moment, they will fall into one another's arms. That's just how it is in my novels."

Dahlia barely heard them, her entire being focused on the man before her. "I know why you demanded my father repay the loan in such a harsh manner."

Kirk's mouth couldn't have been any grimmer, but he said not one word.

That spurred Dahlia on. "It's because I refused your offer of marriage, and you were determined that my family should suffer for it!"

Shocked silence met this pronouncement.

"Marriage?" Lady Charlotte turned her wide gaze on Lord Kirk. "You never mentioned you'd already asked for Miss Balfour's hand."

"She refused me. Therefore, there was no reason to mention it."

His cold, matter-of-fact tone made Dahlia's heart thud sickly, and she had to fight an unexpected desire to burst into tears. "I refused because you gave me no choice." She turned to Lady Charlotte. "He—he—he—" Her voice quavered and, afraid she might indeed indulge in tears, she clamped her lips closed and wished with all of her heart that she had never come into the salon.

The duchess swiftly moved to her side, grasping Dahlia's hand between her own. "He what?" the duchess asked. "What did he do?"

Dahlia ignored Kirk, who stood staring at her with such a blazing expression that she felt she might melt from it. "Lord Kirk asked me to marry him in a way that was—" She shook her head shortly. "I can only say that no woman would ever accept such an insulting proposal."

Lady Charlotte's cupid's-bow mouth formed a surprised "O." "Insulting? Did he— Oh goodness, did he *proposition* you?"

Dahlia had thought that her cheeks couldn't possibly get any hotter, but Lady Charlotte's words proved her wrong. "No, no. Nothing like that!" She took a deep breath. "Lord Kirk said that he wished to marry me in spite of my lack of culture, and the fact that my family was not in a class he wished to associate with."

Kirk had to almost physically bite back his irritation. Good God, the way she presented his proposal, it sounded as if he'd been the veriest cad. "That's not what I said."

Her eyes flashed as she said in a heated tone, "Oh? What *did* you say, then?"

Three sets of accusing eyes fixed upon him. "I spoke nothing but the truth. I said that in spite of the fact that you'd led such a sheltered life—which you have—and are thus ignorant in the way of culture— which you are—and in spite of the fact that your family has little to recommend it as a fortuitous connection—which even you must admit to be true— that I nevertheless wished to marry you."

Lady Charlotte continued to look shocked, while the duchess's expression grew black. Dahlia, meanwhile, glared at him in a very hostile manner.

He scowled back. "Damn it all, what was wrong with that? All I did was tell the truth. And in spite of all of those issues, I still wished to marry Dahlia, which is surely worth something."

None of them looked the least bit convinced.

Dahlia sniffed. "I can assure you, it was the easiest of all proposals to refuse. But had I known the extent to which you were willing to go to punish me for that refusal, I might have—"

"Punish? I did no such thing."

"Then why did you offer my father such a horrid loan?"

"Because he *asked* for one. I didn't pay attention to the conditions, which were not what they should have been, I admit, thanks to my man of business—but revenge had nothing to do with it."

"Ha! You'll never convince me of that, Lord Kirk. *Ever.*"

He absently rubbed his cheek, where the scar pulled. *I've gone through hell and back to change myself, and all she can think about is the past. What a bloody waste of two months.*

It was unacceptable. He hadn't learned how to bow and dress and act like a trussed-up bobkin just to be dismissed within moments. He tightened his grip on the cane knob. "Dahlia, blast you, you know that I would never—"

"Lord Kirk," Lady Charlotte interrupted, her eyes so wide that she looked like a flustered rabbit. "Perhaps we should allow Miss Balfour to retire. I'm certain she's exhausted from her travels." She looked hopefully at Dahlia. "Aren't you?"

Dahlia lifted her chin, her fine gray-blue eyes still frosty, the wide brim of her bonnet framing her heart-shaped face. "Actually, yes. I am very tired from my journey."

"Then you must rest," her grace interceded, sounding relieved. "There are several hours before dinner. A maid should be unpacking your things now should you wish to call for a bath or a light repast."

"Thank you. That's too kind."

Lady Charlotte nodded. "I can't ride in a coach myself without feeling as if someone has beaten me with a broom handle. I'm sure you'll feel better for a hot bath and a nap."

"Thank you." Dahlia curtsied to the duchess and Lady Charlotte. "You've both been too kind." She then gave Kirk a very shallow, very cold bow. "Good day, my lord."

Without waiting for an answer, she turned on her heel and marched out, the picture of fluffed outrage.

Kirk winced as the door slammed behind her.

The duchess turned her sharp blue gaze his way. "Well, Kirk? What have you to say for yourself?"

"Yes, you never mentioned you'd already asked Miss Balfour for her hand in marriage," Lady Charlotte added.

"As I said before, she refused me, so I didn't see the need to say anything about it."

The duchess threw up her hands. "Didn't see the— Good God, how are Charlotte and I to promote your suit if you keep secrets from us?"

"Horrible secrets," Charlotte echoed. "Did you really say such wretched things during a *proposal*?"

"They didn't seem wretched at the time. I was trying to explain that, despite her lack of experience with the world and her family's lack of standing, I thought her so superior as to offer for her hand despite all I could hold against her. How is that a wretched thing to say?"

Lady Charlotte shook her head, her lace cap fluttering. "Did you at least tell her that you found her pretty? Intelligent? Interesting?"

"She knew I thought those things or I'd hardly have offered to get leg shackled to begin with."

"Good God," her grace snapped. "I daresay you didn't even offer the chit a decent ring, did you?"

"I had one that belonged to my mother," he replied stiffly. "It's not very pretty, which I admitted to her. In fact, it's damned ugly—but it was all I had on hand."

Lady Charlotte pinched her nose and shook her head. "Oh dear, oh dear."

"What's wrong with that? It's a family heirloom."

"You poor, poor man. You don't really know, do you?"

"Know what?" he snapped, irritated by the whole situation.

Her grace sighed. "You've much further to go than we thought."

"How much further can I go? Look at me! I'm dressed like a popinjay, my hair has been cut like a damned dandy's, and I've been forced to learn mawkish manners and mealymouthed pleasantries until I can't stand to hear myself speak. And for what? She's not in the room two minutes before she's bringing up the past and telling me in no uncertain terms that she wishes I were to go to Hades. And damn it, after all of this, that's where I wish I were, too!"

"You must give it time. Give her time. It appears she has more to recover from than we realized."

Kirk turned and made his way back to the fireplace, where he stared into the flames. "I told you she wouldn't wish to see me, fine clothing or no. She is furious with me, and I don't blame her. The terms of the loan were horrible."

"How did that come to be?"

"I instructed my man of business to write up the loan. It never dawned on me he would write one that was other than fair."

"Ah. And since you never really expected to collect on the loan, you didn't examine the terms first."

"Exactly. I dismissed him once I found out, but by then it was too late—the loan had been signed, and Dahlia viewed it as evidence that I am a man without a conscience."

"What a coil."

"Indeed." Kirk placed a hand against the marble mantel and leaned against it.

"Still . . . I remain hopeful," the duchess said.

"Then you are more an optimist than I."

"I am more experienced in matters of the heart, Kirk. I have hope for a reason."

His dark gaze turned toward her. "Why? Did you see something?"

"Perhaps." The duchess bent to pat one of the pugs who was staring up at her with a hopeful expression. "For now at least, perhaps you should leave Miss Balfour to Lady Charlotte and myself."

"You think you can help?"

"It's not in my nature to abandon a potential match merely because there are a few difficulties." She pursed her lips. "However, it is a setback that Charlotte and I didn't know the full of your history"—she fixed a hard gaze on him—"which we should have."

"I've already explained that."

"Humph. Because of that, Miss Balfour was not prepared for our meeting. Had Charlotte and I known the extent of the history behind you, we might have softened that blow, but we were not given that opportunity. There's nothing to be done now but press forward. Now that Dahlia has seen you, she won't be surprised again."

"Yes, but she won't speak to me. She hasn't said a word to me in months until today, and you saw how furious she is." He gave a helpless shrug. "She'll have none of me."

"Things will be different here. Good manners will prevent her from ignoring you when you're with the other guests. Those same good manners will force her to speak to you whenever you are together. That should give you time to mend those broken fences of yours, and perhaps forge newer, pleasanter memories."

Kirk rubbed his neck, feeling a dull ache behind his eyes. All he wanted was to bridge this gulf that had grown between him and Dahlia. Why was it so hard? It seemed that the more he wished for it to happen, the less likely it would be so. He looked at the duchess. "Tell me the truth: do you think I have a chance?"

She hesitated, but finally said, "Yes, but it won't be easy. There's much to overcome and not much time in which to do it."

He looked down at his hand, clenched about the cane knob. *Hope. That's all I have. But if there is even the smallest chance . . .* He sighed. "Fine. I will do what I can to make it so."

"Excellent. Charlotte and I shall come up with a plot to allow you some time to speak with Miss Balfour. You, meanwhile, will find a compliment or two you can pay that poor girl."

"Oh yes," Lady Charlotte agreed. "You owe her some compliments."

"Flowers, too," her grace added.

"And a poem, if you can find the time to write one."

"A poem?"

Lady Charlotte nodded. "Yes, but not about her eyes. Everyone writes about a woman's eyes, and really, what can be said other than they shine like a lamp or a star or—"

"Hold. I don't write poetry."

"No? That's a pity, for if you were to write a poem about her mouth or her hair or— It would be the very thing, I'm certain of it." Lady Charlotte peeped hopefully at him. "Are you absolutely *certain* you can't write a poem, even a short one?"

"Bloody hell, no!" Catching the duchess's suddenly stern gaze, he swallowed a growl. "Tomorrow, after I've some time to think it through, I'll ask MacCreedy to procure some flowers. I'm sure I can think

of a compliment or two, as well. But the poetry—
damn it. It's not in me to write an ode."

"That's a great deal too bad." Lady Charlotte
looked mournful.

"You might at least *try* to write one," her grace said
calmly. "Not for tonight, of course. However, there's
plenty of time between now and tomorrow's dinner."

His shoulders ached as if every word they'd said
were weighing them down. With a sigh, Kirk rubbed a
hand over his face. "Good God, is there to be no end
to this?"

"Oh, there will be an end," her grace said, a sharp note
in her voice. "Hopefully it will consist of a proposal and
a happy acceptance. That *is* what you wanted, isn't it?"

For one sweet moment, he imagined Dahlia as
she'd once been, smiling at him, talking about the
last book she'd read, sharing secrets with such open
trust— His heart ached at the thought. *It's been so long
since she's smiled at me. Every day seems a year.* "Fine.
I'll see what I can do, but don't expect a miracle."

"We won't expect anything except your best
effort." The duchess noted the darkness in Lord Kirk's
eyes, and once again she wondered how entangled his
heart had become. He was such an enigmatic man
that it was difficult to tell. "Have heart, Alasdair. This
may be a difficult case, but it is far from hopeless."

His gaze locked with hers and for a moment she
thought he might admit his true feelings, but then he
muttered something about needing to soak his aching
leg, bowed, and limped from the room.

As the door closed behind him, Charlotte blew out her breath in a huge whoosh. "Goodness! That didn't go the way we'd wished."

"No. He was very bad for not telling us all. What a horrid history!"

"They have much to overcome."

"Yes, they do. Both of them, I think."

Charlotte dropped into a chair. "Do you really think there's hope?"

"Yes. I would never waste our time."

"I thought perhaps you were just saying that to be kind."

"There were some positive moments."

"There were?" Charlotte blinked. "When?"

"Miss Balfour had quite a positive reaction on seeing Kirk's transformation. She stared at him as if fascinated." Margaret picked up Randolph and took the chair next to Charlotte's. "I think our Beauty is more taken with our Beast than she realizes."

Charlotte nodded thoughtfully.

"Now we need to provide her with more reasons to be so." Margaret patted Randolph absently. "What would a young lady in love with love wish to see in a suitor? Hmm . . ." After a long moment, she stiffened. "That might work . . . yes. It just might."

"Oh, Margaret, I quite love it when you get that look in your eyes! What do you have planned?"

Margaret smiled, and for the next half hour, they plotted. And when they were done, they were both beaming with hope.

*Four*

**From the Diary of the Duchess of Roxburghe**

I did not place Miss Balfour near Lord Kirk at dinner last night. After the scene Charlotte and I witnessed, it would be an error to allow Dahlia to think for a second that I was promoting Kirk as a potential match. Yet.

If there is one thing I know about the Balfour women, it's that they possess pride and stubbornness in abundance, and must make up their own minds about whom they wish to pursue and be pursued by. That can make assisting them quite difficult. Still, I've never before allowed personal preference, mistaken as it can sometimes be, to get in the way of a good match and I shall not do so now.

Of course, last night was not without some glimmer of hope. Several times I caught Dahlia glancing toward Lord Kirk, and even though it was only to deliver the most burning of looks, it was good that she looked at him at all.

Still, we must change this. Over the course of her stay, we must find ways to remind her of the things she has in common with Lord Kirk. Meanwhile, he must show her that in order to please her, he is willing to leave his least desirable traits behind. If a man or a woman loves another—and I believe Kirk is in love with Miss Balfour, though he has not yet admitted such—he must be willing to *improve*.

We all must do so for those we love.

Bringing these two stubborn souls together will be a daunting task, and yet the match will be all the more worthwhile because of the difficulty—nay, the *impossibility* of it.

"Yer waistcoat, me lor'." MacCreedy placed the garment upon the bed.

Kirk turned from the mirror where he'd just finished tying his cravat, yet another skill the valet had taught him. "Hand me a waistcoat, please. I'm— Oh. Not that one. Find another, please."

"Me lor'?"

"It's red *satin*."

MacCreedy's lips twitched. "Och now, can ye no' wear satin, me lor'?"

Kirk lifted his brows in disbelief. "Do I *appear* to be the type of man who would wear satin?"

"I'll no' be answerin' tha', me lor'." The valet chuckled. "'Tis satin, but 'tis the fashion fer all tha'."

"Which I'm constrained to follow." Kirk couldn't keep the bitterness from his voice. Last night's dinner had been an unmitigated failure. Reluctantly taking the duchess's advice, he'd given Dahlia a wide berth, though he'd wished for just a few moments to speak to her. But judging from her icy glares, the time wasn't right.

This morning, after a restless night during which he'd assigned the duchess's advice to hell, he'd gone in search of Dahlia before breakfast, determined to have a much-needed conversation, but she was nowhere to be found. Later, he learned she'd left with her grace and Lady Charlotte to run errands in town. That had left him to mingle with the other guests, who treated him much as they had last night, with a mixture of awkward glances or morbid stares.

He ran his thumb along his scar, wondering if he'd have to put up with such looks for the entire three weeks.

"Is yer scar hurtin' ye, me lor'?"

"No. I was just wondering how long it would take her grace's guests to stop staring at it."

"Och, 'tis rude o' them."

He shrugged. "It's easier to get used to rude guests than to deal with this damnable neckcloth. It seems that since I've been buried in the countryside, fashion has taken a decidedly French turn. That is not a compliment."

MacCreedy chuckled. "Fer all ye're complainin', fashion has no' changed so much fer gentlemen. Is it possible tha' ye've ne'er been one to dress, e'en afore ye buried ye'self in the country?"

"Perhaps. My first wife frequently lamented I possessed no fashion sense worth mentioning."

"Tha' explains it, then. Ye've been rejectin' dressin' to yer station since th' cradle. I canno' say tha' I'm surprised, fer ye seem verrah set in yer ways, ye do." MacCreedy gave the waistcoat a fond look. "This is verrah much in style, me lor', which is probably why ye instinctively dislike it so."

Kirk grinned. "I've good instincts, have I?"

Humor warmed the valet's craggy face. "I've ne'er seen anyone wit' a better aptitude fer recognizin' wha' is in style, me lor'. The problem is tha' after ye recognize it, ye instantly decide to hate it."

"At least I'm consistent." Over the last two months, Kirk had grown to appreciate MacCreedy's expert assistance. In Edinburgh Kirk had relearned the ways of the polite world, all the things he'd forgotten and many things he'd never known. He now realized that the death of his parents, especially his mother, when he was quite young had deprived him of a certain polish, something he'd never missed until now. He'd never been taught—or over the years had forgotten—basic things such as how to bow with grace, how to greet various members of the nobility, which were appropriate topics of conversation and which were not, and a variety of other foppish duties that no one in their right mind would wish to know.

He'd been quite happy not knowing those things until he'd met Dahlia Balfour, and there were times when he'd questioned his sanity in undertaking this mad quest. *And all for a woman who wishes me to the devil.* A single, slender, fragile strand of hope that somehow, some way, Dahlia Balfour might come to see him as something other than the man who tried to ruin her family pulled him inexorably to this course.

*She'd damned well better appreciate my efforts.* He left his cane beside the dresser and limped to the bed. "MacCreedy, please find a waistcoat that won't make me look like a fop."

MacCreedy wisely didn't argue, but returned to the wardrobe.

Kirk leaned against the bedpost to take the weight off his aching leg. If he were home right now, he'd be sitting in his study reading the latest book on the Egyptian explorations, his newest interest. Either that or he might be trying his hand at the new Beethoven sheet music he'd ordered from London last month. That was one thing he had gotten from his mother, a deep love of music. She used to play beautiful pieces for hours, with a talent he'd never possess.

The thought of the waiting sheet music made him wish he was home right now, where every night Mrs. MacAllis cooked him one of his favorite meals, and his butler made certain that the fire in his study was just so. Instead, here he was, dressed in these damned uncomfortable clothes, hoping that Dahlia would come to her senses and realize they were uniquely matched.

For they were more compatible in thought and action than any other two people Kirk knew. He suspected that Dahlia, young and romantic, didn't realize how important or rare that was. Even if the duchess introduced Dahlia to every eligible bachelor in the kingdom, she'd find no man as well suited to her as he.

That's why he was so determined to win this battle, silly as it was, concerned with satin waistcoats and how deeply one bowed to a duke as opposed to a viscount. But if it took a battle of society to win her hand, then so be it. *She is worth it. More than worth it.*

"I had yer coat pressed." MacCreedy's voice broke into Kirk's thoughts.

"Thank you."

"Och, 'twas fer me own benefit." MacCreedy withdrew a perfectly pressed coat from the wardrobe and placed it on the bed. "A well-turned-out gentleman speaks jus' as much to his valet's credit as his own."

"I'm glad I won't shame you."

"As if I'd let ye." MacCreedy grinned. "I was a topnotch boxer in me day. I'm fairly sure I could take ye now, e'en though I've a score o' years on ye."

"I've no doubt." MacCreedy was unlike any valet Kirk had ever known. After Wellington's valet had been injured during the Spanish campaign and sent home, MacCreedy—the groom in charge of his grace's horses—had been pressed into service for the exacting, crotchety commander. Under the duke's precise direction, MacCreedy had learned the valet arts and was now a master valet. He could black boots to a high gloss, starch cravats into rigid and snowy perfection, and maintain a frosty air with the most impudent of footmen.

Yet because he'd first been a groom and had served the duke throughout the harsh, often desperate conditions of the infamous Spanish campaign, MacCreedy also knew things other valets didn't—like how to clean and fire any sort of pistol, and a thorough knowledge of field medicine. The latter had been of special help, for the valet knew many remedies to ease a sore and aching leg.

Now, though, the valet wasn't helping at all. Instead, he was holding Kirk's dinner coat against the waistcoat. "The red color complements yer black dinner coat." He looked hopefully at Kirk.

Kirk was fairly certain Dahlia would laugh at the ridiculous waistcoat. He had a sudden memory of her laughter—huskier than one might expect, and very attractive. It would be nice to hear her laugh again, anything other than the dark looks she'd sent him throughout dinner last night.

MacCreedy sighed. "Verrah weel, me lor'. If ye've decided, then ye've decided. As ye dinna ha' anyone to impress but yerself, I'll put awa' the satin waistcoat and fetch ye a nice, safe wool one." The valet pulled out a wool waistcoat and placed it on the bed beside the red one.

Kirk looked at the two waistcoats. Beside the vibrant sheen of the red satin, the blue wool looked bland and boring. He sighed. "Damn it, give me the satin waistcoat. I've gone this far to make myself a fop, so why stop now? Besides, I'll be so uncomfortable in these"—he gestured toward his breeches—"that I won't care about the waistcoat."

MacCreedy's craggy face cracked in a smile. "Och, ye're back t' tha', are ye? How breeches nowadays cling?"

"I prefer looser ones."

"Aye, as were the fashion twenty years ago."

Kirk sighed and sat on the edge of the bed, wincing as his leg protested.

MacCreedy eyed him somberly. "I'll order a bath fer after dinner. I've more ointment fer ye to rub into tha' leg, too."

"It has helped."

"I could do more, if ye'd let me. The muscles need to be stretched, they do. Wit' the proper work, ye could turn more easily, perhaps e'en ride. It's e'en possible tha' ye could leave yer cane behind and walk wit'oot a limp."

Kirk looked up at that. "I wouldn't limp? At all?"

"'Tis possible, if ye work hard enou'."

"When this is over, I shall gladly pursue your advice. But for now, I fear that in trying to obtain that goal, you'd leave me limping worse than ever."

"Aye, at least in the beginning."

"Exactly. And I've no wish to look even less capable in front of Miss Balfour."

MacCreedy shook his head. "Och, ye've a bad case o' it, haven't ye', me lor'."

"A bad case?"

"O' love."

"Miss Balfour and I are very compatible. That's far more important than love."

The valet shook his head. "Me lor', I dinna think to hear such nonsense fro' ye."

"It's not nonsense. I was married before and I know love."

"Ah, so ye loved yer wife, but no' Miss Balfour?"

"I loved my wife with the foolhardiness and drama of a youth." He grimaced. "That was fine for the age I was, but no longer. What I feel for Miss Balfour is quite different. We are comfortable, she and I."

"Poor Miss Balfour."

"Why do you say that? Just because I see her without the falseness of a fleeting passion doesn't mean that I don't value her. She's intelligent, pleasant, and pleasing to look upon." More than pleasing, in fact. Her smile was breathtaking and she possessed a freshness that no other woman could match. With her brown curls and the most damnably attractive sprinkling of freckles, he would never tire of just seeing her smile.

Their relationship had been tantalizingly short, but in the months after they'd had their disagreement and she'd stormed out of his home and sworn never to return, he'd found himself missing her far more than he'd expected. Worse, he'd begun wondering about other things . . . like how she'd feel in his arms. If he closed his eyes even now, he could imagine exactly what it would feel like to trace a kiss between each freckle on her nose, across her cheek, directly to those plump lips—

"Me lor'? 'Tis a wee bit past seven. Ye'll be late if we dinna get ye dressed."

The waistcoat seemed to mock his thoughts. *Fine. I may have to endure some foolishness to win Dahlia, but hopefully it won't be much. She's a pragmatist at heart, and she'll soon realize that both of our lives will be more comfortable if we spend them together.*

"Let's get this over with. The sooner Dahlia realizes the silliness of this entire venture, the sooner we can return home and forget this horrendous event."

MacCreedy sent him a humorous glance. "Me lor', 'tis becomin' more and more obvious tha' ye're no romantic."

"Romance is for women and novels."

MacCreedy winced. "Tha' made me cold, it did."

"Well, I'm about to make you ill. Hand me that wretched waistcoat and let's be done with this."

The valet helped Kirk into the waistcoat and then watched as he buttoned it. "I hope ye dinna think I'm pryin', but did ye ha' a chance to, oh, I dinna know, mayhap write some'at this afternoon? A poem, mayhap?"

Kirk turned to look at his valet. "You've been talking to her grace."

MacCreedy picked up the coat from the bed and smoothed one sleeve. "Mayhap I ran into her and Lady Charlotte in the courtyard after I returned fro' town."

"With Miss Balfour, I take it?"

"Sadly, she'd already entered th' house afore I arrived." MacCreedy held up the coat.

Kirk allowed the valet to ease the coat onto his shoulders. "Her grace is a meddling woman."

"Aye, but her heart is in th' right place, me lor'. Ye canno' say tha' aboot many people."

"I suppose. What did you tell her when she asked if I was writing a poem?"

"Tha' I'd seen no evidence of such."

"Nor will you. I'm not a poet. I do, however, know Miss Balfour better than her grace does. Speaking of which, were you able to procure the items I requested?"

"Aye. They're on the table by the dresser."

Kirk limped across the room. Three books sat in a stack. "Ah. An Egyptian history, a study of the Roman ruins found in Bath, and Byron's poetry." He replaced the books. "Well done, MacCreedy. They are exactly what I was hoping you'd find."

"'Twas hard to make a mistake when ye gave me such explicit instructions. The duke's battle orders weren't much clearer."

"It helps that I know the reader's taste so well." This was much better than flowers. "So the money I gave you was enough?"

"Aye, I put the extra in yer lockbox along wit' the bill. The Byron book cost ye a bit more than th' others, which is odd seein' as how it has fewer words."

"The man's work is sappy and dramatic, but since

Miss Balfour's taste runs in that direction, she'll enjoy it."

"She also likes histories?"

"Very much." Kirk remembered her face when she'd found his collection of books on Roman history. Her eyes had widened, her lips parted, her skin flushed— He caught MacCreedy's inquiring look and said shortly, "She'll enjoy all three of these books."

"Are you giving them to her tonight?"

Kirk looked at them thoughtfully. "No, not yet. She's barely speaking to me now. I'll find a better time and place." He limped to the dresser and reclaimed his cane, pausing to look at himself in the mirror. Only a slender margin of the waistcoat showed where his coat opened and, as MacCreedy had suggested, it complemented the black coat well. Two months ago, he'd have never realized that contrast. *Good God, I'm turning into a fop.* Shaking his head, he made his way to the door.

"I'll ha' a hot bath ready when ye return, me lor'. It'll do yer leg good."

"Thank you, MacCreedy." Kirk left and closed the door behind him. Tonight, he would not allow Dahlia to escape without some conversation. One way or another, he was going to break through the wall of chilly disapproval she'd built around herself.

In a bedchamber in the east wing, Dahlia admired her gown in the mirror. Thanks to her sister's skill with a needle, the gown was far better fashioned than many purchased from the famed modistes on Bond Street. The short-sleeved ball gown was comprised of an undergown of blue silk, with an overdress of white silk and silver thread that made it glisten as she moved. White bobbin lace trimmed the hem and the low oval neckline, and the whole was tied with a wide blue sash. "I'm so glad the duchess is offering dancing this evening. I love to dance."

The maid, who was replacing the hairpins on the dresser, smiled. "'Tis a beautiful gown, miss. And t' think Miss Lily made it!"

"My sister is very skilled." Lily's soon-to-be husband, Prince Wulfinski, thought so, too, for he'd encouraged her to open a shop on Bond Street and in Edinburgh's more fashionable district when they returned from visiting his family in Oxenburg. Dahlia imagined her sister's happiness in seeing her wearing the gown, and a pinch of homesickness struck her.

Oh, how she missed Lily. In fact, Dahlia missed both of her sisters, who were off having adventures while she'd been left at home with their distracted father, who was more interested in the growth of his roses than breathing. She smoothed the silk overskirt and sighed. She loved her father dearly—they all did—but he wasn't the most companionable of men.

That was probably why she'd been so fascinated with Lord Kirk when she'd first met him. Although he was a male, he actually *talked* to her, and she, unaware that was the normal way of things, had thought him unusual.

The thought of Lord Kirk brought her spirits even lower. Although she'd known of him for a long time, she'd paid him very little heed until a year or so ago when, in town shopping for some trim for a gown, she had—literally—run into him. He'd been coming out of a store, his hands full of packages, and she'd turned the corner, her vision obscured by her bonnet poke. Their collision had caused him to drop his packages, one of which he'd already opened, and she found herself looking down at the most fascinating array of books on history and architecture, ancient civilizations and—oh, every topic she loved. Although they'd never before spoken, they had fallen into an instant conversation about books, authors, the importance of the new discoveries in Egypt and Greece, and all sorts of things.

Prior to that meeting, she'd barely spared the older, taciturn widower a thought. She knew a little of his tragic story and might have been disposed to view him in a romantic fashion, but his refusal to so much as wave whenever he rode past her or her sisters had left her with little inclination to think of him as anything more than a rude recluse.

But after their conversation about the books he'd purchased, she'd seen him in an entirely different light. Lured by his promise to allow her to borrow any book from his library that she might wish, she'd found herself tramping through the fields between their houses to visit.

Although she'd been hesitant at first, over the next

few months two things had brought her back time and again. One was Kirk's insistence that his housekeeper be present every time Dahlia visited, which made her feel quite safe. The second was the richness of his amazing library. Thus, her fears assuaged, her thirst for new books stirred, she'd found herself returning several times a week, staying longer with each visit.

Dahlia knew she was risking scandal by visiting a widower at his home without the benefit of a known chaperone. But she'd been helpless to refuse such a wealth of books, and if she were honest, there was something about Lord Kirk that fascinated her. He was so alone, so set in his ways, and yet she sensed a darkness to him, a deep loneliness that made her heart ache and quite softened her opinion of him.

For several months, their visits had progressed from discussions of books and history to something subtly more. And Dahlia had dared hope for that more. But to her chagrin, Kirk never offered a single word of encouragement, nor did he touch her. And though she thought she detected a growing warmth in his gaze, he seemed content to leave things as they were.

Or so she'd thought until the fateful day when he'd made his coldhearted proposal, insulting her and her family in the same breath. She'd been deeply hurt, for although it was obvious his feelings weren't involved, hers were. Not very much, for he hadn't exactly been encouraging, but enough that the memory left a bitter sting.

After she'd stormed out, he hadn't once attempted to explain himself or make things better. He'd merely written increasingly more demanding notes, as if he could simply order her to accept his proposal.

It had been a very unsatisfactory end to a very unsatisfactory relationship, if one could even call it that.

Then a short time later, in obvious retaliation, Kirk had made her father that horrid loan. The man's sins were boundless, and she found herself clenching her jaw every time she thought of him.

*That's all in the past,* she told herself firmly. It was irritating that she had to bear Kirk's company while trying to enjoy her time at the duchess's, but overall, that was a very small obstacle now that she was on the road to future happiness.

She pushed the thoughts away and turned in front of the mirror, smiling as the gown flowed about her legs. *Ah, Lily, you are a genius. I wish you could see me!*

The maid sighed. "Ye look as pretty as a picture, miss. E'en prettier than yer sisters."

"Thank you, but I'm not as pretty as either of my sisters."

"Och, ye've a different kind o' bonniness, miss. They are the sort o' beautiful roses sent fro' London-town to decorate fer a ball, whilst ye ha' the prettiness of Scottish heather plucked on a fresh spring mornin'."

"That's quite poetic, Freya."

The maid grinned. "Thank ye, miss. But 'tis still the truth."

Dahlia chuckled. "My sisters are lovelier, but I'm happy with what I have and who I am. I have the luxury of marrying for true love, unlike my sisters. Fortunately for us all, they found love as well, thanks to the duchess."

"She's a smart one, she is." Freya gathered an Indian shawl of blue and pink, and helped Dahlia drape it over each elbow, letting it hang gracefully at her back.

Dahlia noted that the little maid's brow was furrowed. "Freya? Is something amiss?"

"Weel, miss, wha' ye said has me t' thinkin'. Do ye really believe in true love?"

"I believe in it with all of my heart, and I'll settle for nothing less."

"And ye think ye will find it?"

"One day."

"And if ye dinna? Wha' then?"

"Well . . . I suppose it is possible that I won't meet someone." The thought was so lowering that Dahlia instantly shoved it away. "But I'm far more likely to meet an eligible parti here at the duchess's castle rather than hidden away in the countryside at Caith Manor. And if I'm *willing* to fall in love, then it is bound to happen. If it doesn't on this visit, then it surely will the next."

"I'm no' certain I wish fer a husband, bu' I wouldna' turn me nose up a' findin' a beau."

"A beau over a husband?"

"Och, indeed, miss. I'd rather ha' the romance o'

steppin' oot wit' someone, wit'oot the problems o' a marriage. Some o' the downstairs maids are married, and it do seem tha' they be fightin' and squablin' more than the rest o' us."

"Well, I want both: romance *and* a good marriage. Oh dear! I'm late. Pray hand me that fan, and I'm off."

Freya pressed the fan into Dahlia's hand as she whisked herself out the door and down the hallway, the swell of the voices below rising to greet her.

*Five*

**From the Diary of the Duchess of Roxburghe**
Well. That didn't happen the way I'd imagined.

Dinner was a delight. Dahlia was glad she'd again been seated a good distance from Lord Kirk. As usual, the guests were seated men and women alternating. To Dahlia's immense satisfaction, the gentlemen who sat to either side of her were both quite pleasant.

To her left was a rotund young man who sported an outlandish number of rings and watch fobs. While he was rather quiet, he was very polite and offered a smile whenever their eyes chanced to meet. On her other side sat the charming Viscount Dalhousie, whose good-natured tales grew more and more outlandish as the meal progressed, leaving Dahlia and the surrounding guests chuckling.

After dinner, the gentlemen excused themselves for port while the women retired to the salon, which had been set up for the evening's entertainment. The furniture had been moved from one end of the room, where a small quartet played quietly in a corner in preparation for the dancing to come. The women talked and sipped a dessert sherry while waiting for the men to return.

Dahlia found herself near the two young ladies she'd arrived with, Lady Mary and Miss Stewart. From the feathers in their hair to their painted silk slippers, the two women exemplified the latest fashions. More intriguing was the fact that Lady Mary's auburn tresses were cut à la Sappho, a style Dahlia had greatly admired when she'd seen it in *Ackermann's Repository* last month.

She put a hand to her own brown curls and was wondering if she dared ask Lady Mary how difficult the style was to attain when she realized that the two women were whispering furiously, as if in an argument.

It was quite awkward until Miss Stewart gave a sharp nod and turned to Dahlia, a practiced smile on her thin lips. "Pardon me, Misssssss—" Her brows rose.

Relieved the two had finished their disagreement and pleased to be making some new acquaintances, Dahlia curtsied to Miss Stewart. "I'm Dahlia Balfour."

"Miss Alayne Stewart and this"—Miss Stewart inclined her head toward the taller woman—"is Lady Mary."

"Yes, I believe we met in the foyer on our arrival yesterday." Dahlia curtsied to Lady Mary.

Lady Mary barely returned it, her cold gaze flickering over Dahlia from head to toe as if trying to find fault with some aspect of her appearance.

Miss Stewart showed her teeth in a smile. "Miss Balfour, would you mind helping us solve a slight argument?"

"I don't know how I could be of help, but of course."

"Lady Mary and I cannot decide which modiste made your gown. I think it is one of Mrs. Bell's, while Lady Mary believes it to be a creation of Mack and Bennet's."

Hearing the names of two of London's most famous modistes made Dahlia beam with pride. *Wait until I write to Lily and tell her that her gown was mistaken for a Bond Street creation!* "It was neither."

Lady Mary moved forward. "Nonsense. It has to be one or the other— Ah! Of course! It's French."

"Oh my!" Miss Stewart looked at Dahlia's gown with renewed appreciation.

"No, it's not French. Actually, my sister made it." Dahlia couldn't keep from preening just the slightest bit.

Miss Stewart's jaw dropped. "That cannot be true."

"It is true. My sister is an excellent seamstress."

"What's her name?"

"Lily Balfour."

Miss Stewart made a face. "I've never heard of her. Where is her shop?"

"She doesn't have one yet. Once she's married to Prince Wulfinski, they are going to open one on Bond Street."

"Wulfinski?" Lady Mary's gaze sharpened. "Ah!

Balfour. I remember now. Your sister is the last match made by the duchess. Your other sister married the Earl of Sinclair, another match brought about by her grace."

Dahlia inclined her head warily. "Yes."

Lady Mary's smile didn't reach her eyes. "It seems as if the duchess has made a project out of marrying off the Balfour sisters. How quaint."

The note of superiority in her voice made Dahlia say rather hotly, "Her grace treats my family no different from anyone else's. She is kind to everyone."

Lady Mary exchanged a humorous glance with Miss Stewart before the latter tittered and said, "Oh, she's been *especially* kind to the Balfours. You and your sisters have been her grace's most talked-about charity cases."

Dahlia stiffened. "Charity? I beg your pardon, but—"

The doors opened and the men began to enter, talking and laughing, the heavy-sweet scent of cigar smoke hovering about them. Instantly, the quartet changed to a lively Scottish reel as swarms of footmen carrying trays of champagne invaded the room. In the space of a single moment, the air went from feminine quiet to one of boisterous merriment.

"Ah, Miss Balfour! I was hoping to find you here."

Dahlia, still irritated at Lady Mary and Miss Stewart, turned to find Viscount Dalhousie behind her. Instantly, Miss Stewart smoothed her gown and patted her hair in a nervous way. *So, she has an interest there, does she? Well, so do I.*

Lord Dalhousie had been an amusing dinner companion, and he was also pleasingly tall and handsome with gray eyes, light brown hair, and a mischievous smile. Now that Dahlia knew Miss Stewart found him handsome, he seemed even more so to her.

Dahlia smiled at him. "Lord Dalhousie, have you come to tell me more about the time in Oxford when your horse ran away with you, and you ended up in a religious parade where people thought you were St. Christopher? For if you have, I pray you stop right there, for I did not believe a word of your tale at dinner, and I'm even less inclined to do so now."

Lord Dalhousie laughed, his gray eyes glinting. "You caught me! I was going to repeat that very tale, word for word. Now I'm at a loss for anything to say."

Miss Stewart leaned forward, inserting herself into the conversation without a care for politeness. "Lord Dalhousie, you may repeat your story to me, for I've never heard it."

"Oh yes," Lady Mary said, coming to her friend's aid. "Miss Stewart adores nothing more than a funny story."

"I fear this was funny only to Miss Balfour," Dalhousie said, sending a twinkling look at Dahlia before pretending to be mournful. "For me, it was a tragedy, a bitter humiliation that I shall never overcome."

Miss Stewart giggled. "Pray stop teasing, Lord Dalhousie! Do tell us your story!"

Lord Dalhousie sighed. "I would, but I fear the dagger glances that will be shot at me from Miss Balfour's fine eyes."

*Fine eyes?* Dahlia had to bite back a grin, especially after she caught Miss Stewart's fading smile.

The quartet struck up a waltz, the music flooding the room.

"Oh, a waltz," Lady Mary said. "Miss Stewart loves to waltz, don't you, Alayne?"

"Oh yes. I adore a good waltz."

"Then you are lucky there are so many partners available," Lord Dalhousie said, as if he didn't realize the two women were trying to lure an invitation from him.

"Hardly." Lady Mary unfurled her fan and wafted it with practiced languor. "Who do you think might make Miss Stewart an eligible partner? Perhaps aged Lord MacInnis?"

"Aged? Lord MacInnis is a very nice man," Dahlia protested. "He helped Lady Fowley down the stairs before dinner in the most solicitous way."

"Then let *her* dance with him," Miss Stewart said. "He's ancient and smells like licorice."

Lord Dalhousie threw up a hand. "Sadly, after dinner Lord MacInnis retired to his room, saying he was tired and wished an early night and a cup of warmed milk, so he's not here."

"Of course he isn't." Lady Mary's fan wafted gently. "Alayne, perhaps you should dance with Mr. Simmons?"

"I couldn't!" Miss Stewart declared. "Have you seen his hair?"

Dalhousie looked confused. "It's red?"

Miss Stewart opened her mouth, but Dahlia hurried to interrupt in an attempt to move the conversation to kinder ground. "Oh look! Several people have already joined the floor. Perhaps we should move there so we can watch the danc—"

"Mr. Simmons wears a *wig*!" Miss Stewart interrupted without so much as glancing Dahlia's way.

Dalhousie looked surprised. "Does he, now? I've known him for years, since we are both members of the Four Horse Club, and I never suspected."

"Oh yes! When we arrived yesterday, his carriage was beside mine. As I was walking in, he bent to pat one of the Roxburghe pugs and his hair slipped to one side—all of it!"

Dalhousie laughed. "How disturbing."

"Oh, I was horrified! I couldn't possibly dance with him, for fear I might fall into a spate of giggles."

"He won't do at all." Lady Mary's smirk over the edge of her fan couldn't be more pronounced. "What about"—she paused, malice in her eyes—"*Lord Kirk*?"

Dahlia stiffened. She might harbor some anger toward Lord Kirk, but she knew more than anyone else how much it hurt him to be mocked for his scars. Though he'd never said anything to her, she knew from the bleakness of his gaze that every slight ripped at him.

Miss Stewart shuddered dramatically. "I would never, *ever* dance with that scar-faced, gimpy man! *Never!*"

It was then that Dahlia saw him over Miss Stewart's shoulder, just a few feet away. He'd been walking toward them and had frozen at the cruel words, his face taut, leaving the red blaze of his scar more raw than usual, his mouth an angry slash.

His gaze locked with Dahlia's and he inclined his head ever so faintly.

*What does that nod mean?* Her heart ached to think that he might believe her a part of such meanness. "Miss Stewart, that was unkind of you."

"Nonsense, you must admit Kirk is a veritable Medusa, both beautiful and wretchedly ugly at the same time. The first time I saw him I didn't see his scarred side, which was turned away, and I thought him the most beautiful man, didn't I, Mary?"

Dalhousie, having a clear view of Kirk, said in a low voice, "Miss Stewart, it would be best if you didn't speak about Lord—"

"Ha!" She playfully tapped his arm with her fan. "I won't say a thing if you can find me someone to dance with who isn't old or maimed or scarred."

Dahlia felt as if she were caught in a bad dream. The people around them knew of the situation, as they could easily hear Miss Stewart's comments and see Lord Kirk standing behind her. Some reacted with averted gazes and blushes, while others exchanged significant glances and hid smiles.

"That definitely leaves out Kirk," Lady Mary said.

Miss Stewart giggled, oblivious to the rippling reactions about her. "Indeed it does. He can't dance with that horrid limp—"

"Just stop it!" Dahlia hissed, nodding toward Kirk.

Miss Stewart, her mouth still half-open, turned to follow Dahlia's gaze and saw Kirk behind her. She flushed an ugly red and snapped her mouth closed.

Kirk's expression remained stony and cold. To those who didn't know him, he didn't seem to react strongly, but Dahlia knew what the darkening of his eyes meant, and her heart swelled with indignation.

With a smile on her lips, she pushed between Miss Stewart and Lady Mary and swept forward. "Lord Kirk! What a delightful pleasure to see you again. I was hoping for a word with you. It will be so pleasant to talk to someone from Aberdeenshire. Almost a homecoming, one might say."

She spoke clearly, her voice as loud as Miss Stewart's had been as she met his surprised gaze.

A torrent of emotions flickered behind his dark eyes and she wondered if he would rebuff her. *Good God, he is prideful. Will he not accept a friendly gesture?* She said in a low voice, "Please. You must not make a scene or they will have more to gossip about."

His gaze burned into hers. "You were with them."

"Not by choice. Though I've been angry with you for many things, I've never mocked you for anything over which you had no control."

His gaze softened. "That is true." He looked past her and then back. "I've wished to speak to you for months, but not under these circumstances."

"And I've wished to never speak to you again—but I couldn't allow such small people to have such a large say."

His lips quirked and, just like that, Dahlia found herself smiling at him. *I've missed this*, she realized with surprise.

But perhaps it shouldn't surprise her, though, for Caith Manor was so tucked away in the countryside that she'd had no friends to visit, not until she'd befriended Kirk. *And we were friends. He was my only friend, in fact.*

"Perhaps we should find a glass of champagne and watch the dancing? I've never waltzed before, and I would like to observe how it's done." She put her hand on his arm.

He looked down at her hand and covered it with his own, his fingers warm against her skin. "A glass of champagne first, then."

She waited as he signaled a footman, who instantly brought them the tray. Kirk tucked his cane under his arm, took two glasses, and then proffered his other elbow to Dahlia. She smiled at his adroit handling of so many objects and allowed him to lead her away from the watching crowd.

Lady Mary, Miss Stewart, and Lord Dalhousie watched them go. Kirk gave them a cool nod as they passed, and then he led Dahlia to a quiet spot beside an urn of palm fronds. There he handed her a glass of champagne, and then leaned his cane against the wall.

She took the glass and sipped it, curling her nose at the bubbles.

His eyes warmed with amusement. "It tickles, eh?"

"Yes. However, I'm sure that after several glasses, I shall enjoy it quite well."

"Just make certain you don't drink too many glasses at once. Champagne is a thief, and it steals your senses when you least expect it."

"I shall be cautious." She took another sip, careful not to breathe in the bubbles. "I'm sorry if I seemed to be throwing myself at you, but I couldn't allow Miss Stewart to continue."

He shrugged. "It didn't bother me."

"It bothered me. I want you to know that although I haven't forgotten our disagreement, I would never disparage you in public."

"I'd rather you did, if it would help us get over this ridiculous disagreement."

"It's not ridiculous. Your actions were unbearable."

"I was wrong to be so blunt with you, and for that, I apologize."

"At least I know your true feelings—that my family and I are both unworthy of you."

"No, no. I said it totally wrong. I—I was trying to explain that although nothing is perfect, we are so well suited that—"

"We are nothing of the kind. Lord Kirk, that's quite enough. If you continue to bring up this subject, I will be forced to leave your company."

His jaw tightened and he clamped his mouth closed, as if trying to contain words he'd regret.

An awkward silence ensued. Suddenly wishing to be gone, she sipped her champagne quickly. As soon as the glass was empty, she'd make her excuses and leave Kirk to his own devices. But in her haste, she breathed in as she raised the glass and the bubbles tickled her nose yet again. "Oh no! I'm—" She sneezed.

Instantly, a handkerchief was pressed into her hand.

She blinked down at it, seeing Kirk's initials embroidered into the border. It was a gesture her father had made to her and her sisters throughout their lives, but it wasn't something Kirk would have done so quickly or instinctively when she'd known him before. In fact, she'd once sneezed at his house while trying to open a particularly dusty book, and he'd merely watched as she ran for her reticule and found her own kerchief.

He frowned. "What is it?"

"Nothing. I'm just . . . you gave me your kerchief."

"Isn't that what a gentleman is supposed to do?"

"Yes, which is why I was surprised."

He stiffened, but after a moment, he said, "I suppose I deserve that."

"I didn't mean it to be an insult. You are who you are, but . . ." Her gaze took in his clothing and the intricate tie of his neckcloth. "You've changed."

A slight flush colored his face. "I look ridiculous, don't I? Damn it, I knew—"

"No, you look fine. Truly." Better than fine, if she were honest.

He looked down before he met her gaze. "You don't think me ridiculous?"

"Not at all. I just don't understand why you're here. You hate being around people."

"Because I dislike being stared at like a two-headed camel."

"No one likes it." She folded his kerchief and tucked it into her pocket. "I'll have this washed and will return it to you. I—"

"I'm glad to see you."

He said the words in his old abrupt manner, without the stilted politeness he'd been using. Oddly, Dahlia found herself reassured by it.

"I'm glad to see you, too." It was oddly nice seeing a truly familiar face. And she knew his face well. She knew his dark eyes that mirrored his emotions, and his rare lopsided smile that always made her smile with him.

At one time, she'd thought him a dear friend, and when they'd stopped speaking she'd told herself it was for the best, for their friendship hadn't been favored by her family.

Both of her sisters thought of Lord Kirk as ancient. He was older, of course, but as she'd come to know him, the difference hadn't seemed that great and they'd found much in common. Her only real knowledge of him came from a few months' worth of literary and musical conversations, so in many ways, he was still a mystery.

She tilted her head to one side and regarded him closely. "You look very well in your new finery."

He grimaced, but caught himself. "Thank you. You look quite fine yourself. But then, you must know that."

She had to laugh. "I don't feel especially fine among so many well-dressed women. Lily made most of my gowns with her usual consummate skill, but I don't have the jewelry or fans or slippers. I'm woefully lacking in those furbelows."

"You don't need them," he said bluntly. "You're beautiful enough without such silliness."

Her cheeks heated and she looked away. *Where had that come from?*

"I've embarrassed you. I'm sorry, but it's true. Look at the young lady by the hallway doors."

"The one in blue silk?"

"Yes. The one holding the ridiculously large fan made of ostrich feathers. She's hoping that if she waves it enough, no one will notice she hasn't read a book in almost four years. She blithely admitted it during dinner."

"Four *years*?"

"And see the woman with the red hair by the windows? The one who can't help touching that monstrous necklace every few moments?"

"It must be uncomfortably heavy."

"I daresay it is, but she is too parched of common sense to know what to do about it. She eats only potatoes in vinegar."

"She is dieting?"

"No, she saw that Lord Byron was eating such a menu and she decided to copy him in homage to his poetry."

"What do potatoes have to do with his poems?"

"Nothing. Which she would know if she'd actually understood what she was reading, but alas, she allows society to dictate her taste and not her own mind."

Dahlia looked about the room. "There are a lot of silly people here, aren't there?"

"I dare you to find two who've read Reade's *History of the Roman Empire* and can discuss it with anything close to intelligence."

Dahlia wondered if Lord Dalhousie read many books. He seemed intelligent enough. She'd ask him as soon as she was able.

She suddenly realized that Kirk had noticed where her attention had turned and he was also regarding Lord Dalhousie, his expression anything but pleasant. "That man is a fop."

"He is not. He is a very amusing, kind man, which you'd know if you'd attempt to speak to him."

"He's a damn fool." Kirk turned back to her. "Do you know why I came to the duchess's house party?"

"No. It can't be for society's sake; you hate society."

"I came to speak to you."

She blinked. "To speak to me? But . . . why? We have nothing to say."

"We have plenty to say. I've made some errors, and I'd like to repair the damage those errors have done."

"I don't wish to discuss our past."

"I do," he said in a tone that brooked no argument. "And I wish to do it now."

*And there go our new manners.* She finished her champagne and placed the glass on a nearby table. "Lord Kirk, pray excuse me, but I would like to find Lady Charlotte and ask about using the library."

"I'll escort you." He took her arm.

"No, thank you." She disengaged from his grasp. "I prefer to visit her on my own. It was pleasant speaking with you, and I must say it's gratifying to know that not everything has changed about you. Good evening and—"

"I'm not through talking, Dahlia, and neither are you."

She clamped her lips together to hold back a very unladylike retort. After a moment, she managed to say, "You cannot tell me when I'm through talking and when I'm not."

"Like hell I can't. I came all this way, learned all of these societal rules, just to speak with you. You cannot just walk away."

"Yes, I can. I didn't ask you to go to those extensive lengths, my lord, so don't hold that up as a weapon to cudgel me into a conversation. We can be civil acquaintances while we're here at her grace's house party, but I have no wish to reclaim the friendship we once had."

"But I—"

"No. Now if you'll excuse me, I'll say good-bye and—"

His hand closed over her wrist and, without ceremony, he grabbed his cane and pulled her to the nearby doorway.

Dahlia was left with two choices. She could go with him and spare them both the embarrassment of a public fight, or she could dig in her heels and make a scene. It was tempting to try the latter, but although she was furious with his high-handed ways, she was also aware of the critical gazes that followed them, especially those of Lady Mary and Miss Stewart.

Infuriated, she put on a smile and placed her hand over his to make it seem as if they were merely walking into the foyer together under the watchful eyes of the duchess's servants.

As soon as they were out of sight of the other guests, she yanked her arm free. "Look here, Kirk, you can't—"

"Hold a moment." He turned to the two footmen who stood at attention at either side of the doorway. "We need a few moments alone."

The footmen exchanged wide glances. One of them gulped. "Me lor', shall I fetch Mr. MacDougal fer ye?"

"You will fetch no one. Leave the hall for ten minutes. You may come back then. If you do so, I shall reward you each with a guinea."

The footmen exchanged glances and, with a bow, left.

Dahlia, her arms crossed, her toe tapping impatiently, turned to Kirk the second they were alone. "Who do you think you are, forcing me to leave the salon in such a manner?"

"I want to know something." He stuck his cane into the gold umbrella stand that sat to one side of the great doors. "Why did you accept the duchess's invitation?"

"That's none of your business."

"Like hell it isn't."

Good God, how had she allowed her sense of righting an injustice overcome her good sense in having nothing to do with this man ever again? "You are *so* high-handed."

"And you are so stubborn." His gaze flickered over her. "Sadly for me, you appear to great advantage when you're angry."

"You are the most—" She blinked. "I beg your pardon, but what did you just say?"

To her surprise, a grin glinted in his eyes. "Your cheeks flush, and your eyes sparkle. It always makes me wish to kiss you."

She opened her mouth and then closed it. In all of her dealings with Lord Kirk, he'd never once tried to kiss her. "You're just trying to throw me off balance so I won't argue with you."

"If I wished that, I'd merely agree with you. That's all you really want, isn't it?" He grinned, his arms crossed over his chest. "For me to agree with you?"

Her anger instantly began to melt. He was just so handsome when he smiled that way. *Thank God he doesn't do it often.*

Calmer now, she supposed it wouldn't hurt to tell him her plans. Perhaps it would settle this awkwardness between them. "I'm here because I wish to fall in love."

Whatever he'd expected her to say, that apparently wasn't it, for his smile disappeared. "I find it disappointing that a woman of your intelligence believes in such mishmosh."

"Well, I do believe in it. And I asked my godmother to help me, too. Why did you think I'd come?"

"To contract a marriage."

"That's the same thing."

"Hardly. Do you think most of the married couples we saw at the table tonight married for love? If even two of them did, I'd be surprised."

"I don't care about them; I decide my own path. I've no need to marry for money, as my sisters have graciously seen to my dowry. But I want love. I've always wanted love."

He rubbed his scar. "And I want compatibility, peace, and someone who enjoys the books and music that I do."

"I want that, too—but in addition, I want passion." She spread her hands. "Don't you want that, too?"

"Passion is for fools and youth. I've had passion."

"Well, I haven't. But before I leave the duchess's house, I hope to have found it."

"Damn it, Dahlia, you can't just look for love. It has to find you. And when it does, you'll realize that it's a fool's game. It is the opposite of peacefulness and happiness."

"You are so cynical! I don't know how I ever imagined that you could overcome that hard heart of yours, but I clearly see that you cannot."

Kirk scowled. "You don't know me."

"And you don't know me. You think you do, and you think a few months of conversations has given you some sort of right over my future—when it hasn't."

Somehow during their argument, she'd closed the distance between them and they were now standing almost toe to toe, her finger poking his chest with every word she uttered. "You listen to me, Lord Kirk, you with your sour disposition and your cynical determination to spoil the idea of romance—I *will* and *shall* find it on my own."

"You're headed for heartbreak. I only want to spare you—"

"I don't *need* you to spare me. I'm a grown woman."

Kirk could have disputed her on that one, but he wisely held his tongue.

"And I am here to find love"—she poked his chest—"and romance"—she poked again—"and passion! And you will *not* interfere with that. You will cease tossing your depressing predictions in my path and *leave me alone.* Do you understand?"

He had never seen her so animated. Her skin was flushed, her eyes sparkling with—yes, passion. But it was her mouth that suddenly held his gaze. Had it always been so plump and full? Why hadn't he noticed before, when they'd been discussing Homer and Bach?

And was it good that he was now noticing it? Or was it a sign that he should leave well enough alone before this relationship became complicated and difficult and too painful to bear?

In the midst of his thoughts his hands went to her waist, and without consciously making the decision, Kirk yanked Dahlia to him and kissed her.

# Six

**From the Diary of the Duchess of Roxburghe**
Something happened between Lord Kirk and Miss Balfour last night after dinner. What, I do not know, for neither of them will admit a thing—which is frustrating, to say the least. I feel quite slighted that neither will confide in me.

But I'm not the only one who has noticed the change between these two. Although deeply involved in a new novel written by that wretched Maria Clerey (who seems to have nothing to do but pen novel after novel after novel until I could scream), even Charlotte has noticed that Kirk and Miss Balfour look at each other differently.

I find this most promising.

I think.

Oh, I do wish *someone* would talk to me!

The second his lips touched Dahlia's, Kirk was lost. She fit into his arms as if made to be there, her lips soft and pliant under his. God, but she was delicious, ripe and plump and ready to be tasted. Instantly his cock hardened and, with a moan, he pulled her closer.

She rose up on her toes, flung her arms about his neck, and—to his utter surprise—smashed her lips against his, placing all of her weight on his neck.

Pain stabbed his knee and lip at one and the same time. He released her and staggered as he yelled, one hand grabbing his throbbing knee, the other covering his bruised mouth. *Damn it all!* He limped out of her reach, glaring at her.

Her face flooded with color, her eyes wide.

He pulled his hand from his mouth, noting the blood dotting his fingers. "What in the hell was that?"

Dahlia had to gasp to keep from weeping. She clasped her hands together, her heart slowing to a sick thud. "I—I—" She didn't know what to say. Blood seeped from his bottom lip, and he was limping, too, grimacing when his weight rested on his leg. *Good God, I've almost killed the man.* "Your lip is bleeding."

"Of course it's bleeding," he snapped. "You jammed your mouth against mine as if you were a starving hermit and I was a sugar cake. Blast it, woman, who taught you to kiss?"

Dahlia's face felt as if it might burst into flames. "I'm sorry. I didn't mean to hurt you." In the thousands of times she'd imagined her first kiss, she'd never once worried about injuring her partner. Fighting rising tears, she managed to gulp out, "I don't know how that happened. I just . . . reacted."

He touched his lip gingerly. "You've split my lip.

You didn't do my knee any favors, either. Good God, what were you trying to do?"

"That's— I wasn't— I—I—I—" She covered her face and turned away.

Kirk saw her face an instant before she turned, his irritation fleeing before the tears that spiked her long lashes. "Dahlia, don't—"

"No! I—I didn't want to kiss you, anyway!"

His sense of irony made him shake his head. "I find that hard to believe."

"*Oh!*" She grasped her skirts and whirled toward the salon.

"Dahlia, don't—" He grabbed her arm and held her in place. "Please. Just listen. I didn't mean to hurt your feelings."

"You didn't. The kiss—even talking to you—has been a mistake." She jerked her arm free, her cheeks stained with a deep blush. "I'm returning to the salon."

Kirk caught her arm again. "No."

She sent a pointed look at the place where his hand encircled her arm.

He ground his teeth and released her. "Dahlia, please. Be reasonable—"

"*Reasonable?* Since when have I been anything else? *You're* the one who is overreacting!"

"Me? I'm not the one stomping my foot."

"That's only because you can't, or it would hurt your knee. Now, I'm going back into the salon. I shouldn't be here alone with you, anyway. Someone could come along at any minute."

"No one is coming along, and if they did, the door is wide open. Besides, the music just started and they'll all be dancing."

"Which is what I want to be doing, too."

He regarded her somberly. "You want to dance."

"What woman wouldn't want to be swept about a ballroom in the arms of a graceful man?"

He looked down at his injured leg. "I will never be able to dance."

For a second her expression softened, but apparently the memory of their kiss flooded back, for she flushed and then her gaze hardened yet again. "I think we've injured each other enough for one evening, Lord Kirk. I'm returning to the salon."

"Wait. Dahlia, that kiss. It should never have happened like that. I take full responsibility for it. I thought you were more experienced and—"

"Oh! So you thought I was 'experienced'?"

"No, no. I didn't mean it that way. I just—" He rubbed his temple where an ache was building. *Good God, how do I keep getting myself into these situations?*

Her chin couldn't be held any higher. "The kiss was a mistake and should never have happened. I would appreciate it if you forgot it, which is what I intend to do."

"Dahlia, you took me by surprise, so I wasn't braced for your full weight and—"

"My *full* weight?" She couldn't stand any stiffer if she'd been a plank of wood.

"No, no," he said hastily, cursing his unwieldy

tongue. "I just meant I wasn't prepared to lift something as heavy as—"

"*Oh!*"

"No, no! As heavy as *a person.* That's what I was going to say!"

"Humph. Whatever you were going to say, let me assure you that I will never, ever kiss you again. *Ever!*" Her voice was as icy as morning frost. "And while you're cowering in the corner, afraid someone might attempt to kiss you again when you're 'not ready,' I'll be in the salon dancing with every man who will ask me—because *that* is why I came to the duchess's. For romance, Kirk. I came here to experience a grand passion, to kiss someone who won't cringe when I do so, and to dance until I can't dance anymore—all of which I shall do without you!" With that, she marched back into the salon, her back stiff with disapproval.

Kirk glared at the empty door, rubbing his throbbing knee. Bloody hell, could he have handled that any worse? He didn't think so. But good God, she hadn't given him a chance! Now she was so angry . . . how did one speak to a furious woman, anyway? Was there a right way? Things were so complicated, so—

A cough sounded behind him and he turned to find the two footmen had returned. They were both staring straight ahead, their expressions impassive.

"How long have you been there?"

"We jus' returned, me lor'," said one.

Kirk realized that the man was discreetly holding out his hand, palm up. Scowling, Kirk dug into his pocket and grabbed the coins he found there and dropped them into the man's waiting hand. "Split that between you."

The footman glanced at his palm and then gulped, his eyes widening. "Me lor', tha' is far too much—"

"Keep it."

"But me lor', 'tis—"

"Damn it, must *everyone* argue with me? Keep the damn coins. I don't want them." And with that, cane clutched in his hand, his temper boiling over, Kirk made his way to the stairs and limped his way to his bedchamber.

Kirk slammed the door and tossed his cane into the corner. The cane bounced off the wall, hit the rug, and then rolled under the bed.

From where he stood just inside the water closet, MacCreedy stopped adding bath salts to the large copper tub that occupied one corner and peered into the room. He eyed the cane where it was partially hidden under the bed. "Tha' is no a guid sign."

"Pack my bags. There's no use in my staying a moment more."

The valet's bushy brows rose. "Did some'at happen, me lor'?"

"It was a horrid mess. The whole damn night was an unmitigated disaster. *All* of it."

MacCreedy nodded thoughtfully and added a touch more of the salts to the bath before replacing the container on a small table under the window.

"Did you hear me?"

"Och, indeed, I did, bu' I canno' see the benefit in wastin' guid hot water. Can ye?"

The bath did look inviting, and the throbbing in his knee seemed to be growing by the moment. "Fine. We'll stay tonight. But we're leaving first thing in the morning."

"O' course we will, me lor'."

Too angry to sit still yet, even in a hot bath, Kirk limped to the window and leaned against the frame, staring outside with unseeing eyes. He rubbed his chest, where a dull ache seemed to have settled. It felt as if his heart had been stabbed—and it had been, by his own stubborn foolishness.

"Ye look as if ye've lost yer last friend."

Kirk's throat tightened. In some ways, Dahlia seemed as if she were exactly that—his last friend. *Bloody hell, when had* that *happened?*

"May I ask wha' occurred? Surely it canno' be so bad as ye think it."

"Whatever you might imagine, it was worse."

"Ye knocked a candle o'er on Miss Balfour and set her afire," MacCreedy said without hesitation. "And she, panicky like a rabbit, ran outdoors and down the drive, ne'er to be seen again."

Kirk gave a bark of laughter, his despair fading a bit. "Fine. That would have been worse."

"There ye go. Wha'ever happened, so long as it wasna' a fire and she dinna' run away, then we can repair it."

"Not this, I fear. I made the gravest of all errors."

"And wha' was tha', me lor'?"

"I kissed Miss Balfour."

MacCreedy looked impressed. "Did ye now? And how is tha' an error?"

"It's an error when she threw herself upon my neck and nearly strangled me, and bloodied my lip in the process."

The valet chuckled. "Enthusiastic, were she? I'd say tha' was a guid thing."

"Yes, but during her kiss, I not only yelled in pain, for both my lip and knee were afire, but I—" God, he hated to say it aloud.

"Ye?" MacCreedy prompted.

"I asked her what in the hell she thought she was doing. And then, as if that wasn't enough, I pushed her away."

The valet winced. "Och, tha' might well be as bad as a fire."

"I warned you. I didn't mean it, of course, for I was pleased she'd welcomed my kiss. I truly was."

"O' course ye were."

"But she took me by surprise, and my knee twisted and it felt as if knives were being shoved into it, and then she banged her mouth into mine and split my lip, and so—" Kirk absently touched his swollen lip. "Damn my temper. It shall be the death of me yet."

"When ye explain all tha' happened, 'tis no wonder tha' ye reacted poorly."

"Yes, well, explain that to Miss Balfour, for she

wouldn't hear a word from me afterward. And frankly, I don't blame her. Bloody hell, the whole thing was horrible."

Kirk couldn't bring himself to mention the hurt he'd seen in her eyes. That had been the worst part. "I ruined everything, MacCreedy. There's no chance now." His voice was as bleak as his heart. *Damn it all, why can't I learn to speak with more gentleness? I want to be kind to her, but I can't seem to find the way to be so.* "She would be right to never speak to me again."

Sighing, Kirk looked out into the dark courtyard. It was pitch-black, lit by only a faint yellow streak that escaped from a window hither and yon, yet it was no darker than his spirit.

"And the miss, me lor'? Did she say she ne'er wished to speak to ye again?"

"Among other things, yes." Kirk turned from the darkness and made his way to the fire, limping heavily. Once there, he added some wood to the flickering flames. "The entire conversation was a wretched display of my temper, and her reaction to it. I did, however, receive some clear direction from Miss Balfour. She was very forthcoming about her intentions in attending this house party; she is here for one reason and one reason only—to find romance, and I'm not to interfere with her plans."

"Did she tell ye all o' this after ye rejected her?"

"I didn't reject her."

MacCreedy's thick white brows rose.

Kirk flushed. "I'm sure it seemed to her as if I did,

but it's not how I intended it. Damn it all, I'd pay good money for another kiss from her!"

"Ye'd pay?"

"Yes, not that she'd accept it or— Damn it, that's not the point. The point is that although I *sounded* and *looked* as if I were rejecting her, I was doing no such thing. I was merely in pain. That's all."

"Aye, me lor'. 'Tis interestin' tha' she announced why she's here, after ye said wha' ye did."

"'Interesting' isn't the word I'd use. Her words brought me to a standstill, for I can't offer her what she wants."

"No?"

"No. I wish I could, but it's not in me. I find such silliness abhorrent and, damn it, she knows that. She wishes to meet someone who will sweep her off her feet, recite poems, bring her flowers, swirl her across the dance floor—I can do none of those things. I've never written a poem in my life. I suppose I could bring her flowers, but I can't dance with this weak leg and— Damn it, it's just not possible."

"Och, dinna say so." The valet tested the heat of the huge tub and then returned to the bedchamber, where he placed a towel over a chair near the fire to warm. "I doubt things are as bad as ye think."

"I find that difficult to believe." Kirk undid his cravat and threw it on the bed. "At least now I can get out of these ridiculous clothes."

"There ye are, me lor'. Find the bright side o' it. Why dinna ye take yer bath and ha' a nice think whilst ye soak yer leg. Wellington used to say a guid bath was the best place fer strategizin', and it seems tha' is exactly wha' ye need to be doin'."

Kirk tugged his shirt over his head. "Strategy? You talk as if the entire thing were a chess game."

"Och, no. 'Tis no' a chess game but a war, me lor', the oldest war known to man: the one betwixt the sexes."

"At this point, it feels more like a very long, very difficult chore, like mucking out the stables—after the horse has kicked one in the teeth." Kirk sat on the edge of the bed and tugged off his shoes.

The valet chuckled quietly. "I daresay it do. But ye've come this far, me lor'. It'd be sad to quit now."

To be honest, as much as Kirk wanted to pack up his belongings and go back to his peaceful existence at Fordyce Castle, he was quite aware that he couldn't—and damn well wouldn't—walk away. If he did, it would leave Dahlia in a castle full of potential suitors. Just this evening, he'd noticed the way that fool—Dallon? Dalton? Something with a "D"—had been ogling Dahlia when Kirk had approached her in the salon before their argument.

While Kirk didn't care for romance, he understood passion very well and there could be no mistaking the purely physical interest in the callow youth's eyes. *I'll be damned if I leave Dahlia alone to be taken advantage of by such fools and gapeseeds. She's never properly chaperoned, which is something I should discuss with the duchess.*

He tossed his shirt aside and stepped out of his breeches, and limped to where the hot water beckoned.

MacCreedy chuckled when Kirk sighed happily on slipping into the scented water. "Better already, eh?"

"Some." Kirk liked the big tub, which was longer than the one he had at Fordyce Castle. The warm water eased the pain in his knee, although it did nothing to help him stop thinking about Dahlia and his predicament.

He leaned his head against the headrest and slid down until the water covered his shoulders. How could he fix things between them? And while it was certainly true that the duchess wasn't chaperoning Dahlia sufficiently, now that he thought about it, he might be the one to suffer if he mentioned it.

No, better to leave things as they were, but take charge of her chaperonage himself. He'd have to be subtle, but it could be done.

Of course, none of that addressed the real problem—which was how to overcome the breach that had arisen between them after that damned kiss. He didn't even know where to start. He rubbed water over his face and brushed his hair from his forehead. "Women are indecipherable."

"Tha' they are. Some more tha' others." The valet sent him a curious look. "Ye were married afore, were ye no', me lor'? Did ye learn somethin' of value fro' tha'?"

"No, Elspeth was very different from Dahlia. And

so was I, back then. We married young—too young. Because of that, we were both given to drama, and our relationship, while based on love, was stormy."

"Tha' can wear a body oot."

"Yes, it can. Fortunately, I'm far too old for such silliness now."

"So ye dinna think Miss Balfour the type given to drama."

"I know she's not. Or I thought she wasn't." He frowned. "I always knew she had a proclivity toward romance, but a normal amount, not this grand"—he threw out an arm—"whatever it is."

"I dinna know a woman no' given to romance."

"Perhaps it was naïve of me to think her different. I just . . ." He struggled to find the words. Finally he said, "There's a peaceful quality to Dahlia, a spirit that's at ease when all is quiet. It makes being with her very easy." And a complete delight. "Elspeth was never that way."

"Bu' it dinna cause ye problems?"

"I loved Elspeth very much, so I suppose I didn't mind her dramatics the way I would now." He thought about this. "But I'm quite different now, too, especially since the accident."

"When ye lost yer wife." MacCreedy collected Kirk's discarded cravat from the bed. "Mayhap ye dislike the drama now because it reminds ye o' yer first wife and the pain o' losin' her?"

Was that it? Was emotion distasteful to him now because it reminded him of Elspeth, and for so long, he'd wished to think of anything *but* her? "I suppose it's possible that at one time my dislike of this romance nonsense was because it reminded me of Elspeth, but now . . ." He considered his life, and the things he loved. "Now I think I'm simply too used to my own company and my own ways to go back to that silliness."

"Och, 'tis bad to become too used to yer own ways. Ye need people about ye, and tha' means compromise, or ye'll ha' a sad and lonely life."

That was true. He *had* been lonely, and hadn't even realized it. After the pain of Elspeth's death, and brought low by his physical wounds, it had taken him years to overcome his own despair. Later, however, having immersed himself in his books and music, and having accepted his scar and limp and all that came with them, he'd finally found peace and had been satisfied with his life.

Or he had been, until Miss Dahlia Balfour had appeared. After her visits, he'd found himself enjoying her refreshing look at life, the way she passionately delved into every book she read, her bold honesty and all that went with it. Soon he found himself missing her when she wasn't present, thinking about her constantly, and—eventually—admitting he wanted her in his life.

After their argument over his well-meaning but ill-worded marriage proposal and her subsequent refusal to speak to him again, he'd missed her far, far more than he'd expected.

He sighed and idly picked up the soap from where MacCreedy had placed it beside the tub. "Miss Balfour is not your average female. She's a woman of considerable intellect and curiosity, and yet—as contrary as it seems—when it comes to courtship, she apparently possesses a strong nonsensical streak." He soaped the wet cloth, his mind now thoroughly engaged in the trouble at hand. "That's where I made my error before, not recognizing that shortcoming."

"If tha' is a shortcomin', then all of the females o' the world and half o' the males share it."

"Bloody hell, I hope not," Kirk growled. "I hope her madness—for I can call it little else—will resolve itself once our courtship has concluded."

MacCreedy didn't look convinced. "I dinna think tha' will be enou'."

"It will have to be. I shall capitulate long enough to give Dahlia the romance that she wishes—or what I'm able to stomach, anyway—during the courtship phase. Once that's done and we're wed, we can then return to a less dramatic and far more peaceful manner of living."

MacCreedy shook his head. "Lor' love ye, bu' ye dinna know much aboot women."

"I know Miss Balfour, and that is enough."

The valet rubbed his chin, a thoughtful look in his eyes. "She do seem to be a sharp one, I'll give ye tha'. Jus' look wha' she's done already. She had ye turnin' sail and runnin' fra' port wit'oot firin' so much as a shot."

"Oh, she fired a shot. Several, in fact." One of those shots had been her kiss, right before it had gone so horribly awry. There had been one blissful moment when her lips had been soft and pliant under his, so sweet and so innocent . . . a flush of heat wracked him. *I must have her. And if I leave now, some other man will enjoy her kisses, damn it all.* His jaw firmed. "But no matter what, I must stay and fight."

MacCreedy beamed. "Tha' is the spirit!" He collected the rest of Kirk's tossed-aside clothing and carried it to the wardrobe. "The only question now is how."

"You were right before; I shall need a strategy of some sort. One that will win the war and not just one battle. My goal is for Miss Balfour to surrender, completely and without hesitation."

"Now ye sound like his grace." MacCreedy nodded his approval. "The duke would tell ye to plan yer campaign fer the long run, one peppered with encounters and battles, all leadin' to the ultimate victory o'er yer enemy."

Kirk quirked a brow at the valet. "Miss Balfour being the enemy."

"In a manner o' speakin', she is. She's an enemy to ye havin' a day o' peace."

"Sadly, that is true. She does break up my peace." *And stirs my blood.* Before he'd come to the duchess's house party, he'd convinced himself that what he felt for Dahlia was practical, and that it had nothing to do with passion. *I was lying to myself. I want her in my house, and in my bed. Especially in my bed. And that kiss proved it.* "She's both enemy and prize."

"Exactly, me lor'." MacCreedy hung up the coat and waistcoat in the wardrobe. Then he dropped the shirt and neckcloth in a neat pile beside the door to be taken downstairs for washing.

Kirk leaned back in the tub. "So the question is, what do I do next?"

The valet picked up Kirk's boots, collected a small can and a soft white rag from a small box in the bottom of the wardrobe, and sat on a stool beside the fireplace, where he could easily see the tub. "If ye were the king o' a country and ye wished another country t' submit t' ye, what would ye do?"

"I would offer a treaty of some sort—a cease-fire so that we could converse without fuming and fighting."

"Tha' is the spirit, me lor'." MacCreedy opened the small canister and dipped the rag into it and began polishing the boots. "An' wha' would ye offer to entice such a lovely hostile nation t' put down her arms and allow ye o'er the border?"

Kirk considered this as he washed his arms. Finally, he nodded. "Food."

MacCreedy blinked. "Food?"

"Something she—the other nation, I mean—likes, but cannot find. Like pears. She loves pears."

"Och, the duchess loves pears herself, so ye'll see them at many meals here at Floors."

"Damn. They will not be special, then." Kirk considered what he knew of Dahlia. "I'd planned on giving her the books you purchased in town. She'll enjoy those, although there are only three."

"Surely three is enou' to begin wit'."

"No. I want her to know that I'm serious about this endeavor. Three books will not be enough. We've been at war for months. I want my first endeavor to carry some weight."

MacCreedy polished the boot's toe. "Fra' wha' little I know of women—and 'tis a monstrous lil' amount—they like it when ye do something as shows a bit o' effort."

"Effort, eh?"

"Aye. Perhaps if ye add tha' to the books, then ye'll ha' somethin' worth offerin' fer a treaty."

"But what sort of effort? I can hardly show her my skill at chess or backgammon, and I damned well am not able to write a poem, though the duchess thinks that all one needs is a pen and an idle hour."

"Perhaps ye can read Miss Balfour a poem, since ye dinna write them. Ye've a fine voice."

Now, *that* idea held some promise. He used to read to Dahlia when she visited him and she'd always seemed to enjoy it, so that wouldn't be difficult at all. "To make it even better, I would read her some of the poetry she's so mad for."

"Do ye know her favorites?"

"Yes. I'll have to pretend I enjoy them, though, which will be difficult."

"Which is why 'tis an effort, me lor'." The valet dipped the rag back into the blacking mixture. "Och, a

poem along wit' those three verrah expensive books—
how can she say no to tha'?"

Kirk grinned, but then winced and touched his
bottom lip. "Someone needs to teach that woman
how to kiss." *And who else should do that?* "Hmmm.
That would take some effort, too."

MacCreedy chuckled. "Ye think ye can convince
her to let ye do tha'?"

"Perhaps. It'll be tricky, for I can't just walk up to
her and announce, 'You don't know how to kiss, but I
can show you.'"

"Tha' does sound a wee bit off-puttin'."

"More than a wee bit. I've already insulted her
once. She won't be happy if I do so again."

They were silent a moment, and then the valet said
in a cheery voice, "I'm certain ye'll find a way, me lor'."

"I'm so glad you feel that way," Kirk said in a dry
tone.

"Och, I know ye will find a way, fer if ye dinna teach
Miss Balfour how to kiss, 'tis highly likely someone
else mi' do it fer ye." The valet caught Kirk's expression and threw up a hand. "Dinna look so! I'm only
tellin' ye the truth."

Kirk growled, and then held his breath and
plunged underwater. When he came up a moment
later, he pushed his hair from his face and reached for
the soap. "*I* will teach her how to kiss."

"Tha' is verrah wise o' ye, me lor'." MacCreedy
finished polishing one boot and set it before the fire
before he picked up its mate. "'Tis a pity ye canno'

find it in yerself to answer some o' her other wishes. Mayhap I can write some poetry fer ye."

"Can you write poetry? *Good* poetry?"

The valet pursed his lips. After a moment, he asked, "Wha' rhymes wit' 'raven tresses'?"

"Pink dresses."

MacCreedy beamed. "There ye go, then! There once was a lass name Balfour, who——"

"No. And her hair's brown mingled with golden, not raven."

"'Tis more dramatic as 'raven.'"

"I think I prefer your previous plan where I just read some of her favorite verses, hopefully without laughing aloud." Kirk rinsed the soap from his hair. As he straightened, his placed his feet against the tub to stabilize himself. Instantly, ice-hot pain shot through his calf to his knee.

MacCreedy tsked. "'Tis yer leg?"

Kirk nodded, willing the pain away. Slowly, it subsided, assisted by the warm water. He rubbed his shin, eyeing the thick, ropey scar. "MacCreedy, you said you could help my leg? Make it more flexible?"

"Aye. Yer injury is like many o' the grievous wounds caused by cannon injuries tha' I saw in Spain. When ye were hurt, yer muscles drew up, tryin' to protect the ones as weren't injured. When ye returned home, yer leg pained ye when ye used it, so ye dinna move yer leg. So all o' yer muscles lost their strength, e'en the healthy ones."

"My physician warned me not to use my leg. He

said the muscles were weak and should never be taxed."

"Aye, whilst they were healin'. But ye didna stretch yer muscles back oot after they'd healed, so they stayed short and tight. And now they dinna remember wha' 'tis like to be healthy."

"Damn my physician."

The valet shrugged. "If he dinna work wit' war wounds, then he had no way o' knowin'."

"I suppose so." Kirk propped his leg on the side of the tub and glared at the red scar that traveled from his calf, around his shin, to end at his knee. "What if I exercise it now?"

"As it's been a while, 'twill hurt like ye've ne'er hurt before, but wit' time, the muscles will stretch and strengthen again."

"How long would it take?"

"To get back to full strength? A full year, mayhap more."

"What can you do in two and a half weeks? Before the duchess's Christmas Ball?"

MacCreedy whistled. "'Tha' is no' much time." He looked at the injured leg thoughtfully. "Bu' ye walk a good bit, so there still be good muscle. If ye worked hard, ye would see a difference in those two weeks."

"Could I go without the cane? I can walk short distances now, but my knee gives out and I fall."

"We can strengthen tha' muscle, we can." He nodded. "Ye should be able to leave yer cane behind."

"And I'll have more mobility?"

"Tha' ye will. Wit' time ye'll be able to do many things ye canno' do now. Ye could ride, hunt, and stride aboot like anyone else. Ye may limp, but no' much, and eventually e'en tha' may disappear." MacCreedy put the second boot before the fire with its mate and closed the can before he regarded his employer with a long, level look. "Fer quick results, ye'd ha' to work hard, ye would."

"I'm willing."

"E'ery day wi'oot fail."

"Of course."

"It'll hurt 'til ye think 'tis afire."

"Damn it, stop trying to talk me out of it. We'll start in the morning." When MacCreedy didn't answer, Kirk added firmly, "At dawn."

The valet grinned and stood. "Tomorrow 'twill be a loverly day fer war."

"It had better be, for a major campaign has just begun." And he wouldn't stop until Dahlia was his.

*Seven*

**From the Diary of the Duchess of Roxburghe**

It has been two days since Kirk and Miss Balfour stopped speaking to one another, and I still haven't found out why. After dinner last night, desperate to discover the true state of affairs, I even attempted to pull Miss Balfour aside and speak with her. But Lord Dalhousie would not give up his position at her side, so the effort was a total loss.

I suppose I should be glad of that, but while he's an acceptable *parti*, he's not Lord Kirk. Furthermore, the viscount's presence did nothing to satisfy my growing curiosity.

Humph.

Dahlia paused on the crest of the hill, glancing up at the sun where it hid behind the clouds, well above the horizon. The sun had barely been up when she'd slipped from her warm bed, so she surmised that she'd been walking well over an hour, perhaps even two.

The chilly wind tugged her hair free from the brim

of her bonnet, sending a loose curl across her cheek. She shoved the thick strand back into her bonnet and wished she'd pinned her hair more securely. The wind was stronger now than when she'd left the castle, strong enough to stir her skirts even though they were weighted down by a wet and muddied hem.

She shivered and rubbed her arms, and then tucked her mittened hands back into her pockets and walked down the hill toward the castle. Though it was quickly getting too cold for comfort, she'd needed this walk. An endless circle of painful, cringe-worthy thoughts and half-remembered dreams had shoved her from her warm bed at dawn, bundled her into her best wool walking dress and thick woolen coat, and hurried her out of the castle as if pursued. She'd stopped in the kitchen only long enough to tuck a biscuit in her pocket before she'd hurried off, walking as fast as she could without actually running.

But try as she might, it was impossible to run away from her own thoughts. Ever since her unfortunate kiss with Kirk, she'd been unable to stop thinking about that moment, restlessly going back and forth between all the painful memories she wished to forget: the anger in his eyes, the pain when their mouths had bumped, the harsh words they'd exchanged. Yet like a moth to a flame, she found herself reliving the moment over and over.

*Why, oh why, did I kiss him?* she asked herself yet again. She'd never wished more that the ground would open up and swallow her whole than at that moment.

Her first kiss, and she'd ruined it. *He must think me every kind of an awkward fool.*

The thought burned, yet she couldn't stop rethinking it. Before Kirk had botched things up with his horrid proposal, she'd enjoyed his company and had grown to value his opinions. During her visits to his library, they'd discussed books and authors, politics and religion, culture and history—he knew something about almost every topic. Over the course of those discussions she'd come to respect him and his intellect, which was why it had hurt so much to discover his low opinion of her and her family. His arrogance should have killed her growing feelings for him, but her reaction to their botched kiss had made her realize that, ludicrous though it was, she still cared what he thought.

The whole episode made her angry: she was angry with Kirk for being so ill-tempered and rude, and she was angry with herself for allowing her inexperience to show so clearly. *What he must think of me*— She grimaced. *Oh, just stop thinking about it! Just. Stop.*

But she couldn't.

She'd had a glorious walk over the green hills and through the yellowed leaves, the ground spongy and fragrant, but although she was now chilled and pleasantly tired, it still wasn't enough to quiet her thoughts. Scowling, she hurried on, tucking her chin down so that her coat collar provided some shelter from the wind.

Perhaps the reason she cared about Kirk's opinion wasn't because of some hidden morass of feelings, which was a ridiculous idea, but because of something far simpler. She knew him better than anyone else at Floors Castle, so in a way, perhaps he represented home.

She paused on the pathway and considered this. That actually made sense. *Finally, a thought that is helpful! I should also remember that, despite his ridiculous reaction, I didn't permanently maim the poor man, either.*

For her imagination had gone that far and beyond. She'd actually been relieved when he'd come limping into the foyer on his way to the breakfast room the following morning, looking only slightly the worse for wear. True, his lip was slightly swollen, and she saw him wince when he sipped some orange juice, but other than that, his limp was no worse than usual, nor did he appear with a black eye or any other horrifying mark from their kiss.

The true tragedy was that the kiss, so wretched and imperfect and horrid, had been her first kiss ever. She'd dreamed about that first kiss, and yearned for it, imagining every moment to be perfect, lovely, and breathlessly sweet. Never once, in the thousands of times she'd imagined it, had she seen herself grievously injuring the man who'd kissed her.

Dahlia grimaced and tried not to reimagine his exact expression, which seemed to be burned into her memory. *What was I thinking, to allow that kiss to begin with?* But she hadn't been thinking. Not even a little. He'd kissed her, and the last thing she could do was think, so she'd kissed him back with every drop of enthusiasm she'd possessed.

Now that she thought about it, that bothered her even more than her humiliation. *I liked his kiss. But how can that be? I don't even like* him. *He's rude and opinionated and—* She shook her head. *He's also handsome, and intelligent, and even funny when the mood strikes him. Heavens, why is this so* complicated?

The wind picked up, rustling the grass and making her shiver as it tugged at her bonnet. She hurried on down the path, glancing up at the sky. During her tramp the clouds had gathered, pushed by a growing wind, and the distinctive taste of snow was in the air. The unusual warmth they'd been blessed with during the earlier part of the week was gone, and the bite of winter nipped at her nose and cheeks.

She crossed a small rise and came up behind the castle, the beautiful sweep of lawn glistening like a discarded ribbon of green silk. On one side was a sparkling lake, topped now with small whitecaps as the wind teased it. The trees on the island were almost bare of leaves, so she could see a glimpse of a folly. Leading up to the small lake, a winding river sluggishly rolled, disappearing into a thick wood. Here and there, the duchess's army of gardeners had placed gorgeous flower beds and trees that exquisitely augmented the natural slopes.

Dahlia's gaze moved back to the castle, her trepidation returning.

She'd avoided Kirk since their unfortunate kiss,

but it was only a matter of time before he found an opportunity to speak to her. And he wished to do so; she could tell by the way he watched her. Fortunately, the duchess had planned activities for practically every minute of every day—pall-mall one afternoon, followed by a pleasant evening of whist, and a carriage ride the next afternoon to see the ruins of old Roxburghe Castle, followed by a late tea beside the maze. Although guests were encouraged to partake of only the events they'd enjoy, Dahlia had attended every one. To her surprise, Kirk had done the same, and each time seemed bent on speaking to her. She'd made certain he hadn't, though, for she had no desire to discuss something she wasn't even certain she understood.

Thankfully, Lord Dalhousie had been of assistance, too. For some reason, the young lord had attached himself to her side and Dahlia had been happy for it, as his presence offered a determent to private discussion. She tugged her coat closer and eyed the castle, which still looked majestic even under the graying sky, roiling clouds gathered over it. She supposed she should return now. Her biscuit was long gone and she wanted nothing more than to take a long, hot bath before having to rejoin the other guests.

She headed down the slope to the garden maze that decorated the expanse of lawn behind the castle. Dahlia slipped into the garden, quickly made her way down the side of the maze, and found the side gate that would allow her to reach the kitchens without passing by the main windows of the castle. Heavens knew she didn't wish to see anyone until she had time to wash and change.

She was walking past the lane that led to the stables, her head bent against the wind, when from the path before her came an all-too-familiar voice.

Deep and rich, it sent a different sort of shiver through her. "Ah, Miss Balfour. Just the person I wished to see."

She looked up, slapping a hand on her bonnet just as the wind tried to steal it. Kirk was dressed as he used to, in loose breeches and unpolished boots, a kerchief knotted about his neck. The wind tugged at his long greatcoat and mussed his dark hair, giving him a more rakish appearance than his new finery did.

She inclined her head, holding her bonnet on as best she could, the wind swaying her damp skirts against her. "Lord Kirk, how unexpected."

He bowed and then said dryly, "I'm certain that, had you known I was here, you would have used another path to reach the castle."

There was something peculiarly unpleasant about being predictable. "I'm sure I would have done no such thing," she lied.

His gaze flickered over her, lingering on her face. "You've been walking again, I see."

There was neither approval nor disapproval in his voice, but their recent encounter made her stiffen. "I always take walks. Why are you out in this weather?"

"It is cold, isn't it? I'm on my way to meet my valet."

She looked past him to the direction in which his path led. "In the stables? Why would your valet meet you there?"

Kirk gave an impatient flick of his hand. "It doesn't matter. Dahlia, I'm glad we met. I've been wanting to talk to you for two days now, but you've been avoiding me."

She started to deny it, but he lifted his brows in a silent challenge.

Dahlia flushed. "Fine. I didn't wish to speak to you after— I don't need to rehash it. You know what happened as well as I."

"Yes, but this has nothing to do with that. Well, it does, only— Dahlia, I want—" He halted midsentence as if something had occurred to him. When he spoke again, his tone was more measured and polite. "Dahlia, I find myself in a very difficult position. I find that I need your assistance."

"*My* assistance? With what?" She couldn't keep the suspicion from her voice.

"Our kiss. It was wretched."

Heat flooded her face, which said a lot considering the coldness. "Kirk, I—"

"You don't need to say anything. And it was obvious from the very first second that the fault for that kiss was mine."

"The fault . . . was . . . yours?"

"Of course it was. My impetuous behavior tromped all over the moment, and— It was inexcusable. After the fact, I pretended otherwise and blamed you—" His gaze met hers, direct and open. "But it was my fault and no one else's. I am too proud sometimes. I have suffered from that, and will continue to do so unless I find a way to overcome it."

Well, she certainly couldn't argue with him about that.

The wind whipped his hair about his head, and the silver streak at his temple, usually so distinct, mingled now with the dark brown. "I've been thinking of nothing else for two days, hating my own behavior and wishing I could redo the whole thing. There is no excuse, I know; I must take responsibility for ruining what should have been a delightful moment."

What did one say to that? "Kirk, please. There's no need to—you weren't as at fault as I was. It—it was my first kiss and I did not know how . . . things worked."

His looked appalled. "Your first kiss?" He cursed long and loud. "And I acted like— Dahlia, can you forgive me?"

"There's nothing to forgive." And yet there was, for both of them. Still, hearing him apologize and—better yet—admit that the kiss had disturbed him, too, for some reason relieved some of her own angst. "We should forget it and move ahead—"

"No. You may be able to forget it, but I cannot." He hesitated a moment, and then said, "It isn't often that moments like that arise, when a kiss is a natural event to be shared. Those moments are rare and should be treasured. And to do that"—his gaze locked with hers—"you must be prepared for those moments."

Were they rare? She hadn't thought about it, but she supposed that was true. "But how can you prepare for such a moment?"

"It's possible to learn any skill if you put your mind to it. Sadly, those same skills are perishable, too. In the years since Elspeth died, I've been alone. Very alone. And over that time, I've lost some of my skill when it comes to wooing."

Her heart gave an odd leap and she heard herself say in a stiff voice, "You . . . you wish to woo someone?"

"Of course. I had hoped that you and I might mend our fences, but I am beginning to doubt that happening. But that does not change the fact that I need a mate."

"A mate? That sounds so cold."

He shrugged. "I asked you to marry me, and you refused, so here I am. You may not have me, but perhaps I can find someone who will. Someone who also enjoys reading and music, and the things we enjoyed."

"Kirk, no. You don't have to wed. You're happy alone. You've said so many times."

"I was wrong." His gaze locked with hers. "Your visits made me realize what I've been missing. You showed me, and I foolishly allowed you to slip away."

It was the kindest thing he'd ever said to her. She had to clear her throat in order to free her voice from the tightness that held it. "That is all in the past now."

He inclined his head in agreement.

"And—and I'm sure you'll find someone to your liking. Someone better than I ever was." Although she said the words, Dahlia discovered that she wasn't nearly as happy thinking about Kirk finding a wife as she was about finding a husband for herself. At some point in time, she'd come to think of him as hers. *Stop being silly. I'm living in the past, when I'd hoped— imagined—there was something more between us.* She pasted a smile on her lips. "You said you needed my assistance with something?"

"Yes." He brushed back his hair, and she was once again reminded of his beautiful eyes. Sherry brown and surrounded by thick black lashes, they reflected his every mood like a mirror.

Right now, caution shone through his gaze. *That's odd. What does he have to be cautious about?*

"I never want to bungle a kiss like that again, so I wonder— God, this is difficult, but if you could see your way to help me, I would be grateful. Deeply so."

"Help you do what?"

"This castle is filled with people we don't know. But we know one another well. Better than anyone else here, in fact."

"True, although our relationship has hardly been genial of late."

"Because I made a stupid error. I should never have asked you to marry me."

Dahlia opened her mouth and then closed it. "Of course."

"You've no interest in me, and I should have accepted it. And then, being a prideful fool, I made things even more difficult with that damned kiss—"

He scowled as if furious with himself. "I never meant to kiss you; it just happened and I regret it."

*He regrets it?* She didn't like that, not even a little. But trust Kirk to say what he thought. She only wished it didn't affect her so. "Of course it was a mistake. *All* of it was a mistake." Perhaps. Maybe. *Oh, blast it, I don't know.*

"I was in a passion over what you said, and then you were there, and we were alone and—I lost my head. But I can promise you this—I won't succumb to an impulse like that again."

She should feel much better now. Shouldn't she? But she didn't. In fact, she felt worse. Still, she managed a frosty smile that matched the wind whipping about them. "So what do we do now?"

He smiled and limped forward and held out his hand. "Let us be friends again. Whatever happens, we should at least be that."

She looked down at his hand. He had beautiful, masculine hands, and at one time, she'd loved seeing him play the pianoforte that graced his library. *Funny, but I didn't allow myself to remember that until now.* She knew she should be glad they were moving past their argument. She had so few friends here, and knew so few people—why not?

Slowly, she placed her hand in his. Even though her fingers were covered by her gloves, the second their hands touched, a jolt went through her, stealing her breath and making her knees tremble faintly. *What is* that? she wondered.

Kirk seemed completely unaffected. He shook her hand in a brisk, friendly fashion, and then released it. "There. Friends again. That wasn't too difficult, was it?"

Dahlia had to swallow before she could answer. "No. Not a bit." She felt deeply cheated in some way. As if in reacting so instantly to his touch, while he seemed completely unaffected, he'd stolen something from her.

His dark gaze met hers and in their depths, she saw the reaction she'd missed before. There was a tightness, too, to his jaw. *Ah, so you're just better at hiding it.* A satisfied warmth made her smile. "Of course we're friends. What else could we be?"

She'd said the words to challenge him to . . . Well, she didn't know *what* she wanted from him, but she found herself wishing that he'd express some of the heat she saw in his eyes.

Instead, he inclined his head and said in an almost formal manner, "Good. For, as a friend, that leaves me free to ask a favor."

There were times she lamented his new politeness. It veiled so much. She forced herself to smile and say just as politely, "Of course."

He regarded her somberly, although she detected the hint of a twinkle deep in his eyes. "Dahlia, my one and only friend, will you protect me, a poor widower with no prospects, from embarrassing myself again?"

She blinked. "I'm sorry, but how am I to do that?"

"Before I throw myself into finding another mate,

I must relearn how to kiss. And you could help me do that."

She opened her mouth, and then closed it. *Surely he hadn't just said—*

He laughed, his face crinkling with amusement. His scar, though bold and wide, must not have been a deep wound, for his smile was perfectly normal and transformed his face, softening the hard lines and making him seem younger, almost carefree. "You should see your expression." His voice was rich with laughter. "I couldn't have shocked you more."

"No, you couldn't have. I am beyond bemused."

"I will explain. If I'm to find a bride, then my next kiss—unlike the one we shared, which was just between friends, after all—will be of the utmost importance. The next kiss could possibly convince my bride to accept my offer." He looked at her expectantly. "I daresay you've thought the same thing about your next kiss, as well."

Her throat tightened. Actually, she'd been too busy wondering what horrible things Kirk must be thinking about their kiss to consider what might happen next, but she supposed he had a point. Sooner or later, someone would try to kiss her again, and it might be someone she wished to impress. What if her awkwardness chased the next man off, and he was one she hoped to marry? *Good God, am I doomed by my own ineptitude to never have a decent, romantic kiss—or relationship? Ever?*

She realized that he was closely watching her and she tried to smile, and failed.

"You hadn't thought about it, had you?"

She shook her head. "Not yet, but now that you mention it . . . Oh dear."

"Yes. And there will be another kiss. If not from me, then from someone else."

His voice sharpened at the last phrase and she sent him a questioning look. Quickly, he said, "And so we must help one another. Together, when no one is around, we must work on our technique."

"Work on our . . . There's a technique to kissing?"

He slanted her the most wicked of grins, which made her heart pound even harder in her chest. Suddenly, the day wasn't nearly as cold.

"There's a technique to everything." His deep voice seemed to caress the words.

Heavens, why hadn't anyone told her? Dahlia wished that she'd discussed this with one of her sisters, but Rose and Lily had always considered her too young for such conversations. And now, when she was old enough and found herself with a million questions, they were both far away. She pressed her mittened hands to her cheeks and tried to calm her racing thoughts. "So you think that we could help one another by . . . practicing?"

"Exactly."

"Would it . . . would it take much?"

He shrugged. "Perhaps. Perhaps not. We won't know until we attempt it."

"I see. And this . . . practice. It would be just that, and no more."

"Of course," he said at once. "Only practice. We must do this, Dahlia, for if we don't, then our next kiss—whomever it is with—will be just as much of a disaster. We could lose so much more then, too. *Both* of us."

She bit her lip. She should have a million objections to make to this proposal, but somehow, basking under his warm, brown gaze, her fingers still tingling where he'd held her hand through her mittens, she heard herself say, "I suppose you're right."

"Of course I'm right."

She could almost hear his *I always am* attached to the end of his sentence. "My father always said practice makes perfect."

"There you have it, then."

"But . . . do you think it would take much time?"

"A half hour, perhaps more. We might need more than one, er, session, too. So we can think about our progress and how to better our performance."

"I see."

"So we'll plan to practice once or twice, perhaps three times if the need arises, so we're ready whenever the next kiss happens."

*He certainly makes it sound reasonable. And perhaps it is just that simple. A lesson or two wouldn't be amiss, would it?*

Kirk watched as Dahlia's even white teeth worried her plump bottom lip. Instantly, the heated blood that had been beating a determined path through him since he'd held her hand now made itself known in other areas that made him glad he was wearing a heavy coat that cloaked his breeches. Damn, but she was beautiful.

He realized that he was holding his breath. She looked so lovely that his heart had literally jumped when he'd seen her, and hadn't stopped since. Her cheeks were pink with cold, her hair tumbled around her face beneath the brim of her bonnet. But it was her mouth that drew his attention.

With every breath, a faint puff of mist came from her parted lips. It took every ounce of strength he possessed not to reach down and capture her lips and her warm breath and mingle it with his own. The whole thing was ludicrous, for there'd been only a hint of passion in their relationship before, nothing like what he felt now each and every time he saw her. Now just seeing her cheeks pink with cold made him long to cup them with his warm hands while showering her lips with enough kisses to steal her breath. *Good God, what has happened to me?*

She pushed a curl from her cheek with her mittened hand. "We mustn't get caught—"

"We wouldn't. I'd make certain of that." *If only she will agree to this! It could be a new beginning for us, a chance to know one another in a better manner than before.* But he could see she was wavering, doubt shadowing her beautiful eyes, so he hurried to say, "This is my last chance, Dahlia. If you do not meet the man of your dreams, there will be other invitations to the duchess's house parties. But not for me."

"I'm certain her grace would invite you back."

"I could never accept. You know I'm not given to putting myself up for ridicule more than once. Though you may not be aware of it, my life has become less since you left it. That encouraged me to come here and try to be more convivial—although I hate every bloody second."

Her lips twitched. "Is it that difficult?"

"Yes," he said bluntly. "It pains me like a rock in my shoe, cutting into my sole with every step."

She chuckled. "You are a sad case."

"I know, but I am who I am. I've tried to conform to society's demands, which is why you see me trussed up like a dandy, but it's not really who I am. I will do my best these next two and a half more weeks, but that's all I can do. If I fail to find a suitable lady in that time—" He shrugged. "I shall return home alone and stay there."

Her smile faded as her gaze searched his face. "You don't give yourself much time."

"I can't do more." He saw her worried gaze and added, "Now you know why I must do better with my next endeavor. The first kiss is important. *Very* important."

The wind lifted the ribbons of her bonnet bow and they danced across her face. She pushed them aside, making the bow lopsided. "And only I can help."

"Who else do I know? Besides—and I mean this with no hint of criticism—you could use some assistance in this area, too."

She sighed. "I know. I was—" She shook her head. "I'm going to regret this, but I can see no other way for either of us to accomplish our goals. I accept your suggestion, Kirk."

He had to bite his tongue to keep from letting out an exultant cry.

The wind gusted and Dahlia shivered. "So how would we— I mean, where would we—"

"Leave it to me. And it will be private and discreet. I promise."

"Very well, I'll—" Another gust of wind yanked Dahlia's bonnet loose from the lopsided bow. The bonnet swirled behind her, the ribbons dangling. Dahlia reached for it, but the wind filled it like a balloon, taking it higher.

Within seconds, Kirk was pressed against her, his chest to hers, one arm around her waist, his other arm high over her head—and her bonnet ribbon clamped between his fingers.

Too surprised to think, Dahlia could only stare up at him. Her gaze took in his firm chin, the chiseled line of mouth, the faintly aquiline nose, and his warm brown eyes. Her body seemed to soften, to melt against his, to fit in a way it never had before. She wasn't breathing, but she didn't seem to need to. All she could do was soak in the firmness of his body against hers; the faint, heady scent of his cologne; the long hard line of his leg against her hip.

She tried to think of something witty to say, something to break the frozen tableau, but no sound came from her lips. She could only savor the length of his body pressed to hers, deliciously warm and strong. How was it that in all of their time together before, she'd never noticed how wide his chest was, or how firm his thighs and—

Her gaze widened at the feel of him pressed against her. Their eyes met and, flushing deeply, Kirk set her from him. Instantly, the cold swooshed over her and she shivered, both from the heat he'd generated as well as from the instant icy cold.

Kirk held out her bonnet. "I— This is yours."

She plucked it from his hand. "Thank you. That was very kind— Thank you so much— You have been— I—I really must get back to—" Words seemed to tease her, but none would come to rest on her tongue.

"Yes, yes. Of course. We'll— I'll speak with you soon about that other matter, and we'll meet as soon as I can arrange something."

"That will be nice— I mean, not nice, but necessary and I—" She gulped. "I really must return now and—" She turned and nearly ran down the path, leaving Kirk standing behind her, his dark gaze locked on her.

*Eight*

**From the Diary of the Duchess of Roxburghe**

Normally when my guests arrive for the house party prior to the Christmas Ball, the castle is already decorated. This year, however, we thought to do something different, as variety is the lifeblood of a thriving social calendar. This year, for fun, small parties of guests will plan and oversee decorating the main sections of the castle.

We have not yet announced this, as I think it should be a competition with lovely prizes for the winners, but Charlotte fears that would make the event unnecessarily complicated, which is a ridiculous thought. How could such a simple event go wrong?

Really, Charlotte worries far too much . . .

Dahlia hurried down the cobblestone path to the kitchen door, her heart pounding. Safely out of sight, she stopped, glanced back to make certain she wasn't being observed, and then slipped between two large shrubberies and leaned against the stone wall. Protected from the wind, she took some time to compose herself before entering the castle.

Good God, but she'd never been more confused in her entire life. *What had just happened?* She had no idea. It wasn't a romantic meeting. No, those involved pretty words, not a request for help between "friends"—yet she couldn't imagine feeling this way about a mere friend.

She tried to re-tie her bonnet, but her hands were shaking too much. The whole thing was ludicrous. Somehow, between apologizing and asking for her help, Kirk had talked her into agreeing to hone her "skills" with him.

Yet she had to admit the idea held some appeal. A lot of appeal. *Perhaps too much appeal.* She let out her breath in a long sigh and stuffed her uncooperative bonnet into her pocket. When he'd held her, his— dear heavens, what *was* the polite term for that? She only knew the farm terminology, which seemed too crude when referring to a person rather than a bull. Should she call it a "manhood"? A "private member"? Or, as the grooms referred to it for horses in the stables, "cock"? Whatever it was called, it had been quite hard and had pressed against her hip in a very insistent way.

Having grown up in the country, she knew how animals mated. So she realized Kirk had been aroused.

*By me.*

A surprised smile tickled her lips. She instantly covered her mouth, only to find that the smile was followed by a giggle. *He was aroused by* me.

She was flattered. Yes, flattered that such a critical, unyielding man should desire her. And despite being mussed and muddied, Dahlia suddenly felt *pretty*, the feeling as intoxicating as champagne.

As irritating and overbearing as Kirk was, one never, *ever* forgot that he was a man, and an attractive one at that. *His mouth is so lovely and quite warm—* She pressed her mittened hands against her eyes. *I really must stop this. He is not for me, nor am I for him. I've spent far too many hours over the last two days thinking about him as it is.*

She resolutely pushed all thoughts aside and decided that what she really needed was a hot bath and some breakfast, although perhaps not in that exact order. She made her way back to the path and reached the kitchen door. Once there, she removed her muddied boots and, holding them by the strings, she stepped inside.

The air was redolent with the scent of ham and fresh bread as Cook shouted out orders to a row of white-smocked undercooks. Dahlia slipped out of the way of a bevy of black-frocked maids who carried various bowls and items to the long wooden table where a line of breakfast trays awaited. Dashing between the cooks and maids, footmen assembled the glassware for each tray.

No one paid Dahlia the slightest heed. With her

unruly hair whipped to a frenzy by the wind, her cheeks red with cold, and her gray woolen gown as plain as any maid's, she looked far more like a lost servant than one of the duchess's revered houseguests. Glad for her anonymity, she skirted the room, ducking out of the way when a footman came rushing around the corner carrying a tray filled with rattly teacups and saucers.

Just before she left, she grabbed a roll from a basket and then raced up the stairs to the main floor. If she was lucky, the foyer would be empty, allowing her to dash upstairs before anyone could see her. Fortunately, it was quite early and the chance of anyone having already been awake and dressed was quite low.

As she expected, she found the foyer empty and silent. With her muddy boots held to one side, she swiftly crossed the floor. As she passed the dining hall, she peeked through the ajar doors and saw a number of footmen bustling about, setting out boxes of Christmas decorations, the butler gently pressing them on. Dahlia hurried past and reached the steps.

She'd just put her foot on the first one when the outside door burst open. A wild scampering of paws and the huffy panting of a herd of dogs told her who'd just entered before the duchess had a chance to say a word.

"Ah, Dahlia! Just the person Lady Charlotte and I wish to see."

Dahlia turned around to curtsy, hiding her boots behind her back as the pugs rushed up to sniff her muddied hem. "Good morning, your grace, Lady Charlotte."

"Good morning." The duchess stripped off her gloves. "I hope you slept well."

"Very well, your grace."

"Oh, Dahlia!" Lady Charlotte came forward, a beautiful bonnet on her head, the rosettes on the brim matching the ones on her blue-gray pelisse. "We had the loveliest idea this morning before we went to visit the vicar. We're going to decorate the castle in groups and—" Her gaze locked on Dahlia's hair and the words simply stopped.

The duchess followed Lady Charlotte's gaze. "Goodness, but it was windy today, wasn't it?"

Dahlia's face heated. "I'm sorry. I went for a walk and I'm not fit for company just now." She held up her muddy boots. "I was trying to sneak up to my room before anyone saw me."

Lady Charlotte untied her bonnet and cautiously lifted it from her soft curls. "A walk sounds *lovely*. I always say fresh air is good for the complexion, don't I, Margaret?"

The duchess undid her pelisse. "Indeed, you do. And every time you say it, I inform you that you're wrong, and that walking outdoors will expose you to all sorts of illnesses." Her grace's sharp blue eyes took in Dahlia's flushed face. "I must say, though, that Miss

Balfour has set my worries to rest. She looks wondrously healthy."

"She glows, doesn't she? Where did you walk, I wonder, for I find the hills far too fatiguing."

"La, Charlotte, let the poor girl breathe!" The duchess glanced about the foyer. "Where are my footmen?"

Dahlia answered, "I believe some of them are in the dining room organizing some boxes, your grace."

"Ah yes, the decorations. I forgot that I'd asked them to be brought down from the attic. I've— Oh, MacDougal! There you are. We just returned from the vicar's."

"So I see, yer grace. I dinna hear ye come in, but fortunately Randolph came and found me." The butler smiled down at the gray-nosed pug that sat at his feet, its tongue lolling out of one side of its mouth. MacDougal took the duchess's and Lady Charlotte's pelisses and handed them to the footman who'd followed him into the foyer.

He looked inquiringly at Dahlia, whose pelisse was mud spattered from her adventures.

"No, thank you, MacDougal. I will put it into the care of my maid. She'll clean it for me."

"Very guid, miss."

Lady Charlotte relinquished her gloves and bonnet to a footman. "MacDougal, the duchess and I noticed that the weather's turning bitter. We'll have to plan other amusements for our guests this afternoon."

"Other tha' decoratin' the castle fer the Christmas Ball?"

"Oh, everyone will wish to discuss how they'd like their assigned area decorated before they actually begin, so I doubt they'll be putting anything up right away. No, we need an activity that our guests can enjoy today." She turned to Dahlia. "We were planning to row boats across the lake to the island to visit the folly for lunch, but it's far too cold."

"And it looks like rain," the duchess added in an ominous voice. "We *never* plan events on the island if it looks like rain."

Lady Charlotte explained, "The weather once caught us while our guests were on the island and mayhem ensued, so we no longer take chances."

MacDougal nodded his agreement. "A guid idea, me lady. The weather tastes o' snow, it do, which would be even worse. I wouldna' be surprised to discover tha' 'tis goin' to come upon us afore nightfall."

"Excellent. Snow adds such a festive air to our Christmas Ball." The duchess adjusted her wig, which was slightly askew. "But for today, once the footmen have sorted the decorations and prepared the dining room for our luncheon, pray set up two battledore courts in the arboretum."

"The arboretum?" Dahlia exclaimed.

Lady Charlotte beamed. "It's a lovely place for a game of battledore. Wait until you see!"

"Verrah guid, me lady." MacDougal turned to a waiting footman. "Ye heard her ladyship." The footman bowed and hurried off. Another footman instantly took his place.

"Did someone say battledore?" came a man's voice from the salon door.

Dahlia tucked her stocking-covered toes back under her skirt as Lord Dalhousie sauntered into the foyer. Dressed in his riding clothes, his cravat a testament to complicated knotting, he looked dapper and handsome. "I haven't played battledore in a year or two, but I enjoy it vastly."

"So do I." Miss Stewart followed Lord Dalhousie, accompanying Lady Mary and another young lady whom Dahlia had met just the night before, a Miss MacLeod, all of them wearing riding habits, as well. "But in this weather? It's much too cold to—" Miss Stewart caught sight of Dahlia's hair. "Good heavens, what happened to *you*?"

Dahlia didn't even try to smooth her hair, for she knew that nothing but a comb and an hour of untangling would set it to rights. "I just returned from a walk."

"We can tell," Lady Mary said. "*Just* returned."

Miss MacLeod smiled kindly at Dahlia. "You and I share the same type of hair, Miss Balfour. Without pins—" She threw out her hands hopelessly.

"Yes, well, I think you look lovely," Lord Dalhousie said, although without much conviction.

Dahlia managed a smile. "Thank you."

Lady Charlotte looked at the small group of young people. "You are dressed for riding. Are you leaving now? For it's getting quite cold."

Miss Stewart made a face. "We had planned on

leaving a half hour ago, but the weather convinced us otherwise."

Lord Dalhousie sighed. "As embarrassing as it is to admit, we only made it to the doorway when an icy blast sent us running back to the warmth of the fire in the salon."

Lady Charlotte tsked. "I do wish it had stayed warm a bit longer, but I suppose we were lucky to have such pleasant weather at the beginning of the week. Fortunately, I think you will all enjoy the excitement of a battledore tournament, which we're having set up in the arboretum."

"I beg your pardon, but did you say it would be in the arboretum?" Lady Mary asked.

"Oh yes. We've done it several times now. We'll have two full courts, and there will be a viewing stand with the chairs from the Blue Salon."

"The viewing stand was MacDougal's idea." The duchess bent to scoop up the closest pug, which immediately licked her cheek. "He's brilliant at adding those little touches. We shall put up the courts and leave them for the duration of our guests' stay, so that you may all enjoy a game whenever you wish."

"It sounds lovely," Lady Mary said. "But how do you set it up?"

"Oh, that's quite easy. The footmen place the net poles in the very large pots that hold our giant ferns."

"They are almost as tall as my head," Lady Charlotte added. "They hold the nets better than planting them in the lawn."

Miss MacLeod looked impressed. "What a unique idea."

"The foliage also gives the game a truly festive feel," her grace added. "Almost as if one were playing in a jungle."

Lady Mary smiled. "The arboretum must be quite large to hold two battledore courts and a viewing stand."

"*Two* viewing stands," Lady Charlotte corrected gently. "Roxburghe has never been one to build small."

"I, for one, cannot wait." Miss Stewart turned to Lady Mary and Miss MacLeod. "Shall we fetch our hats and then retire to change into something suitable for battledore?"

"Yes, please," Lady Mary said. "But before we change, breakfast would be most welcome. I am famished."

Miss MacLeod turned to Dahlia. "Do you come with us to the breakfast room, Miss Balfour?"

Dahlia smiled. "No, I believe I'll have a tray in my room. But I hope to see you in the arboretum this afternoon."

The three women curtsied and, after making their good-byes to the duchess and Lady Charlotte, headed toward the salon, whispering to one another as they went.

The duchess turned to the viscount. "What about you, Lord Dalhousie? Are you not going in to breakfast?"

"No, I am perfectly satisfied here, with you, Lady

Charlotte, and Miss Balfour." He bowed to Dahlia, his gaze flickering to her hair and then away.

She bit back a wince. From now on, she'd make sure she carried a comb in her pocket during her walks.

Kirk hadn't seemed to care, but then, he was immune to fashion. For the first time, she realized there might be a benefit to that flaw.

The duchess sighed sadly. "I had thought about setting up an indoor pall-mall game, but there's simply no challenge to it when the floor is flat. The footmen tried to make it more entertaining by putting piles of rags here and there under the carpet to simulate a lawn, but it didn't work."

Lady Charlotte leaned toward Dahlia and said in a low voice, "It was an utter disaster. The balls hit the little hillocks and, as they had no grass to soften the roll, they shot into the air. We lost two vases and a chandelier—an Italian one—before her grace put a stop to it."

"Charlotte, please don't remind me." Her grace kissed the pug's forehead before she put him back with his brothers and sisters, who were stretched out upon the floor in various piles. "Fortunately, battledore works quite well indoors. Better, perhaps, than outside."

"There's no wind," Lady Charlotte explained. "So you don't have to chase the bird if it gets gusty outdoors, which it always does. Scotland is filled with bad weather."

Her grace frowned. "We have delightful weather in the summer."

"On occasion," Lady Charlotte agreed, not at all put out by the duchess's apparent displeasure. "Between rainstorms, and fog, and wind, and—"

"Thank you, Charlotte. I've had to deal with the weather enough today, if you please. And now, if you'll excuse me, I believe I'll meet with Mrs. Cairness about lunch." Her grace started to turn away, but then paused. "Miss Balfour, perhaps you'd care to join me in the salon in a half hour for a bit of tea?"

"I wish I could, your grace, but I must get ready for the luncheon, and my hair will take at least an hour to fix."

The duchess looked disappointed. "I suppose you must. Well, then, I'll be certain to catch you later this evening, before dinner. I wish to make certain you've sustained no injury from your walk."

"You are too kind, your grace. I walk all of the time, and as you can see, I'm perfectly fine."

"We'll see about that. Until this evening, then." The duchess turned. "Angus!"

A footman stepped forward, and Dahlia recognized him as the one who'd assisted her out of the carriage when she'd first arrived.

The duchess pointed to the oldest pug. "Poor Randolph is panting so. Perhaps you could carry him for the rest of the morning?"

"Aye, yer grace." He bent and scooped up the elderly dog, who took the opportunity to lick the footman's chin.

"Thank you, Angus." Her grace turned to the other

dogs. "Come!" They all rose, stretching and yawning, but looking quite happy to be hailed. With a gracious smile at her guests, the duchess went in search of the housekeeper, Angus following and the other pugs trotting behind.

Lady Charlotte sighed. "Poor Margaret. She hates it when someone criticizes anything that has to do with Floors Castle."

Lord Dalhousie smiled, his eyes twinkling. "Apparently even the weather."

"Yes. You should have seen her when MacDougal mentioned that a stiff east wind always makes the fireplace in the dining room smoke. You'd have thought he'd insulted the Roxburghe name." The huge clock rang the hour. "Oh dear, look at the time! My new novel is waiting and if I hurry, I've just enough time to read the first chapter before I change for lunch. Miss Balfour, if you and Lord Dalhousie will excuse me——" As she spoke, the tiny lady hurried off.

Lord Dalhousie chuckled. "Lady Charlotte is right; her grace does not like to hear anything about the castle being less than perfect. Yesterday, during tea, someone dared to say that they thought the garden could use some of their prize roses to 'fill out the flower bed,' and that they'd be glad to send some to her grace. She was offended that someone dared suggest that the gardens were not perfect as they are, and it made for quite an awkward moment."

"She's very protective. Still, I understand. It's very

easy to become sentimental over buildings. I'm very fond of Caith Manor, where I grew up, and if anyone says a cross word about it, even if it's true, I get very defensive."

"What style of house is Caith?" Lord Dalhousie asked, looking far more interested than he should have.

"It's a hodgepodge—part Tudor, part Gothic, part something else. But to me, it's the most beautiful house ever."

"Oh?" He leaned against the newel post at the foot of the stairs. "What does Caith look like?"

"It's not overly large, is rather square, but with a beautiful arched doorway, and a parlor that overlooks the prettiest garden. It's two stories with an ornate staircase that creaks horribly and—" Dahlia bit her lip. "I'm sorry, I don't mean to go on and on."

"Oh, you weren't. To be honest, I—"

Lady Mary and Miss Stewart returned arm in arm, Miss MacLeod trailing behind.

Miss Stewart cast a blinding smile at the viscount. "Dalhousie, Lady Mary and I were hoping that after lunch, you'd play us in battledore."

He sent a regretful glance at Dahlia before he turned a polite smile on Miss Stewart. "I will need a partner, then."

"Very true," Lady Mary conceded. "Perhaps Lord MacKelton would do."

"If he can stay awake long enough to play. Why, he must be seventy years old."

"Eighty-three. I know, for I asked Lady Charlotte just this morning."

Miss Stewart glanced at Dahlia from under her lashes before saying in a challenging tone, "How about Lord Kirk?"

"Oh yes," Lady Mary agreed. "With his perpetual scowl and that horrid scar—" She shuddered.

Dahlia had to unclench her jaw before she could speak. "He cannot help being injured."

Lady Mary didn't look the least regretful. "He can help how much he scowls. I never see him without getting the feeling that he wishes everyone in the room to perdition."

"As do I," Miss MacLeod said. "Although I think him a bit of a tragic figure, like one from a play. There he is, beautifully handsome and yet marred by that scar. I heard he got the scar fighting pirates. How romantic!"

Dahlia frowned. "There were no pirates."

Miss Stewart turned a curious glance her way. "Oh? Do *you* know how he got his scar, then?"

"He and his wife were returning from the Indies, and their ship caught fire. They were carrying gunpowder and the entire ship blew up. His wife was killed."

"What a tragic story," Miss Stewart said.

"Yes, but he has recovered, which is a testament to his character."

"Oh my," Lady Mary said, eyeing Dahlia. "It seems that Lord Kirk is not without his admirers."

Surprisingly, Miss MacLeod interjected, "Of course he is not; he's an intriguing and mysterious figure."

"A scar does not add a caveat of mystery, at least not to me." Lady Mary didn't look pleased. "The man has a wretched temper; one can see it just by looking at him. If Lord Kirk were to play us in battledore, I'd be shaking in fear so much that I wouldn't be able to hit a stroke."

"Then he is the perfect partner for me," Dalhousie exclaimed. "I shall ask him immediately."

"He is the perfect partner only if you don't *look* at him. Although I must say his eyes have a peculiar beauty." Miss Stewart's sharp face softened. "The very shape of his—"

"That is quite enough!" Dahlia almost didn't recognize her own voice as four shocked faces turned her way. "Pray stop speaking about Lord Kirk in such a way."

Miss Stewart blinked. "I was complimenting him."

Dahlia's face heated. "Yes, well, before that you were mocking his appearance."

Lord Dalhousie's smile had slipped, but he rallied. "You're quite right, Miss Balfour. Lord Kirk cannot help being injured."

"We meant no harm." Miss Stewart looked quite put out. "I did admit that his eyes are lovely."

"But he does limp horridly." Lady Mary sniffed. "*If* that's actually a leg. Why, it might be a peg, for all we know."

Miss Stewart feigned shocked. "A *peg leg*! Oh, can you imagine—"

"No." Dahlia stepped forward. "Miss Stewart, Lady Mary, if you'd like a game of battledore, allow *me* to challenge you to one."

Lady Mary arched her brows delicately. "Miss Balfour, I feel I must warn you that Miss Stewart and I are excellent at battledore."

"So am I. Quite good, in fact."

Miss Stewart couldn't have looked more astounded than if Dahlia had announced that she was the pope. "You can't play us *both*. There's only *one* of you."

"Actually, I can do just that." She'd played both of her sisters many times, and had won almost every match. "Well, Lady Mary? Miss Stewart? Do you accept?"

Lady Mary's gaze narrowed. "You sound as if you were challenging us to a duel."

Lord Dalhousie brightened. "Then I claim the honor of being Miss Balfour's second."

Miss MacLeod bounced in place. "I'll be a second for Miss Stewart and Lady Mary!"

Dalhousie bowed to Miss MacLeod. "We shall set the details after lunch. We will plan the duel for—shall we say, tomorrow? That will give us time to prepare the rules for our wager."

Miss MacLeod curtsied, laughing as she did so. "I look forward to it! We will make certain all is fair."

"Then it's settled. Our fair opponents shall play tomorrow afternoon."

"It will also give Miss Balfour time to practice," Miss MacLeod offered.

"I shall have no need of it," Dahlia said, filled with a determination to win. "I look forward to the match." Suddenly, she was tired of the house party, tired of defending Kirk's honor, tired of hearing people malign someone they didn't know—all of it. "If you'll excuse me, I must change." She turned and, boots in hand, marched loudly up the steps in an attempt to drown out the excited chatter of what were surely two of the most spoiled women on the face of the earth.

# *Nine*

**From the Diary of the Duchess of Roxburghe**

The battledore courts have been a rousing success and there have been games nonstop since they were set up yesterday, which is a good thing, for the weather has gotten worse.

Meanwhile, this morning, I noticed two of my footmen sporting the gaudiest watch fobs I've ever seen.

I shall ask MacDougal to count the silver.

Dahlia winced. "Ow!"

Freya clucked her tongue. "I'm sorry, miss, bu' if ye wish yer hair to stay oop, then I must brush it guid and well."

"I know, I know. But do be careful. No matter how lovely you make my hair, the effect will be ruined if it gives me a headache and all I can do is frown." Dahlia's stomach growled and she pressed a hand to it.

"Ye should take yer breakfast on a tray in the mornings, like the others."

"I had a biscuit earlier, when I came back through the kitchen after my walk. And while certain others may enjoy lazing about until noon, I do not."

"Och, no. Ye're oop wit' the birdies, ye are."

"I love mornings. Besides, the more interesting guests are up early, and we've had some excellent conversations over the breakfast table. Lady Grantham has been telling me the most fascinating tales of the history of their family seat. And Miss MacTintern raises the most exotic animals—she has *two* monkeys, both quite tame, and she's promised to show them to me if ever I visit Edinburgh."

A discreet knock sounded on the door.

Freya put down the box of pins and went to the door.

A footman holding a silver salver bowed. "From Lord Dalhousie. I'm to wait fer an answer."

Freya took the missive and brought it to Dahlia with a mischievous look. "Fro' Lord Dalhousie, miss."

Dahlia's face heated. She slipped her silver comb behind the seal and broke it, and then opened the missive. The entire page was filled with flowing script.

Aware of the waiting footman, she scanned it quickly. "Pray tell his lordship that I will be happy to meet him in the portrait gallery at ten."

"Aye, miss." The footman bowed and then left.

As soon as the door closed, Freya clapped her hands together. "Och, miss! Not here a whole week and already gettin' love letters."

"It's not a love letter." However, it *was* a very nice

letter. Dalhousie had invited her to a viewing of the Roxburghe portrait gallery, which he'd planned for their amusement. He was most effusive about the idea, and had closed with "I eagerly await your answer." She smiled and folded the letter and placed it the dressing table.

"Viscount Dalhousie is quite a handsome mon." Freya slid a sly look at Dahlia.

"He's very charming." Dahlia remembered how Miss Stewart had looked at him the day before. "Half of the ladies here are already in love with him."

"The duchess ne'er invites someone to her house party wit'oot havin' a plan fer them. I wonder who she wishes to match to Dalhousie?"

That was an interesting question indeed. Dahlia's stomach growled again and she glanced at the clock. "It's a quarter past nine. I should hurry to breakfast if I'm to reach the portrait gallery by ten."

Freya placed two more pins in Dahlia's hair and then stepped back. "There now. See if tha' is no' wha' ye had in mind."

Dahlia tilted her head this way and that. Her thick brown hair had been pinned in a series of loose knots with silken tendrils falling in loose curls at her ears. It was a far cry from the tangled mess she'd come in with after yesterday's walk, that much was certain. "It's perfect. I hope it will stay up."

"If it dinna, then jus' come back to the room and ring fer me. I'll come in a trice and fix it."

Dahlia stood. "Thank you, Freya. I must say, I'm

excited to see the Roxburghe portrait gallery. Her grace said at dinner last night that some of the paintings were by very famous artists."

"So I've been told. I'm surprised Lord Dalhousie knows the Roxburghe history enou' to be a guide fer ye."

"I daresay that what he doesn't know, he will feel free to invent. He has a vivid imagination and a rich sense of humor." No one made her laugh more than Lord Dalhousie.

Freya grinned. "Mayhap he's jus' tryin' to get ye alone. He's a verrah fine gentleman, but I do hear tell tha' he has a rovin' eye."

"Well, if dalliance is his purpose in inviting me to view the portrait gallery, then he is doomed for disappointment, for there will be footmen placed every six feet or so. How many footmen are there at Floors Castle, anyway? One cannot turn around without running into one."

"If ye ask Lillith, the upstairs maid, there is no' enou'," Freya said darkly. "When the footmen were setting oop fer the battledore tournament, she wouldna' leave them alone, commentin' on their muscles and flirtin' so much tha' the housekeeper sent her back to her post!"

"I daresay she was annoying the footmen."

"As to tha', I canno' say, fer she's—" Freya cupped her hands out before her breasts.

"Ah. She has a figure, does she?"

"Aye, miss. More tha' she can handle."

Dahlia looked at her own figure in the mirror and sighed. "I've always wished I were thinner, for then one can wear the latest fashions without draping oneself from head to foot in enough cloth to hide what one doesn't wish noticed."

"Och, ye are beautiful, miss. E'eryone says so."

"You are too kind. By the way, later this afternoon I shall need your help getting ready for the battledore tournament. I'm scheduled to play at two." Judging by the number of people who'd mentioned the game to her after dinner, there would be quite a large number in attendance. That was fine; if there was one skill Dahlia was certain about, it was battledore.

A knock sounded on the door.

Freya went to answer it. As she opened the door, a pug scampered between her feet and bounded into the room.

Freya gave a shout and lunged for the dog, but it was quicker, dodging her grasp and running as fast as it could around the entire room. Finally it collapsed upon the rug before the fire, panting, a silly grin on its muzzle.

Freya whipped about to glare at the footman. "Angus, ye falpeen fool! Wha' do ye' mean, bringin' tha' beastie into a lady's room like tha'? And I'll ne'er catch tha' one, fer she's faster than all o' the other combined!"

The footman grinned. "She is, isna' she? Small and wiry, to boot."

"Dinna say tha' as if it's funny, fer 'tis no' funny at

all. Especially when the beastie goes to chewin' on the misses' shoes."

Dahlia looked around at that. "Oh dear. Does she do that?"

"Aye. And she's no' the only one as has tha' problem, neither." The maid glared at the footman. "Did ye come jus' to make trouble, or are ye here on an errand o' some sort?"

Recalled to his duty, Angus straightened and held out a salver, a note in the center. "I've a note fer Miss Balfour. I was tol' I dinna need to wait fer an answer."

Freya took the note. "Fine, but ye are takin' tha' dog wit' ye."

"I'm no', fer I've someplace to be, but I'll come back later and fetch her when she's no' so excited. And, Freya, do no' chase her aboot. Ye're bad aboot tha' and it only makes her harder t' catch."

"Och! Ye're a fine one to talk, Angus MacLellan! I've seen ye chase the pugs all o'er the front lawn, I have."

"Only when her grace asked me to. Other than tha', I dinna take a step toward 'em unless they welcome it."

"Why, ye lyin'—" Freya caught herself and, with an apologetic glance back at Dahlia, straightened her narrow shoulders and faced the cheeky footman. "We'll discuss this another time." She curtsied. "Thank ye fer bringin' the missive."

"Ye're wel—"

She slammed the door. A muffled word came from

the hallway, but she ignored it and brought the note to Dahlia, who instantly recognized Kirk's familiar back-slanted handwriting.

The maid had the grace to look shamefaced. "I'm verrah sorry fer slammin' the door, miss. I shouldna' ha' done tha', but tha' mon is a lazy bit o' bone and blood, he is. E'er since the duchess asked him t' be the one t' carry puir ol' Randolph oop an' down the stairs when he refused t' do it hisself—"

"Pardon me, but who is this Randolph?"

"Och, Randolph is the oldest o' the Roxburghe pugs, miss. He's ancient, he is, bu' full o' life. Mac-Dougal thinks 'tis all a trick and tha' Randolph can manage the stairs fer all tha' her grace thinks he canno'. Angus, meanwhile, has been lordin' it o'er everyone belowstairs, actin' as if he'd been crowned king."

"King of the pugs, is he? Men can be so infuriating."

The note was pleasantly heavy in her hand, as if it held something of great value. *So you've made arrangements for us to meet privately, have you?* She'd wondered when and how he'd manage it. A faint shiver rushed over her, a wave of invisible heat.

Aware of the maid's eyes upon her, Dahlia tossed the unopened missive onto the dressing table and said, "I believe I'll wear the blue slippers."

"Aye, miss. They'll look fetchin' wit' tha' gown. I'll fetch them fro' the dressin' room."

"Thank you." Dahlia waited for the maid to leave before she picked up the missive. Yesterday, when Kirk had suggested that they practice their skills so as not to embarrass themselves again, she'd found herself in complete agreement, swayed by both his reasoning and his presence. But the cool logic of a night spent thinking away the hours had brought to light several flaws with this plan, not the least of which was the impropriety of it. Beyond that, there could be unexpected outcomes from their continued contact.

As it was, she was having a difficult enough time forgetting their kiss. Those first seconds had been beyond anything she'd ever dreamed, which was why she'd reacted so strongly. So how would she be able to forget a kiss from Kirk that was exceptional from beginning to end? *Could* she forget it? Would she want to?

She picked up her silver comb and, just as she'd done to Dalhousie's missive, she slid it under the flap and broke the seal. She replaced her comb on the dresser and then unfolded the stiff paper.

The paper was remarkably fine. Only the best for the master of Fordyce Castle. She smiled as she opened the vellum.

> *The library at ten. Do not be late.*
> *Kirk*

She frowned. *Short and to the point, with no time taken for pleasantries. Worse, he doesn't even ask, but announces it as if I'd have nothing to say about it.* As could be expected from Kirk, the missive was vastly unsatisfying.

She scowled at the letter. Why had she agreed to his request to hone her kissing skills with him, of all men? It was ludicrous. She'd come to the duchess's to find love and romance, something Kirk couldn't understand, nor did he wish to. Why, even common courtesy seemed to stretch his resources.

A rational woman would have avoided him, and would certainly have never agreed to his proposition. But yesterday, she hadn't been able to do either.

Something had happened when Kirk had lunged for her bonnet and she'd found herself in his arms. Even now, if she closed her eyes, she could feel the split second of heat caused by that innocuous embrace and smell the faint hint of cologne that had lingered on his coat.

Of course, now that time had passed, she realized that his seeming embrace had merely been a way to steady himself. Equally disheartening, she also realized that his scheme to advance their kissing skills— something she would have suspected as an attempt at flirtation had another man proposed it—was exactly as he'd declared it: he wished to avoid another embarrassing moment and he was woefully without practice.

Perhaps it was kind that he thought to include her, but it still confirmed that there was nothing the least bit romantic about his efforts.

As always, Kirk's request had been based on cold,

hard practicality and his own needs, and she deeply regretted agreeing to participate. And yet somehow she had.

But perhaps she shouldn't be so hard on herself. She'd been raw from their horrid encounter; then after he'd held her, she'd fallen under some sort of spell cast by his dark gaze and the feel of his strong arms about her.

Well, her reason had returned. She would meet with him at ten o'clock and explain why she was no longer interested in "perfecting" her skills.

She tossed the letter on the dresser where it came to rest beside Dalhousie's longer, more eloquent missive. The viscount had *requested* the honor of her presence, not rudely assumed that he would have it. There were many other things to recommend Dalhousie's letter over Kirk's, as well—his warm tone, the politeness of his request, the time he'd taken to plan an amusement for them both—all of it pointed to a deepness of thought and consideration that was completely lacking in Kirk's abrupt, demanding missive.

A cold, wet nose touched her elbow.

"*Oh!*" Dahlia looked down at the pug, who was wagging her curly tail with abandon. "Your nose is like ice."

Freya stuck her head out of the dressing room. "Och, is she botherin' ye, miss? I can try to catch her and—"

"No, no. She's fine."

"Verrah weel. I mus' say tha' I'm glad, fer she dinna take kindly to bein' chased."

"None of us do."

Freya twinkled. "Unless 'tis by the right mon, miss. I've found yer shoes bu' they needed a mite o' polish. I'm jus' finishin' them oop now."

"Thank you, Freya."

"Ye're quite welcome, miss." The maid disappeared back into the dressing room.

Dahlia regarded the dog sitting at her feet. "I wish you could go to the library for me. If there's one thing I'm certain of, it's that Lord Kirk is going to be angry when I tell him no."

Meenie cocked her head to one side.

"Oh, I know, he stomps about and snaps like a dragon. He meets almost everything with irritation—a change in the weather, a book that has had the corners of the pages folded, a cravat with too much starch—the list is endless. Which is why, when he huffs and puffs, I shan't pay him the slightest heed."

Meenie wagged her tail.

Dahlia was heartened by this positive reaction. "Yes. I will simply tell him I don't need to hone my skills. I need to hone my *reaction*." She reached down to pat the pug. Its hair was velveteen soft and made her smile. "You are a sweet one. Come sit on my lap."

The dog barked once, and then ran away as fast as its legs would carry it, making wider and wider circles around the room until, once again, she collapsed in a panting, grinning heap before the fireplace.

Freya came out of the dressing room carrying the shoes. "Ye canno' pick tha' one oop, miss. No' unless she decides she wishes ye to do so." She placed the shoes on the floor before Dahlia. "So Lord Dalhousie sounds as if he might be interested in ye, miss. Do ye like him?"

"I don't know." Dahlia opened her jewelry box and selected her favorite garnet earrings. "He's fun and lively and he flirts outrageously, but . . . we shall see." Compared to Kirk, who didn't like to do many things at all, Dalhousie was the most attractive of companions.

Still, for no reason at all, she couldn't help but wonder what a real kiss from Lord Kirk might be like. A kiss born and sustained by passion, one uninterrupted by her own inexperience.

*But Lord Kirk has no passion. As he pointed out yesterday, we knew each other before, so naturally we're comfortable when we're together and enjoy a feeling of familiarity.* Yet there had been that decided flare when he'd held her. That was stronger than mere familiarity.

"Why are ye scowlin' so, miss?"

Dahlia realized that her maid was watching her in the mirror. "I was just thinking of how difficult it is to know one's own feelings."

"Aye. I've been thinkin' aboot tha' meself of late." The maid hesitated, and then asked, "Miss, I hope ye dinna mind me askin', but wha' do ye think aboot an older mon?"

Goodness, how did Freya know Kirk was— She caught the maid's gaze and gave a relieved laugh. "You have an older suitor!"

The maid's face pinkened. "I was jus' askin', miss. Sometimes I think it might be well on to have a mon who is experienced in the ways o' the world, and no' a young foo' who's more interested in makin' himself happy. Young men know passion, but an older mon knows how to woo a girl proper."

That wasn't true about Kirk. He didn't know how to woo anyone. "Who is this older man?"

"He's a valet. And verrah nice and—" The maid shook her head and, with a smile, fetched a shawl from the wardrobe. "It dinna matter. Ye'd best be on yer way or ye'll miss yer meetin' wit' Lord Dalhousie."

Dahlia allowed Freya to settle the shawl over her elbows.

"Off wit' ye, miss. And let me know wha' sort o' nonsense Lord Dalhousie tells ye aboot the Roxburghe family. It might make fer guid tellin' at the servant's dinner table."

"I shall. And remember, I'm to play battledore at two, so I shall need a looser gown."

"I'll be waitin' fer ye at one, miss."

Dahlia left, pausing to pat the pug one more time. Whatever was going to happen with Kirk would happen, and she'd be ready for it. Straightening her shoulders, she turned and left—ready for come what may.

*Ten*

**From the Diary of the Duchess of Roxburghe**

I expect certain things from my guests: good manners, a pleasant demeanor, a willingness to be entertained—odd as it may seem, these simple skills are not always found where one expects them to be. While I'm certain Kirk would not appreciate my interference, I refuse to allow two spoiled misses to mock a man on such a noble mission. I was prepared to take a stand and bring up the issue, but Lady Charlotte feels it would be best to allow Miss Balfour's plan to play itself out before I act.

If, as Charlotte hopes, Dahlia succeeds in pointing out the folly of such rudeness, I'll leave well enough alone. But if I find myself dissatisfied with the outcome, I shall speak—and speak loudly.

It is during these moments that I miss Roxburghe the most, and wish he were here and not out doing the prime minister's bidding. Roxburghe always knows how to remind people of their obligations with the lightest of words. Meanwhile, try as I might, my words fall like sledgehammers upon railway spikes—loud, forceful, and perhaps, at times, a bit firmer than necessary.

Although Dahlia would have relished a quiet breakfast before meeting Kirk, she arrived in the breakfast room to discover that far more than the usual dozen early morning guests were gathered about the table. She thought she might slip in and sit off by herself a bit and avoid discussion, but within moments of arriving, Mr. Ballanoch—a gossipy old man much inclined to present himself as an admirer of Lady Charlotte's, although she never seemed to notice him—brought up the afternoon's battledore tournament and (with an impertinently arch look) announced Dahlia's challenge to Lady Mary and Miss Stewart.

All conversation from that point on centered upon the coming game and battledore in general. Battledore was all the rage ever since soldiers returning home from adventures in India had brought the game with them. The Duke of Beaufort had confirmed the game's prominence by orchestrating tournaments for his guests.

The game had been a marvelous way for Dahlia and her sisters to pass desultory hours. As they were three girls with no other playmates within reach, they'd played two against one. At first they'd traded teams, but when it quickly became evident that Dahlia was far more talented than her sisters, she was consigned to her own team more and more often, which was how she liked it, anyway.

Judging by Lady Mary's and Miss Stewart's smug expressions yesterday, they thought they were quite talented, too. But Dahlia knew a few tricks, and because of the circumstances of their match, she was more than willing to use them. Of course, her determination had nothing to do with the fact that disparaging comments had been made about Lord Kirk, but rather because Miss Stewart and Lady Mary had dared mock someone from Dahlia's beloved Aberdeenshire.

All too soon, the clock in the breakfast room chimed a quarter of ten, and Dahlia finished her tea and excused herself, slowed by the rounds of hearty good wishes for a successful game. It was odd how enthusiastic the other guests seemed to be. As she hurried down the wide hallway to the library, she mentally rehearsed a very chilly and flat statement about why she no longer wished to participate in Lord Kirk's flawed plan.

She slowed when she arrived at the library. Two footmen flanked the doors, both standing at attention as if they were palace guards. She eyed the one closest to her. "Pardon me, Angus?"

Surprised she'd remembered his name, Angus sent her a startled glance. "Aye, miss?" He couldn't have spoken more cautiously if she'd been a Bow Street runner and he a smuggler.

"Lord Kirk asked me to meet him in the library."

"Aye, miss. He's waitin' on ye now. We're to let ye in."

"I see. And then what are you supposed to do?"

Angus and Stuart, the other footman, exchanged warning looks. Angus offered a tentative smile. "We're merely doin' our duty, miss."

Stuart nodded vigorously.

"So is guarding the library doors a part of your regular duties? Shall I ask Lady Charlotte how—"

"Och, no! There's no need, miss. Indeed, I—" Angus gulped and then fell silent. He'd known from the first moment he clapped his peepers on Miss Balfour that she was a sharp one. *I should ha' asked Lord Kirk fer mo' than a guinea once't he said we was waitin' on Miss Balfour.* She had her arms crossed now, too, and he could see her slippered foot tapping away as if it was itching to kick his shins. Worse, her expression reminded him far too much of his oldest sister, who was a wee thing, but as mean as a stirred badger.

He straightened his shoulders. "Miss, as ye ha' surmised, Lord Kirk paid us to stand guard."

"I see. And once I've entered, what are you to do?"

"We're to keep oot anyone as may wish to interrupt ye."

"Aye," Stuart agreed. "Like guards, we are."

"I see. Do guests often pay you to do such things?"

"All of the time." Stuart blushed when her brows rose. "Oy mean, er, no miss. Ne'er."

"Stuart, dinna tell the miss such a tale." Angus had

no doubt she'd see right through any pretense, so it was best to simply speak the truth up front. "It happens all o' the time, miss. Although no one has ever paid as much as his lor'ship."

"How nice of him to be so generous. Sadly, I must inform you that you are no longer needed."

Angus was suddenly glad Lord Kirk had paid them in advance. He had plans for that money, he did. There was a certain pert maid he wished to prove something to, a Miss Freya of the Smart Mouth That Needed to Be Kissed. Or, if she didn't offer him a few kinder words, he might just spend it all on himself.

He turned to Stuart. "Tha' is it, then. Miss Balfour says we're no' needed, and so we're no'."

"Bu' his lordship—"

"His lordship will understand how 'tis. Now open the door fer Miss Balfour and leave it open, and then we'll be off. I've a notion, anyways, tha' I will be needed to carry the auld pug oop the stairs soon, fer Lady Charlotte was takin' it wit' her fer a walk."

"Verrah weel." Looking unhappy, Stuart opened the door wide and then stood to one side.

Dahlia took a steadying breath and, trying to still her racing mind, she entered the library. Now was the time to stand firm. She only wished her heart didn't ache so, as if she were hurting it herself.

She stepped onto the ornate rug and paused. It was a cloudy morning, leaving the pale swath of light that entered the terrace doors gray and wan. No lamps had been lit, so the only other light in the dark room came from the fire, which snapped and crackled cheerfully, as if aware it had to put forth more effort.

And yet the air remained gloomy, and Lord Kirk was nowhere to be seen. Dahlia took a few more steps into the room, her shoes silent on the thick rug. All about her, shelves of books—normally the most welcome of all sights—loomed. The library was an impressive part of Floors Castle

She was just about to call Kirk's name when the large wing-backed chair before the fireplace creaked and she caught sight of his left hand as he gripped his cane and rose. He saw her, and then glanced at the pocket watch he held in his other hand. "You're late."

Dahlia'd just bent her knee in a curtsy, but at his words, she froze and then slowly straightened. "I beg your pardon, but did you just announce that I'm late?"

Kirk opened his mouth to answer, but the flash in Dahlia's gaze made him pause. He'd arrived in the library a good half hour early, as eager for their meeting as a callow youth waiting for his first tryst. He'd spent the time imagining how he wished the events to play out, what her reaction might be, how he might best draw her to him—every thought lighting his already heightened awareness. But none of his imagining had included Dahlia staring at him with such a martial light in her eyes.

He slipped his watch back into his pocket. "I was merely commenting on the time. It's ten after."

Her gaze narrowed.

He hurried to add, "Not that it matters, of course."

"No, it doesn't. Kirk, before you say anything more, I must inform you that I'm not here because you commanded me to be."

Kirk frowned. "Commanded?"

"Your note—if I can even call it that—was as rude and insensitive as the remark you just made about my being late."

"I merely gave you the time and place. It was as all notes should be—informative and to the point."

"It *was* informative, for it allowed me to see that this"—she waved a hand in a circle—"scheme of yours, or whatever you wish to call it, is a waste of time. *My* time."

*Ah. So she's getting cold feet, is she? I should have expected as much.* "Fine. If you feel that way, then there is nothing more to be said."

His capitulation seemed to surprise her, for she frowned. "So you think it is the case as well?"

"No, but—" He shrugged. "If you are decided, you are decided. I would never—" He narrowed his gaze. "You are rubbing your arms. Are you chilled?"

"A little," she admitted. "As large as this castle is, I daresay it is impossible to keep it warm in the winter."

"It's cold outside, and getting more so, and you can feel it. Here, let me stir the fire." He grasped his cane and started to turn.

"No, no. There's no need."

"Don't be foolish." He made his way to the fireplace. When he bent to pick up the log, he had to hide a grimace caused by his aching leg. His morning sessions with MacCreedy were more painful than he'd expected, despite the warnings the valet had given him. He tossed in the log and straightened. "There."

"Thank you. That is very kind."

"It's not kindness to do what should be done." Dusting his clothing, he turned to face her. "That should warm the room up soon enough."

"I can already feel it."

"Move closer to the fire and you'll feel it even more."

She glanced toward the door as if it called her.

"Come, Dahlia. We know each other too well to leave things unsaid. If we do so, we'll only mull it over until we can't sleep. We're the sort of people who think, often too much. A good conversation now could give us both a better night's sleep later on."

She smiled. "My father has accused me of over-thinking."

"Many, many people have said the same of me. So we must talk."

"I suppose you're right." She walked around the settee and came to stand near the fire. "I've no wish to cause you to lose any sleep."

"Good." He watched as she held her hands out to the flames. Such delicate hands, too. Hands he'd seen caress a book as if it were human. His body tightened at the thought, and he had to put his weight on his aching leg to refocus his wayward imagination. "Let me make this easier: you no longer wish to participate in my 'scheme,' as you put it."

She flushed. "You are going to speak very baldly, aren't you?"

"You would have me speak through a filter of politeness?"

"No, not at all. Pray continue."

"Thank you. I did make a suggestion, but it was no scheme. I'd no wish to experience that sort of awkwardness again, and I assumed that neither did you. Or don't you want to find a mate?"

She grimaced. "I hate it when you use the term 'mate.' It sounds so vulgar."

"Isn't that what we're doing? Two peacocks preening before the opposite sex, hoping one or another will notice us?" He flapped his arms as he talked.

Her lips twitched, but she said in a severe tone, "That's not any better."

"The truth is rarely pretty. Not in this case, anyway." He limped back to his chair and sat. When he noticed her lifted eyebrows he said, "I should stand? My leg hurts."

"You could have invited me to take a seat, as well."

"But you were cold and wished to be near the fire."

"Kirk, when you're being polite, you sometimes ask things even though you know the answer."

"That sounds like a damn waste of time."

"And you shouldn't curs—" She sighed. "Oh, never mind."

She turned and moved closer still to the fire, the amber light warming her skin, bringing out the faintest hint of red in her brown curls, and catching the red light of the garnet earrings that hung from her delicate earlobes. The earrings must hold special meaning, for she rarely wore any others.

*They're pretty, but garnets aren't good enough. She deserves rubies. Rich, red, bold rubies.*

Kirk smiled to himself at the thought. She really was a pretty woman, his Dahlia. Beautiful, even, if not in the showy manner preferred by the shallow-hearted followers of fashion. No, her beauty consisted of a purity of line of nose and jaw, and the ripe curve of her lips. Her skin, not the colorless white so favored by the maidens here, seemed fresh and young, dusted with a smattering of freckles that begged a man to trace them with his lips.

She lifted her skirts the tiniest bit and extended one daintily slippered foot toward the fire. As she did so, she moved to one side and suddenly, the light from the fire silhouetted her slender legs through the material of her gown.

His heart slammed an extra beat and he found himself unable to look away. *God, but she's gracefully shaped, with rounded calves and thighs that beg for a man's hand. She has none of this scrawny thinness that's so fashionable. Who could even think of such bone-baggery when faced with such generous, lush curves?*

She turned her head and met his gaze, catching him in midstare. His face heated and he blurted out, "You are standing too close to the flames. You'll catch your skirts afire." His voice was harsh, rude even, and she flushed, but after a stilted moment she moved away and he was spared the torment of seeing her fair form outlined before the flames.

He examined the line of her mouth and knew he'd angered her once more. "I'm sorry if I spoke too harshly, but the thought of you bursting into flames is untenable." *Actually, I'm the one who's the most likely to burst into flames.*

"I wish you'd regulate your tone. You always sound so angry."

"I'm not angry."

She didn't look convinced.

"Really, I'm not. I was merely concerned." *And aroused beyond all belief.* "So about my 'scheme,' as you call it."

"Yes. I've changed my mind about participating because it wouldn't be wise. Besides, perfecting such a skill with you wouldn't necessarily transfer to another man."

That was a very good point, for kissing someone else wouldn't be at all like kissing Dahlia. For one thing, he couldn't give a damn about anyone else he'd met, and didn't expect to.

But Dahlia . . . she was a different matter altogether. Not that he was—as so many emotionalists seemed to think necessary—"in love," for he wasn't. He was too mature for such nonsense now, but he was far from dead and had to admit that, besides their compatibility, he was beginning to recognize that a certain physical attraction flowed between them as well—which convinced him even more that they should pursue their former relationship.

He regarded her from under his lashes. "I worry for us both should we bump foreheads and teeth while trying to attract someone."

"It won't happen again. Next time, I shall be more cautious."

The thought of her "next time" not being with him made him want to leap to his feet and roar, but he forced himself to shrug. "That may satisfy you, but I've no wish to appear foolish and am determined to overcome my awkwardness in this area. I suppose if you don't wish to assist me, then I will just have to ask someone else."

It had been a shot in the dark, but her gaze instantly locked with his. "Who?"

"I don't know. I hadn't thought about it, since you and I had our agreement, but I'm sure I'll find someone." He held his breath and waited.

But instead of recanting her decision, she sent him a blazing look and marched past him, moving so quickly that her skirts swirled about her ankles.

"Wait!" He climbed to his feet and limped forward. "Dahlia, please, just— We had a purpose in meeting today. I cannot allow you to walk away."

At his words, she stopped. Her head bent and he could see where her thick brown hair had been swept up to reveal the delicate nape of her neck. God, but he longed to press his mouth to that tantalizing spot. She would shiver with longing, and then—

"Dahlia, *please*. I'm trying—" He sighed heavily.

Dahlia pressed a hand to her forehead. His sigh tugged at her heart, although she knew it shouldn't. Not everyone at the duchess's understood his abrupt ways, and already there were those who mocked him. Her hand curled into a fist. He'd been through so much already, losing his wife and fighting the injuries that had maimed and scarred him. At the very least, he deserved respect and politeness, but he would get neither unless someone assisted him.

She took a deep breath, and then turned to face him. "If we are going to continue to be friends, then you must stop—" She spread her hands. "You must stop all of this."

"All of what?"

"To begin with, you cannot order me about as if I'm one of the footmen you had standing guard."

"I didn't order them; I bribed them."

"Then you've paid them more courtesy than you have me."

He raked a hand through his hair. "I'm making a damned mull of this, aren't I?"

Despite herself, she was caught by the bewildered look in his eyes. "Yes, but it wouldn't matter if you weren't, for I'd already decided not to continue with this improper plan of yours. We should not be alone even now."

"The door is open."

"True. That saves us a bit, although someone could come along and assume that . . ." She gestured with a hand.

"I see." He rubbed the scar on his cheek.

Dahlia wondered if he even knew he did it. She'd noticed months ago that whenever he was perplexed by something, his fingers traced his scar, as if in doing so, it might clear his thoughts.

Her heart softened the tiniest bit more. He was trying so hard, and he'd already made so many changes—his clothing, his hair. And rough as they still were, his manners were vastly improved. Even the fact that he'd noticed she was chilled was a step forward from the totally self-absorbed man she'd known before, one who'd lived alone for so long that it never dawned on him that other people might feel cold, or hunger, or—well, anything, unless he was feeling it, too.

*He is trying. That's worth a lot from someone who has never made an effort.*

She sighed. "Kirk, please try to understand."

"I only want success—for both of us."

"Sadly, your idea of practicing a kiss can only lead to disaster, whomever you decide to practice with." For some reason, that last bit left a bitter taste on her tongue.

Humor glinted in his dark eyes. "Kisses can lead to many places, my dear. A disaster is but one." His voice deepened. "'*When age chills the blood, when our pleasures are past—For years fleet away with the wings of the dove—The dearest remembrance will still be the last—*'" He lifted his brows.

"'—*our sweetest memorial, the first kiss.*'" She was unable to keep from smiling. "While I can easily resist you, I'm no match for Byron."

"He is one of your weaknesses. Personally—" He curled his nose.

She sent him a rueful look. "As you've told me many times before. You must want to win this argument very, very badly to quote a poet you don't even like."

"I must. A first kiss is of the utmost importance in building a relationship."

"Sadly, with your manners, you'll never get close enough to any woman to offer a kiss."

To her surprise, his grin merely became more wolfish. "It would surprise you, what passes as flirtation among the romantic of your sex."

*What does that mean?*

Before she could consider it, he stepped forward and said, "Come, Dahlia, let's start this conversation over." When she hesitated, he added, "Here. I'll begin." He came to stand before her and bowed. "Good morning, Miss Balfour. How are you?"

His tone and manner were perfect, but so . . . odd and unlike him that while she knew she should be complimentary about them, a small part of her sighed as if she'd lost something.

*Don't be ridiculous.* She curtsied. "Good morning, my lord." As she stood, she leaned forward and said in an undertone, "Your bow is perfect."

"I have a good teacher. My new valet was once in the Duke of Wellington's employ."

"Was he? How did you come by him?"

"The duchess, of course. Our godmother is a woman of many resources."

"So he's been instructing you in—" She gestured lamely.

"I believe the phrase you are searching for is 'the gentlemanly arts.' That's what Lady Charlotte would call it."

"Ah. And for how long have you been receiving this tutelage?"

"For two months now, although apparently it wasn't long enough."

She had to smile. "No, no. You're much better than you were."

He grimaced. "Ouch."

"I didn't mean it that way."

"Of course not. If MacCreedy were here now, he'd tell me that a good dose of small talk would be just the thing. Perhaps we should discuss the weather. I've been told that's a safe topic." He looked at the windows, which were covered with frost. "It's cold."

She waited, but he seemed to think he'd done his job well, for he merely turned his gaze back to hers. "Well?" he asked finally. "Don't you think it's cold?"

She had to chuckle. "You don't enjoy this, do you?"

"I hate it," he agreed promptly. "Why waste words on the obvious? I can make no sense of the reason, thus I cannot do it well."

"It does seem redundant at times."

"Worse, it's boring and stupid and— Don't get me started."

"It's only meant to fill the silence until you can think of something of merit to say."

"I'd rather skip to the observations that have merit. For example, I've noticed that you dance very well."

"You've never seen me dance."

"I have, too. The night of our argument. I came back downstairs."

*And watched me.* For some reason, a little thrill raced through her. "Thank you. I'm flattered."

"It's merely dancing, which is hardly a skill worth mentioning."

She threw her hands in the air. "And there you go, ruining a perfectly nice compliment."

He looked astounded. "That ruined it?"

"Yes. Completely."

"But I didn't realize you could dance at all."

She could either laugh or cry, and frankly, his obvious astonishment was too comical to ignore. "Oh, Kirk, please. For both of our sakes, say no more."

"I was going to add that you were even graceful." He looked offended at her laughter. "Damn it, did I spoil it again?"

"The word 'even' made it far from a compliment."

"Good God, one word and I'm awry. It's all nonsense, I tell you."

"Perhaps." Taking pity on him, she tucked her hand in his arm. "Come, let us stroll to the window and look at this weather."

He fell into step immediately, sending her a quizzical glance. "So this is part of the inane business of 'small talk'?"

"It can be."

"That's good to know, for I like looking at the weather much better than talking about it."

They stopped by the window, where a steel gray sky sat atop trees and the grass was rippled by a cold wind.

Dahlia went to pull her hand from his arm, but Kirk placed his hand over hers and held it there.

Such a move wasn't at all within the boundaries of polite behavior, but there was something nice about his hand resting over hers, so warm and cozy, as if it belonged there.

He glanced down at her. "When did you learn to dance? I can't imagine you had much practice while living at Caith Manor."

"There were local assemblies and some small balls."

"In our neighborhood?"

"Yes—which you'd know, if you ever left your home or made yourself available to your neighbors."

"I detect a note of censure."

"You, sir, are a hermit."

"I like my own company."

"You're a hermit, and are the most happy when you're alone. You should admit it and be done with it."

"That's not true. There's one person whose company I prize more highly than my own." His gaze never left hers.

Dahlia didn't know where to look. "Only one?" she heard herself ask breathlessly.

"Only one."

If any other man had made her such a compliment, she'd have accused him of being a hardened flirt. But there was no guile in Kirk's eyes, no curve to his lip to assure her he was teasing. There was nothing but the bold intensity of a look that was far too direct, a hand that fit far too well over hers, and a soul far too tender to play the games society demanded.

*He means every word he says. He always has. And therein lies his vulnerability. He won't understand when others aren't so forthright.* She wished she could warn him, but before she could say anything, his fingers tightened over hers and he drew her closer still.

She suddenly found it difficult to breathe and her gaze locked with his once more. His eyes were of the richest brown swirled with gold, which made her think of the luxurious sable coat her sister had worn at her wedding. For one wild moment, Dahlia wondered what it would be like to have those eyes gaze upon her every day.

Kirk saw the softening of Dahlia's mouth and his body tightened instantly. "You know I'm not happier alone. If I were, I'd never have proposed to you."

Her lashes lowered and she said, "Perhaps 'happy' isn't the right word."

"It's the damned wrong word, is what it is."

She broke into a sudden, soft laugh.

He stiffened. "What?"

Her eyes twinkled up at him. "You cannot help yourself, can you? Every other word is a curse word, and every other sentence is a rude declaration of some sort."

"Actually, it's more like every fifth word. I know, for MacCreedy has been keeping count."

"That's very kind of him."

"No, it's not, but he enjoys it."

She chuckled and said in a gentle voice, "We were supposed to be talking about the weather."

"I'd rather talk about something that matters. About us, in fact."

Her expression closed, the laughter fading from her lips. "Kirk, there isn't an 'us.'"

He had to bite back a fierce desire to sweep her to him and kiss her until they couldn't breathe. *Not now and not like that,* he told himself firmly. *But soon.* "We know one another; it's to our benefit to look after each other's interests."

"I don't think it's wise."

"You're wrong. But if you wish, then you can assist me out of the mere kindness of your heart."

"And you'll leave my goals alone?"

"To find 'true love'?" At her nod, he grimaced, but said, "I'll try."

"I suppose that is better than nothing."

"Good. Now, about me—" He glinted a smile at

her that was at once so mischievous and so masculine that her lips trembled to return it. "Since you won't have me, I shall now start searching for a mate—"

"I do *hate* that word."

"Fine, then, a wife. I'm searching for a wife."

She didn't look happier, but she said, "That's much better."

He could feel her heart beating through the delicate veins in her wrist beneath his hand. "And you?" he asked. "You're looking for true love, but what else? What other attributes should this mystery suitor possess?"

"Hold. I thought you were going to leave me out of this completely."

"I'm merely asking a question. Do you have any ideas? Tall? Short? Thin? Athletic?"

She sent him an exasperated look. "There you go. You've moved out of the acceptable area of small talk and completely into the impolite realm of the 'too familiar.'"

"If I were to talk about the blasted weather, it would bore us both and then I'd say something foolish, and you'd get angry—with reason, but still—and then I'd try to apologize, but you wouldn't accept—" He shrugged. "We might as well skip all of that and discuss something that assists us both." When she hesitated, he said bluntly, "You're worried about something. It's in your eyes."

She sighed, and as she did so, she leaned a bit against him, her breast warm against his arm. "I shouldn't talk to you about this, but I suppose it wouldn't hurt."

"You've no one else to talk to."

"True. I admit I'm a bit worried about this undertaking."

"I don't blame you. There is no more serious undertaking than marriage."

"My sisters are happily married, both of them. My parents were, too. It's quite a challenge to follow in their footsteps. I can only hope that I'll make someone a good wife, for I truly wish to be happily married, too."

He watched her from under his lashes. She would be an excellent wife. She was beautiful, amusing, intelligent, well read, appreciated the arts, played the pianoforte with a passion that made his heart melt, was compassionate and gentle—he had to bite back a desire to demand how she could think she'd be anything but an excellent wife. "Don't be foolish."

Surprisingly, this didn't seem to calm her concerns.

He added, "Any man would be damned lucky if you so much as looked his way, much less agreed to wed him."

Her eyes widened. "Kirk, that's the nicest thing anyone has said to me since I arrived."

"Bloody hell, are the men here dead?"

She laughed although she shook her head. "Two things—one, as you know but cannot seem to remember, a gentleman never curses before a lady, and two, no, the men are not dead. Some have been very kind and said some lovely things, but I know you don't often praise, so it's worth a good deal when you do."

"I meant it." He did, too. And any fool with a pair of eyes and a brain would think the same way. She wasn't perfect, but to him, even her foibles—her impetuousness, her stubbornness, her innate desire to always better the people about her—added to her charm, even as they frustrated him to the ends of the earth and back. He supposed he was cursed, but there it was.

"In fact"—she tilted her head to one side, her gaze roving over his face—"what you said was actually quite romantic."

"I don't believe in romance."

"You don't believe in a good many things that you should." She sent him a half smile. "*Away with your fictions of flimsy romance, those tissue of falsehood which folly has wove. Give me the mild beam of the soul-breathing glance, or the rapture which dwells—*'"

"'*—on the first kiss of love.*'"

"Exactly! You—of all people—have memorized that poem. Lord Bryon should be honored."

"Perhaps you don't know me as well as you think."

"Perhaps not." Her voice was thoughtful, and she gave him an appraising look. "When I came to the library, I was determined to tell you that your scheme was impossible, but now . . . Perhaps you are right."

"About the kiss?"

"Yes."

Hope leapt but he held it at bay, afraid it might

show on his face and frighten her away from the line she was about to cross. "So perhaps . . ."

"Perhaps we *should* practice that all-important first kiss. Where you could not convince, Byron has."

"For once, I find myself liking him."

She sent him a laughing look, and with it, she had him completely at her mercy.

Unaware of her power, she slipped her hand from his arm and faced him. "So . . . how do we proceed?"

For a wild moment, he couldn't move or speak or even breathe. But then a quirk of her brows brought him to life. "Slowly. There will be no rushing this time." He set his cane against a chair and then turned to face her and gently took her hands in his.

It was such a simple gesture, to grasp her hands, yet it gave rise to a new tension—one so thick and instant that he was surprised it didn't shimmer in the air about them.

Dahlia gave him a nervous laugh. "I—I don't know what to—"

"This time, just hold still."

"But I—"

He captured the rest of her words with the gentlest of kisses, his lips barely possessing hers.

Dahlia stood stock-still, her eyes wide, Kirk's warm lips over hers. He didn't move, didn't break contact, but his lips held her in place. Her entire body seemed to focus on her lips, and only that surface had any feeling, any sensation. But oh, how *much* they felt. She was drawn to him through that kiss, and a slow heat began to simmer, deep within her. She pressed forward, leaning toward him and—

He lifted his head and broke the kiss.

Dahlia closed her eyes as tremors of awareness flooded through her, making her skin prickle and—of all things—her breasts tingle. She felt alive, and naughty, and excited—so many feelings at once. She touched her lips with her fingertips and opened her eyes to find Kirk watching her, his gaze dark.

She sighed. "That was—"

He kissed her again, only this time, he pulled her close so that she was pressed to his wide chest, his arms wrapped about her. This kiss didn't ask, but took. His mouth possessed hers, demanding more. And she was ready to oblige, her body awakening under his touch.

He plundered her mouth ruthlessly, taking what he wanted, and she gave without reflection, drowning in the wild feelings that coursed through her. When he sucked on her bottom lip, she shifted restlessly against him, agonizingly aware of wanting more, needing more. She could no longer think, no longer hear, no longer do anything but *be*, and it was a wild, untrammeled feeling that thrilled and frightened at the same time.

Somewhere along the way, she'd slipped her arms about his neck and now she kissed him back, giving back embrace for embrace. Mimicking him, she took his bottom lip between hers and gently sucked.

He moaned and his hands cupped her bottom urgently in a way that should have alarmed her, but only made her hold him tighter. He deepened the kiss, running his tongue over her lips until she opened for him as—

*Woof!*

Dahlia and Kirk froze, their gazes suddenly open and locked with each other.

*Woof! Woof!*

Dahlia pulled away and looked down.

An old pug sat not a foot away, grinning up at them as if aware of the impropriety of the moment, his gray muzzle spattered with orange marmalade. As if he realized he wasn't prepared for company, his long tongue flicked out and removed the marmalade and he resumed his grin.

Kirk gave a muffled curse. He sent Dahlia a lingering, heated look and then he stepped away.

The chilled air instantly took the place of his warm arms and she was aware of a deep loss, as if all of the excitement of the day had been whisked away, leaving her feeling alone and vulnerable. She found it difficult to swallow.

Kirk cursed, "Damn it, wherever that dog goes, there's sure to be—"

"Oh!" came Lady Charlotte's breathless voice from the doorway.

Dahlia's face heated as she turned toward the doorway and dipped a curtsy. "Good morning, Lady Charlotte. It's a bit early for you, isn't it?"

"Oh la, I've been up since dawn."

"Dawn? Really?"

"Actually, no. It was closer to nine, but it sounds better when I say 'dawn.'" Lady Charlotte came farther inside, her lace cap hanging askew, a stack of books clutched in her plump hands. Her bright blue gaze flickered between Dahlia and Kirk. "I hope I'm not disturbing a private tête-à-tête?"

"Don't be absurd," Kirk said in a husky voice. "Miss Balfour and I were just discussing the works of Byron."

Lady Charlotte looked disappointed, but she quickly rallied. "I do love Byron."

"Then you have excellent company in Miss Balfour."

"But not you?"

"I have never been a follower, although I must admit some of his poems speak so true that they cannot be ignored."

Dahlia knew exactly the one he spoke of, and her cheeks heated yet more.

Lady Charlotte nodded, her cap flopping over her ear. "There are times I feel that exact same way about passages in certain books, and I wish others could hear them as I do in my mind." She blinked, looking much struck. "Lord Kirk, you have a lovely voice; I've noticed it before."

She waited for him to thank her for her compliment, but when he merely continued to regard her much as one might a snake found suddenly upon one's terrace, she continued undaunted. "Would you mind reading for the other guests one evening after dinner?"

"No." At Dahlia's exasperated glance, he added in a reluctant tone, "No, *thank you.*"

Lady Charlotte merely smiled. "I'm certain you'll enjoy it. Oh, this is so fortuitous! Just this morning, her grace and I decided that an evening listening to the best voices among our guests as they read their favorite works of poetry and perhaps an improving essay or two might be just the thing. We could alternate between humorous, romantic, and other works." She sent an arch look at Dahlia. "For variety, we thought we might even add a few performances on the pianoforte, if someone were so inclined?"

"I fear I'm not proficient enough to—"

"Of course you are, dear! I shall put *both* of you down for our entertainment and—"

"No," Kirk broke in. "Lady Charlotte, I do not read aloud. Perhaps another—"

"You've read aloud to me," Dahlia said promptly. "You do it quite well, too."

Perhaps, just perhaps, if the other guests heard him read, they'd see him the way she'd come to see him all of those months ago. It was the one time his passions had shown through, and no one would ever again wonder if such a scarred and caustic man had any feelings left to hurt. They'd know he was a man capable of great emotion.

He scowled. "That was months ago."

"I doubt you've forgotten how to read." Dahlia curtsied to Lady Charlotte. "We'll both be glad to assist with the evening's entertainment, but I'll need to borrow her grace's pianoforte for a bit of practice."

"Of course, my dear. And Lord Kirk, pray stop scowling. I'm certain you'll do quite well. When we mentioned our idea to a few of the younger guests this morning over breakfast, the females were quite taken with the idea and instantly offered to read their favorite poems and such. But no gentlemen offered his services, so you are quite necessary to the success of our evening. Once the other gentlemen hear that you've agreed to read, I'm sure they'll be more amenable. Will you read a poem from Byron, perhaps?"

Dahlia glanced at Kirk. He sighed heavily, but then said, "Fine, fine. I'll do it. You have worn me down with your insistence."

Nothing could have been more ungracious, but Lady Charlotte couldn't have looked happier. "I'm very, very good at that."

Reluctance stiff in his shoulders, Kirk bowed. "I hope you don't mind, but I must leave. I'm expected elsewhere." Without waiting for a response, he walked toward the door. As he passed by Dahlia, he paused. "Tomorrow after breakfast."

It wasn't a question. Because of that, and for other even more important reasons, she knew she should protest. She should leave this room and vow to never again be alone with him, no matter the cost.

But instead, her lips still tingling from his kiss, she replied in a very faint voice, "Yes. Of course."

His hot gaze flashed over her and then he was gone, the elderly pug waddling after him.

Lady Charlotte tsked. "That was certainly abrupt. He's better than he was, though. And Randolph seems to have taken a liking to him, which is surprising."

"Indeed," Dahlia murmured. Bemused, and awhirl with feelings she'd never known existed, she found it difficult to listen as Lady Charlotte began talking about a book she'd just read that had a scene set in a library that almost perfectly matched the duchess's.

Dahlia barely waited for Lady Charlotte to take a much-needed breath and then quickly excused herself, saying she had to get ready for the coming tournament.

"Of course, my dear," Lady Charlotte said graciously. "I'm sure you'll wish to compose yourself before then. But there's one thing I must mention." She glanced at the doorway and then said in a low tone, "Her grace and I heard about the circumstances of your challenge to Lady Mary and Miss Stewart. It's unfortunate that gently bred young women would speak so disparagingly of Lord Kirk's scars."

*Good God, if the duchess and Lady Charlotte know the particulars of our wager, then so must everyone else.* She sighed. "It seems that what I thought a rather private matter is no longer private at all. From what I gathered at breakfast, several people plan on attending, too."

"More than you might realize. Her grace was not

happy to hear how Lady Mary and Miss Stewart spoke ill of Lord Kirk, and she is not one to mince words about such happenings. In fact, she was going to speak to both young ladies in question just this morning, but I assured her that you had the matter well in hand." Lady Charlotte leaned forward. "You do, don't you? Have it *well in hand*?"

"I'm certain I'll win the tournament, if that's what you mean."

"That's exactly what I mean." Lady Charlotte couldn't have looked happier. "You are to be commended for standing up for Lord Kirk."

"He's a neighbor of mine. I would do the same for anyone from Aberdeenshire."

"That's quite loyal." Lady Charlotte gave Dahlia a curious look. "I don't suppose you had any other reason for coming to his defense?"

"No."

"None?"

"Not a one."

Lady Charlotte looked disappointed. "Oh well. I had hoped that— But that's of no matter. I don't suppose he knows about the tournament or the circumstances surrounding it?"

"He didn't mention it."

"Ah. That's probably best. He would be so angry, you know."

"Why? I'd think he would be most grateful to discover that so many people were willing to look out for his interests."

"Grateful? A man that proud? That's not likely. So if you please, do not say anything to him about it. If we're fortunate, he'll never know how many of us—including you, my dear—stood up for his cause."

Dahlia glanced at the door. *Would he be angry? Truly angry?* She turned back to Lady Charlotte. "Thank you for your advice. I shall heed it, of course."

"And you'll win the tournament?" At Dahlia's nod, Lady Charlotte added, "And if you could possibly win by at least five points, I'd be extremely grateful."

*Why would the number of points matter?* Dahlia wondered. Still, she inclined her head. "Of course."

"Excellent, my dear! Excellent!" Lady Charlotte beamed. "Now, off with you, for I've no doubt you've preparations to make."

"Thank you." Dahlia curtsied and made her escape, aware of the oddest feeling, as if her feet weren't touching the floor. Even after being interrupted by a dog, being importuned by Lady Charlotte, and being quizzed about the coming tournament, she still felt the effects of the kiss coursing through her veins.

When she reached the hallway, she found it blessedly abandoned and, finally, she was alone. She slipped beside a huge, ornate wall clock which hid her from view, and leaned against the wall, pressing her fingertips to her lips.

*So that was what a kiss was supposed to be.* Her entire body still quivered, wildly alive and energetic, as if she were ready to run up a hill or take on a monumental task—*anything* to answer this flush of power that trembled through her.

She trailed her fingertips from her lips to her throat where her pulse beat wildly. She was still panting slightly, her breasts oddly heavy, her nipples strangely sensitive. It was as if no part of her body were the same. *All from a kiss.*

She pressed her hands to her heated cheeks. *I had no idea a simple kiss could be so . . . significant.*

Her only regret was that her sisters were not here to discuss this amazing discovery, something they probably already knew. If only—

The sound of voices approaching made her smooth her gown and hair. She composed her expression to one of polite civility and stepped into the hallway, glancing at the clock face. She was late for her meeting with Lord Dalhousie in the portrait gallery, but she was in no frame of mind to hear about the Roxburghe portraits today. She'd send a footman with a note bearing her apologies, and reschedule for a better time.

With that in mind, she hurried to the foyer and gave instructions and a coin to one of the footmen waiting there, and then hurried toward the staircase. But just as she placed her foot upon the bottom step, an entire gaggle of women swarmed out of the salon.

"Ah, there's Miss Balfour now!" called a matron wearing a purple turban adorned with an ostrich feather held in place with an emerald pin. Mrs. Selfridge came to slip her arm through Dahlia's. "This is so fortunate, for we were just discussing your coming battledore match."

"My— Oh yes. It's not for some hours yet."

"Yes, but we were just wondering about your *skills*."

"In battledore? Well, I've played with my sisters quite a bit."

They all looked at her expectantly.

"And?" Lady Hamilton, her wiry carrot-colored hair pinned with blue flowers, leaned forward. "Surely you've played in some tournaments?"

Dahlia shook her head.

Miss Spencer shook her head. "Don't believe a word she says; she's just being modest. Come, Miss Balfour, let's retire to the Blue Salon and discuss this further."

Dahlia tried to resist, but they'd have none of it, demanding "only a moment" of her time. Then they were carrying her into the Blue Salon, leaving her feeling like a leaf swept away by a flooding stream.

## Eleven

**From the Diary of the Duchess of Roxburghe**
Just now, whilst on my way to change into something suitable for viewing the battledore tournament that my guests have suddenly developed a madness for, I realized that Charlotte was right and everyone is too distracted to decorate their assigned portions of the house. I shall have to be vigilant in making certain the castle is in full holiday bloom when the time comes for the ball. In the meantime, I must hurry to the battledore courts, for—as Charlotte and some of the other guests have taken to calling it—the Battledore of Honor begins shortly . . .

Half an hour later, Dahlia was still caught in the salon, trying desperately to make her escape. The worst of her captors were Mrs. Montrose; her chattering daughter, Miss Slyphania; and the indomitable Mrs. Selfridge. They'd all quizzed her relentlessly about her battledore experiences, the number of games she'd played with her sisters, and her "strategies," which they apparently assumed to be many and complex.

The rumor mill had caught the tone of her conversation with Lady Mary and Miss Stewart, and Lord Kirk's name was mentioned more than once, although Dahlia managed to avoid any direct comment. But the realization worried her. Was Lady Charlotte right in predicting that Kirk would be furious with Dahlia for interfering in something he might see as his own personal business?

Whatever he thought, she couldn't back down— not now, not with so many people involved. She was at a loss to know why everyone seemed so enthused about the tournament, for she was certain no one cared about Lord Kirk's honor the way she did. But they all seemed deeply engaged with the potential outcome, one way or another.

Dahlia felt relief when Miss MacLeod stuck her head in the door and brightened on seeing her seated amidst the group. "Miss Balfour! Just the person I wished to see."

Dahlia almost leapt to her feet. "Ah, Miss MacLeod! I was just leaving. I—I'm to meet Viscount Dalhousie for a tour of the portrait gallery."

Miss MacLeod crossed the room in a rustle of pale green jaconet muslin, gathered with a lemon-colored ribbon and matching slippers. "Don't worry about Dalhousie. I saw him wandering about the gallery like a lost soul and explained that you must have been held up."

"He's not angry, is he?"

"Lud, no. Miss Stewart was with me and she kindly offered to take your place. Dalhousie was explaining the portrait history to her as I left."

All eyes turned to Dahlia as a silence fell over the group. *Goodness, they wish to see me react to that, and ask even more questions. Well, they're to be disappointed.*

"How pleasant for them both. I was sadly worried that he'd be bored, left alone. I'm glad Miss Stewart was available."

"Just what I thought." Miss MacLeod slipped an arm through Dahlia's. "Now come, I must speak to you about the match. Dalhousie and I have much of it planned, but there are still a few details that must be addressed." With a wave to the protesting ladies, she led Dahlia out of the room.

As soon as they reached the foyer, Miss MacLeod led Dahlia into the dining room.

"Miss MacLeod, I really should rest before—"

"Yes, but this won't take long." Several footmen, setting up tables for a cold luncheon and arranging festive springs of mistletoe and red candles down the center of the table, stopped what they were doing on seeing the two young ladies, but a friendly "Carry on" from Miss MacLeod freed them to continue their duties.

Miss MacLeod pulled Dahlia to a windowed alcove where they might not be overheard.

"I vow, but every guest at the castle has become enamored of this one match," Dahlia said.

"I know. It seems odd to me. And you can't tell me they've all suddenly developed a fondness for Lord Kirk and are glad someone is standing up for him, for I've seen their reaction when he enters a room."

"They scatter like fish before a crocodile."

"Exactly. I wish the motives of our fellow guests were more noble, but I fear they are concerned with something far more base: they all wish to win."

"Win what?"

"Their wagers."

Dahlia blinked. "Wagers? On me?"

Miss MacLeod chuckled. "Yes, some of them. Some of them, not."

Dahlia saw nothing to laugh at. "I can't imagine her grace would countenance such a thing."

"Then you don't know her grace well. The Duchess of Roxburghe is quite a gambler. In her heyday, it was the fashion for women to wager at high stakes. Look at the Duchess of Devonshire."

"Who brought one of the greatest fortunes in the history of England to its knees? I hardly think she is a good example. I can't imagine my godmother throwing away a fortune."

"And she never would; she's Scottish and knows the value of a coin. So while there is to be gambling, her grace has limited all wagers to no more than a guinea—so you won't see any fortunes changing hands. The enthusiasm you see is for bragging rights rather than fortune, but it's enough. I believe every guest present now has a finger in the pie."

"Oh no." Dahlia pressed her hands to her cheeks. All of her earlier euphoria was now gone. "Good God, this has gotten out of hand. It was just to be a friendly wager between the three of us—"

"Friendly? Miss Balfour, I was there. Lady Mary and Miss Stewart deserved a challenge."

There was no mistaking the plain look Miss MacLeod sent her way. Dahlia frowned. "You are their friend."

"No, I'm not. I know them, yes. But friends?" Miss MacLeod shook her head. "Sadly, one cannot truly be friendly with Lady Mary. If there is anyone I would count as a friend, or would wish to, it is Miss Stewart. She has always been very kind to me, although she's far too ready to please Lady Mary."

"I've noticed that." Dahlia was silent for a moment. "So they sent you to speak to me as their second. I don't suppose they wish to offer their apologies and ask for the whole thing to be forgotten. If so, I am quite ready to—"

"Oh no. They asked me to bring you their compliments and to inform you that no quarter will be given."

Dahlia stiffened. "That was hardly necessary."

"I thought so, too." She shook her head. "Miss Balfour—"

"Please, call me Dahlia." She sat upon the window seat and patted the cushion beside her, feeling drained. "Pray join me. I cannot stand another moment."

Miss MacLeod did so, smiling a little. "I hope you regain your energy before the match."

"Oh, I shall. I will order some luncheon on a tray delivered to my room, and will be right as rain with a little quiet." *I hope.*

Miss MacLeod tilted her head to one side. "I hope you don't find this forward, but I feel that we shall know each other quite well before this is over."

"That would be nice. I don't know many of the guests."

"It *will* be very nice. And you should call me Anne. I'm here because Lord Dalhousie asked me to speak to you and explain a bit about Miss Stewart and Lady Mary."

"You've come to help me?"

"If by 'help,' you mean 'assist in winning,' no. I am still their second. Besides, I've never played a game of battledore in my life, so I wouldn't know where to begin in offering assistance. Dalhousie thought you should know why Lady Mary and Miss Stewart are the way they are."

"Why does he wish that?"

Anne smiled. "I suspect he believes it will assist you in your efforts, although I'm not so certain." She adjusted the folds in her skirts and said in a thoughtful tone, "The viscount is a good man, you know. Better than most. And he's known Lady Mary since he was in short coats."

"I had no idea."

"Oh yes. Lady Mary's father, the Earl of Buchan, and the late Viscount Dalhousie were great friends." Anne plumped a pillow and leaned against it. "I think they'd always hoped that Lady Mary and Lord Dalhousie might make a match of it, but it never came to fruition. Lady Mary is quite wealthy and her family is significant, which I'm sure you know, for she cannot take more than two breaths without mentioning that she can trace her lineage all the way back to William the Conqueror. But despite her bravado, she's an only child, and was sickly for most of her life. That has shaped her character, and not always for the best."

"You'd never know it to see her now, for she's in the bloom of good health."

"She cast off the remnants of her childhood ailments when she left the schoolroom. I believe it is because of the riding we did at our boarding school. Miss Latham, the headmistress, is an accomplished horsewoman and she was determined that all of us would be, too. However, Dalhousie thinks it is because the countess, Lady Mary's mother, was no longer able to coddle her daughter so."

"I'm sorry to hear of Lady Mary's misfortunes."

"It's good to know your opponents. Miss Stewart, on the other hand, is far from Lady Mary's equal.

It's been rumored that Miss Stewart's only claim to society is Lady Mary's sponsorship. Some people say Miss Stewart's father was once"—Anne glanced at the footmen, and then leaned closer and whispered— "Lady Mary's head groom."

"She dresses very well for someone without funds."

"Lady Mary's castoffs. Every one. Lady Mary loves to lord it over Miss Stewart, and reminds her of it frequently. I feel for her, I truly do."

Dahlia's heart had been sinking as Anne revealed more and more. *Had I known all of this, I would never have challenged either of them, Lady Mary because she's not worth the attention, and Miss Stewart because her life is difficult enough without my complicating things.*

"Miss MacLeod—Anne, do you think I should step back from the challenge?"

"Lud, no! Everyone is going to be there, so it's too late for that. Besides, to be honest, Lady Mary could use a good setdown. Since yesterday, she has been relentless in mocking Lord Kirk. Just this morning she said that Lord Kirk's manners were no better than a groom's, although she doubted that such a maimed and lame man could even ride, being nearly an invalid. Naturally her comment cut both Lord Kirk and, to some extent, poor Miss Stewart."

Dahlia's jaw tightened. *How dare that woman? I should—*

"Ah! There's Dalhousie now, peeking through the doorway." Anne waved. "He must wish to confirm our arrangements for the tournament and— Oh dear." She lowered her voice. "Lady Mary and Miss Stewart are with him."

Dahlia barely heard, for she was still fuming. Maimed and lame, indeed! Kirk may have a faint limp, but he was far from being "maimed." As for lame, he was every inch a healthy man under his well-pressed coats, a fact she knew better than anyone. This morning, she'd felt nothing but solid muscle under her fingertips when they'd kissed. The memory, instant and sensual, warmed her face, and her shoulders, which had drawn up as she'd gotten angry, relaxed a little. *I know him and they don't. Therefore their opinions don't matter.*

"Ah, Miss Balfour!" Dalhousie took her hand and bowed over it, looking through his lashes as he spoke. "I missed you in the gallery this morning."

Dahlia had no doubt that look had gotten him excused from many a transgression. "I'm so sorry, but I was detained. Did you receive my message?"

Dalhousie pressed his other hand over hers, capturing it firmly. "Yes, but it did little to reconcile me to your absence."

Dahlia, aware of Lady Mary's tight expression as she looked on, found herself unable to think of a single response. The viscount was being gallant, and Dahlia was quite certain she'd enjoy his flirtation under more normal circumstances. After all, she'd come to the duchess's house to find romance, and who wouldn't enjoy a handsome, titled gentleman offering compliments with such a whimsical smile? Why, she'd dreamed of just such a thing.

But right now, all she felt was a stab of irritation, and the fact that Lady Mary was glaring over his shoulder didn't add an iota of pleasure to the moment.

Dahlia had to admit that Lady Mary looked stunning in a morning gown of blue muslin finished at the hem à la Van Dyck, her Greek kid spring slippers of gold complemented by her gold and ruby bracelet and earrings. She was every inch the daughter of a wealthy, powerful house.

Now, she stepped forward and slipped her arm through Dalhousie's, effectively drawing his hand from Dahlia's. "We *all* missed you, Miss Balfour." There was no mistaking the falseness of Lady Mary's tone. "Dalhousie gave the most amusing tour."

Miss Stewart, dressed in a spring muslin featuring tiny roses, nodded—ever eager to assist her friend. "He'd asked Lady Charlotte to tutor him on the portraits, so he was well prepared. Why, the story about the third Duke of Roxburghe was so amusing! Apparently he—"

"Alayne, enough!" Lady Mary's brows rose. "As amusing as it was for us, I'm sure Miss Balfour doesn't wish to hear about our tour of the gallery, and would instead like to speak about our upcoming match."

"An excellent idea!" Dalhousie slipped his arm from Lady Mary's grasp. "Last night Miss MacLeod and I went over the rules. You will each be able to choose a battledore paddle from the duchess's large selection. Miss MacLeod and I have already picked out the best shuttlecocks for the game. As for the points—" He bowed to Anne.

She smiled. "Since battledore may be played in two ways—count each hit as a point, or count the drops—Lord Dalhousie and I had to make a decision. As this is a two-to-one game, it is only fair to count the drops. Every missed hit, or drop, will count as a point for the other side. Whoever is first to reach twenty wins the game. Any questions?"

Lady Mary shrugged. "It suits me."

Dahlia nodded. "I agree."

"Good," Dalhousie said, looking relieved. "So now we must set the wager itself. Lady Mary and Miss Stewart, do you have anything in particular you'd like to wager?"

Miss Stewart sent a quick glance at Lady Mary, then turned to Dahlia. "What about your earrings? We've noticed you always wear the same pair."

Dahlia wore the small garnet and gold earrings frequently. They were family heirlooms, given to her by her mother and once owned by her grandmother. She was just about to shake her head when Lady Mary sniffed.

"I don't have anything to match against garnets." She said the word "garnets" as if she thought they were the most unworthy gemstone upon the planet. "Perhaps this." She unrolled her glove and peeled it off, and then held it toward Dahlia.

"Your gloves?"

"Oh no. Just one. I want to be fair. This glove came all the way from Paris and is embroidered with Belgian lace."

Dahlia looked at the glove dangling so carelessly from Lady Mary's hand, too shocked by her sheer rudeness to reply.

"Mary," Anne murmured reprovingly. "Pray be polite."

"I'm being perfectly polite. You can't tell me this glove isn't worth both of those earrings."

Instantly Dahlia heard herself say, "I agree to wager my earrings. But I want something other than a glove when I win. What I want is a promise."

Dalhousie and Anne exchanged glances. "A promise?" he asked.

"If I win, then Lady Mary and Miss Stewart will stop mocking Lord Kirk for the rest of their stay at Floors Castle."

Lady Mary drew her glove through her hand, her eyes narrowed unpleasantly. "Miss Balfour, you overstep yourself."

"Why? Because I'm asking you to stop abusing a man who is a very kind and decent person?"

"Kind?" Lady Mary couldn't have looked more surprised. "He's rude."

"Very," Miss Stewart agreed. "Just this morning, I passed him in the hallway and said good morning, but he just kept on going, ignoring me completely."

"He can be as rude as he wishes, but you will not mention it. Nor will you discuss his limp or scars, nor say anything about him other than kind, good things."

Miss Stewart looked outraged. "You can't tell us what to—"

Lady Mary silenced her friend with a wave of her hand. "Miss Balfour, we'll accept your conditions. But I must warn you, after we've won our match, I may feel even more compelled to mock Lord Kirk, *especially* in your hearing."

Dahlia had to fight the urge to throw a pillow from the window seat right in Lady Mary's smug face. "Fortunately for Lord Kirk, I shan't lose."

"You're that confident that you'll win?"

"Yes."

"So confident that you'll spot us . . . say, five points?"

Dahlia hesitated. *Five points? Do I dare risk it?*

Lady Mary laughed. "I thought not. I'll—"

"Yes." The word flew from Dahlia's lips before she could stop it.

Lady Mary's look of triumph could not be mistaken. "Then we are set. Your earrings against our comments regarding Lord Kirk. I look forward to the game. I look even more forward to giving your earrings to my maid. She'll look pretty in garnets."

Hands clenched to hide her fury, Dahlia stood and bowed. "We shall see, Lady Mary. Now, if you'll excuse me, I need to get ready." Without a backward glance, she left the group by the window seat, passing by several footmen who were setting out Christmas-themed china for the luncheon. It wasn't until she reached the landing on the grand staircase that her actions fully settled in, and she had to pause and press a hand to her head where a dull ache had formed. *Good God, I can't afford one misstep. Not one.*

# *Twelve*

**From the Diary of the Duchess of Roxburghe**
I've seen many battledore games on these grounds,
but none equal in intensity or pure enthusiasm.
However, it wasn't just the game that left our guests
reeling, but rather what occurred immediately
after . . .

Dahlia opened the door to her bedchamber and
found Freya hanging up a pressed gown. "Freya, I'm
promised to play battledore this afternoon—though it
is more like going to war."

"Och, miss, verrah guid. Shall I order ye some luncheon whilst ye get ready?" At Dahlia's nod, the maid
tugged the bellpull that hung by the fireplace, her eyes
bright with curiosity. "If ye dinna mind me askin',
who are ye goin' t' war wit'?"

"Lady Mary and Miss Stewart. If they win, I forfeit
my earrings." Dahlia touched one of them, a pang in
her heart at the thought of losing them.

Freya clicked her tongue. "Ye ne'er wear any others."

"They're very dear to me." She forced a smile. "But the risk is worth it. For if I win, they are to stop gossiping so unkindly about Lord Kirk."

The maid looked surprised. "Lord Kirk? But ye—"

A knock sounded on the door and the maid went to answer it. She spoke quickly to the footman outside, and then closed the door. "A tray will be brought oop shortly, miss."

"Very good."

Freya returned to Dahlia's side. "So ye're challengin' Lady Mary and Miss Stewart to a game o' battledore to keep them from speakin' ill o' Lord Kirk?"

"You wouldn't believe the horrid things they've been saying. They were so rude, whispering that he was maimed and lame—I couldn't stand by and accept it. I *had* to do something." Whatever happened, she couldn't allow Kirk to defend himself against such unjust comments. While he'd have swiftly put Lady Mary and Miss Stewart in their place, Dahlia was certain he'd do it in the most heavy-handed and rude way possible. She shuddered to even think of the things he might say, all of which would be repeated and cause yet more talk. It was better for all concerned that she handle this small incident herself. If all went well, Lady Mary and Miss Stewart would be effectively silenced for the duration of their visit, and Kirk might never know.

Dahlia smiled at Freya. "I need to change into something that allows me to move easily. Somewhere in my wardrobe is an older gown of gray muslin that barely reaches my ankles. I hung it there a day ago when I got back from a traipse through the north fields. The higher hem doesn't drag on the ground as much as some of my others."

"Aye, miss. I'll look now." The maid hurried to the wardrobe and peeked inside. "'Tis kind o' ye to wage a battle o' honor o'er Lord Kirk."

"I suppose you could call it that, although I very much doubt Lord Kirk would think it so. He does not know yet of the wager. I hope he never finds out, though that may be a vain hope." She dropped into the cushioned seat before her dressing table. "I must win."

"I'm sure ye will, miss."

Dahlia fidgeted with her silver backed brush. "Lord Kirk might be very angry if he ever found out."

"How would ye know if he was angry or no', wha' wit' his scowlin' and growlin'?" At Dahlia's surprised look, Freya flushed and hurried to add, "No' tha' he's no' a nice mon, fer I'm sure he is, but he dinna wear happiness as oft as one might wish."

Dahlia had to chuckle. "That's very gently said, Freya, but the truth is, he's a curmudgeon and a grump. He's always been that way." *But when he smiles . . .* She could picture the rare twinkle in his eyes, and the way his face transformed, and she found herself smiling, too. "Whether he gets angry about my assistance or not, I've committed myself to doing this."

Freya held up the gray gown. "Is this the gown ye wished, miss?"

"Yes! Thank you."

The maid started to bring the gown, but then something caught her eye and she frowned. "Och, there's a bit o' mud on it. It shouldna be hangin' dirty in yer wardrobe."

"It's only a little muddy, and I planned on going for another walk in the morning, so there was no sense in asking you to clean it just yet. Pray bring it here."

"Yes, miss."

Soon Dahlia was dressed in the plain gown, her feet encased in a pair of worn leather boots that fit her feet perfectly. She held one out for Freya to examine. "They may not look like much, but they fit like a glove and lace over my ankles."

"They'll do ye well during the match, miss."

"Very well. Better than slippers, which I expect my opponents will wear. Slippers may be prettier, but they fall off when one leaps." She tucked her foot back under her skirts before turning back to the dressing table. "Now, my hair. I cannot play without having it well secured." She met the maid's gaze in the mirror. "I shall place myself in your capable hands for that."

"Och, miss, I'll make certain 'twill no' fall." Beaming, Freya pulled out the crystal jar that held the hairpins and began to work her magic.

Dahlia, meanwhile, reviewed every game she'd ever played with her sisters. What tricks might her opponents resort to? What plays might help her win her cause? She wished she hadn't allowed her pride to goad her into spotting the other side with five whole points.

Dahlia's jaw firmed. She would *not* lose this game.

For her own sake, as well as Kirk's, she couldn't afford to.

Six hours later, a spontaneous round of applause met Dahlia as she entered the dining room. Guests crowded around her, offering their congratulations and making jocular comments.

Mr. Ballanoch, ever ready for a good snippet of gossip, pushed through the crowd and took her hands in his. "My dear Miss Balfour, what a match! It shall go down in the annals of battledore."

Mrs. Selfridge patted Dahlia's shoulder. "And that lunge at the very beginning of the game—masterful, my dear! I told Lady Hamilton that you were like Diana the huntress, and no amount of wild parries would force you to give up the shuttlecock."

Lady Hamilton added, "The play that stands out in my mind was the final one. It was simply spectacular. There you were, waiting for the shot." She stepped back and stared into the sky, an invisible paddle in her hands. "It came, but went awry, flying wide to your left." Lady Hamilton jerked to her left, her eyes following the imaginary shuttlecock. "Anyone else would have allowed it to fly by, but you knew it was the winning point. You *had* to hit it. So you stretched out as far as you could, and leapt full into the breach and—" Lady Hamilton lunged to one side and swung her imaginary paddle, almost knocking over a footman holding a tray of drinks. "Pop! You *got* it!" Lady Hamilton clasped her hands together. "Ah, sweet success!"

"That was a perfect shot," Mr. Ballanoch agreed. "You returned it right between Lady Mary's eyes. She didn't have a chance to raise her paddle in defense."

"I didn't mean to hit her with the shuttlecock." Dahlia's ears still rang from the screams. "I'm glad it only made the faintest of marks."

"Oh, it'll bruise, I've no doubt, for I was on the other side of the room and I heard it hit." He shrugged. "But those are the chances one takes in such an endeavor. It was a brave victory!"

"So it was!" Lady MacKintoch nodded, all three of her chins wagging in agreement. "Brave indeed, though your opponents were none too happy with the outcome."

"I'm certain Lady Mary didn't mean anything she said after the match."

"Not after her grace got through with her." Mrs. Selfridge giggled. "Of all the house parties I've attended here, I've never seen her grace take anyone by the ear and march them from the room as if they were a child of six—but by God, that's what she did!"

Mr. Ballanoch leaned closer. "Tell us, Miss Balfour, is it true that your wager with Lady Mary was for her to stop speaking so harshly of Lord Kirk ever again and—"

"The wager is a private matter between Lady Mary, Miss Stewart, and myself," Dahlia said quickly, glad Kirk was nowhere in sight. It had dawned on her that, had she thought it through, she would have arranged to meet with him in private right after the match and explain how the wager had come about, but she hadn't had time to think properly. "I would rather not discuss the wager."

"Nonsense," Mrs. Hamilton said. "You should be lauded for standing up for poor Lord Kirk. Such a pity about his face."

Mr. Ballanoch grimaced. "I shudder every time I look at—"

"As I said," Dahlia interrupted in a frosty tone. "I will not discuss the wager. In fact, I don't plan on mentioning the match again. I'm quite fatigued."

"Of course you are," Miss Spencer agreed, taking Dahlia's arm and leading her to one side. "Come and let's find some champagne. The duchess ordered it especially after your match and—" She came to an abrupt halt as a tall figure blocked their path.

Dahlia knew without looking up which broad-shouldered male now stood before her, too close for comfort and sending off palpable waves of fury. *Oh dear, he's every bit as angry as I feared.* Gulping back a wince, she glanced up at him and forced a smile.

Miss Spencer was quicker. "Lord Kirk, there you are! Have you come to thank Miss Balfour for performing such a duty to your good name?"

Wincing inwardly, Dahlia peeked at him through her lashes. His face was white, his lips pressed into a straight line, his eyes ablaze as he leaned upon his cane. "No," he said in a blunt tone. "I didn't come to thank her. She did nothing in my interest."

Lady Hamilton's smile faded. "You're quite wrong. She—"

"Lady Hamilton," Dahlia said quickly, "please don't bother explaining things to Lord Kirk. He will make up his own mind about events; facts do not interest him."

Kirk's expression darkened. "Pardon us." He reached out and captured Dahlia's wrist and limped away, pulling her after him, his cane thudding furiously on the carpeted floor.

Dahlia had to scamper to keep up with her captor. "Blast it, Kirk, you can't just pull me around like a horse!"

"Be glad you're no horse of mine." He reached the wall, pulled her around to face him, and then released her. "You have a lot of explaining to do."

She rubbed her wrist. It wasn't sore, for although he'd tugged her along, he hadn't held her too tightly. Still, her skin tingled where his long fingers had been. "I have nothing to explain."

"Oh? Then what in the hell was that blasted game about? And don't tell me it didn't concern me, for I know it did."

She shrugged. "It was just a game."

His eyes blazed anew. "It was not just a game. Every person in this room placed a wager on it."

They had, too. She'd been astounded when she'd seen the amount of notes changing hands after the final stroke. "I didn't expect that. We were just playing a friendly game of battledore and—"

"There was nothing friendly about that game." His gaze narrowed. "What were the stakes?"

She found it suddenly difficult to meet his gaze. "The conditions of that particular wager are private."

"Don't be a fool." He bent closer until his eyes were level with hers. "I know damn well what you wagered, all of you."

She sighed. "I had hoped you wouldn't hear."

"Your hopes have been dashed. I may be horridly scarred, and as lame as a three-legged dog, but my ears are excellent."

There were other parts of him that qualified as excellent, too. Even blazing with anger, his dark brown eyes were beautiful, the lashes ridiculously long. Why was it that men always seemed to have a surplus of eyelashes, which they most expressly did not need, while women—who longed for thick, long lashes— often had the scrimpiest ones on earth? She bit back a sigh. "I didn't expect to be thanked—"

"You're not delusional, then."

She wished she wasn't so aware of the sensual curve of his firm mouth. It was perfectly made, carved as if from a statue of a Greek god, and made her ache for his touch. The scar that ran to the corner of his mouth and beyond merely accentuated it. With supreme effort, she pulled her gaze from his mouth. "While I didn't expect to be thanked, I *did* expect you to be understanding."

"Of what?"

"Of my lack of control once my temper was raised.

You, of all people, should understand the consequences of that particular flaw."

He frowned. "What does your temper have to do with this wager? From what I heard, Lady Mary and Miss Stewart were mocking me, not you."

"They were and it made me angry, so I took care of it."

His mouth went white. "I don't need your pity."

"Pity? For you? Don't be ridiculous. I just hated that they felt they could freely malign someone they don't even know. I'd have done the same had they been mocking anyone else I know. You're not a special case."

He didn't look as if he believed a word, and she let out a frustrated sigh. "Oh for the love of— Kirk, Lady Mary and Miss Stewart do nothing but mock people. Heaven knows whom else they talk about, although I suspect the answer is simply everyone. I can't stop them from doing that, but I was able to keep them from mocking you, at least while they are under this roof."

"What will you do now? Challenge them each and every time they talk about someone you know?"

"If I must, yes." She allowed herself a small smile. "Although after today, they will not be so quick to accept my challenge."

He didn't return her smile. "I didn't ask you to stand up for me, Balfour."

"You didn't have to; I did it of my own accord."

"And now everyone is talking about it, and me, and how I am indebted to you."

Dahlia looked past him and found that almost every eye in the ballroom was upon the two of them. Her heart sank. She'd known her wager would cause some interest, but nothing like this. She shifted a bit, putting a little more space between them. "Kirk, my disagreement with Lady Mary and Miss Stewart had very little to do with you; I merely wanted to put them in their places. And now I will look forward to hearing their fawning pleasantries over the next few days, knowing what it will cost them."

"Fawning pleasantries? Do not tell me that was part of this ridiculous wager."

"Well, yes. I thought the least they could do was be especially nice to you."

Kirk muttered a curse under his breath. "You—" He cast a glance around and then grabbed her wrist once again, and limped toward the door.

"Kirk, stop! Everyone is watching and will think—"

"I don't give a damn what anyone bloody well thinks." He pulled her out of the door, through the foyer past two startled footmen, and into the Blue Salon. As soon as they crossed the threshold, he kicked the door closed, tossed his cane onto a chair, grasped her arms and yanked her to him, their chests now touching.

Dahlia's breath caught, acutely aware of the strength of his hands where they encircled her arms, of the warmth of his chest where it rested against hers, of the way her toes barely touched the ground as he held her in place as if she weighed no more than a feather.

Through clenched teeth he snapped, "Damn you, Balfour, I will *not* be pitied! Neither Lady Mary nor Miss Stewart nor their vapid words would ever embarrass me the way you've done so through this stupid wager."

"I admit that it's caused far more talk than I envisioned, and for that, I'm sorry. But you cannot keep accusing me of pitying you, for nothing could be further from the truth. If there's one person I *don't* feel sorry for, it's *you*. You're wealthy and independent, and can do anything you wish to: how could anyone pity a life like that? No, there is only one person who feels sorry for you, and that's—" She poked his chest.

"Me?" He looked astounded, as if she'd just said the sky was green and the grass blue. "You think I feel sorry for myself?"

"Why else have you eschewed society for the last seven years, hiding away and pretending you wouldn't be accepted?"

"I didn't pretend. People were not kind after my accident."

"They stared. So what? I can't believe you really care about such fustian."

"I have my pride, you know."

"Too much pride, if you ask me."

If that wasn't the pot calling the kettle black, he

didn't know what was. "I was also in mourning. Have you forgotten that?"

"That reason suffices for the first year, perhaps two. After that, it was nothing but self-pity that shackled you to Fordyce Castle and your books."

Kirk didn't know whether to shake the senseless words out of her mouth or kiss them away.

"Well?" she asked. "Are you going to admit that you've been feeling sorry for yourself?"

"No, I'm not, because it's not true. I've *never* felt pity for myself."

Her brows rose.

He flushed. "Not after the first few months, anyway." He suddenly realized how tightly he was holding her arms, and he slowly lowered her to her feet and released her. Red fingerprints marked her arms, and he winced. "I'm sorry."

She shrugged. "They're not bruises; it will be back to normal in a moment. Had you held me too tightly, I would have said something. I'm not shy, you know."

For some reason, that almost made him smile. "No, you're not shy. Far from it, damn you." He found himself wishing he hadn't released her, but had pulled her into his arms instead. Now that he'd released her, he felt oddly bereft. *God, what a mull.* "I saw your blasted battledore match."

Her gaze flew to his. "You were there?"

"Yes."

Pink stained her cheeks. "And?"

"It was magnificent."

Her plump lips curved. "Thank you. My sisters have trained me well."

"I'm sorry I lost my temper, although I'm not happy with what you've done. I was unprepared to discover the nature of your wager."

"I stupidly hoped you wouldn't even hear about it. Then it very quickly grew into a public matter and I knew—" She wet her lips nervously. "As I said, I'm sorry for that part of it. It was supposed to be a far more private matter."

He found himself staring at her lush mouth as a pang of pure, hot desire flashed through to his core. *Bloody hell, my passions are surface high today.*

"However, since we are here, there is one thing I wish to know." She slanted him a look from under her lashes. "It's rather personal, though."

He shrugged. "I've no secrets, especially after your little wager."

"Do you think of her often?"

"Think of who?"

"Your wife."

The suddenness of the question almost floored him. *Why does that matter?* "Not as often now, no."

"But you loved her."

"Yes, but that was long ago and I was someone quite different then." He raked a hand through his hair, trying to pull his wayward thoughts from her lips and back to her words. "Dahlia, why are you asking about Elspeth?"

"I didn't play that game out of pity for you, but in your honor. I played it because I know you are a good person, no matter how rude you might be. But even I must admit that you sometimes refuse to follow the dictates of society, as if you're angry with everyone."

"And you think that's because of the death of my wife?"

"Yes."

"Perhaps it's something simpler—a refusal to bend my knee to a society that doesn't accept me as I am now, scarred and 'maimed.' I'm not in mourning, Dahlia. I haven't been for a long, long time. Nor am I flattered you don't think me capable of dealing with nobodies like Lady Mary and Miss Stewart."

"They're not nobodies. People listen to them."

"Do you?"

"No."

"Then no one I care about will pay heed to a word they say."

She flushed, but quickly rallied, a light in her eyes. "If you don't care, then you should. You are looking for a wife, aren't you? Whoever that is might care a great deal about what is said about you."

She had him there, and for a moment, he couldn't think of a response.

Dahlia smiled. "I'm right, aren't I? Admit it."

He had to fight not to return that smile. There was something about her—perhaps the intelligence in her fine gray-blue eyes, or the smattering of freckles across the bridge of her nose, or the pert way she tilted her head to one side when she looked at him, as if she were focused on him and no one else. Her cheeky twinkle was damnably taking, and he had to fight to remember why he was upset. "Don't pretend you thought about that when you made this ridiculous wager. Somehow, forcing these two women to be polite to me stroked your vanity."

"I will admit to feeling a certain satisfaction when I triumphed, yes."

"*That* is why you made the wager, not because of me."

"Certainly not because of any pity you seem to mistakenly believe I felt."

"You, madam, are trouble. You need a keeper. Someone who will monitor those high spirits of yours and keep them in check."

"My spirits don't need checking, nor do I need a keeper." Dahlia looked at him through her lashes, noting that he looked less angry now, but far more perplexed. "I wouldn't mind having a partner, though."

"A partner in crime?"

"Among other things, yes." Something glimmered in his dark eyes.

She met his gaze evenly. "The wager was made to soothe my pride. I've known you longer than anyone here, and I will not tolerate fools who would mock one of my friends."

"You made an error with this challenge."

"I know. I lost my temper. It won't happen again."

"That's not enough. Before we leave this room, you will admit you are not my keeper. Nor my champion."

"No? Then just what am I?" The heat of his gaze sent a tremor of awareness through her and suddenly, she wished they weren't standing two steps apart.

"This is what you are." He reached out and pulled her back into his arms and kissed her.

The kiss made their previous ones look meek. Those kisses had explored and surprised, but this kiss raged; it devoured and consumed. It took everything she had and gave her more than she could withstand. He molded her to him, holding her against him so that she felt the hard plane of his chest, the ripple of his muscles as lifted her from her feet. His hands never stopped roaming over her, exploring her curves and waist, finding the fullness of her bottom.

She wiggled against him, holding him closer, accepting and giving at the same time as he plundered her mouth over and over—

"Where are they?" came the duchess's voice from the hallway.

Dahlia broke the kiss, her gaze locked with Kirk's. Passion had darkened his eyes, his lips damp from their kiss. The air about them shimmered with unspoken passion.

"We can't leave them alone; there will be a scandal! Someone must find them."

With a heartfelt grimace, Kirk lowered Dahlia to her feet, but instead of releasing her, he merely rested his forehead against hers. The only noise in the room was of their breathing, still harsh and desperate. Dahlia could only be glad that he was as affected as her.

"They will find us." She couldn't keep the disappointment from her voice.

"This time." He cupped her face between his warm hands and kissed her nose. "We are not done with this. Not by a long shot." He dropped his hands from her face, picked up his cane from where he'd discarded it, and limped toward the long windows.

She followed. "Kirk, what are you—"

"I'm saving your reputation." He threw a window open and swung his leg over the casement, smiling as he rested half in and half out of the room. "Now we are even. You've 'saved' me from vicious gossips, so I've done the same. Return to the others."

"Dinner will be served soon and you will be missed."

"I'm ordering a tray for my room. I've had enough stares for one night."

She nodded, an odd ache in her chest. "Fine, but before you go . . . Kirk, your kiss. Was this another session?"

He paused a moment. When he spoke, his voice was deeper than usual. "No. That kiss was for me."

Their gazes locked and she found that she couldn't breathe. "Kirk, I—"

The duchess's voice could be heard closer to the door now. "I shall look here."

Kirk frowned. "Go, Dahlia. And if anyone says a bad word of me, for the love of God, let them."

"But what if—"

But he was gone. She stared through the empty window as the blackness of the evening swallowing him from sight.

Dahlia sighed and closed the window, pausing to touch her tender lips. What an embrace. Even now, she burned from it head to toe, an odd ache in the pit of her stomach. Every time he touched her, this feeling returned, and each time it was stronger. And oddly, when she was in the throes of passion, she wished it to never end. *It's as if I'm starving for his kisses, which is ridiculous, for I rarely think of such things.*

As soon as she had the thought, she realized it was a lie. She thought about Kirk—and his kisses—often. Even in her sleep, which was her most private time of all. *But why am I doing that? He's the same man he's always been—rude, demanding, impulsive. I know it, and yet something has changed. Or perhaps it's someone. Could it be me?*

The duchess's voice raised again, this time outside the door. Dahlia turned away from the window just as the door opened and the duchess appeared, Lady Charlotte and the pugs following. The duchess's sharp blue gaze flickered over Dahlia, and then past her to the window, but the older woman never said another word about it. Instead, she and Lady Charlotte exclaimed over finding her alone. Dahlia told them that Kirk had yelled at her and then stomped away, a plausible enough story given his temper when they'd left the others.

Her grace and Lady Charlotte accepted Dahlia's story, but neither was happy, and all of the way back to the dining room, they chided her for allowing Kirk to make a scene.

Dahlia didn't hear a word they said, for try as she might, her thoughts were lost in a kiss.

# Thirteen

**From the Diary of the Duchess of Roxburghe**

Even the most novice of matchmakers knows that a relationship that develops too quickly, and burns with too high a flame, will soon die out. After Lord Kirk nearly caused a scandal two days ago by dragging poor Dahlia from the dining hall in such a forceful manner, and then abandoning her in such an obviously well-kissed state, Charlotte and I decided that their relationship needs a day or two to cool. To that end, we've taken great care to ensure that Miss Balfour hasn't had a moment alone.

Neither Miss Balfour nor Lord Kirk has appreciated our efforts, for they've stabbed us with a number of dark glances, but we will not budge until tomorrow. Then, and only then, will we allow them to resume their flirtation.

All in all, things seem to be progressing well, although I cannot help wishing that Lord Kirk would gain more address. He is much improved in manners, but he is still painfully abrupt, and on occasion says the most outrageous things. While aware that Dahlia is fond of Lord Kirk, Charlotte and I fear he doesn't have the address to raise romantic feelings in the breast of one who longs for such overtures.

It is a difficult case indeed.

Kirk walked down the hallway to his bedchamber, his mood as dark as the dimly lit castle corridor. For two days, he'd tried his damnedest to find a way to speak to Dahlia alone and had yet to succeed. Their assignation in the library had been canceled because when he'd arrived at the appointed time, he'd discovered her grace had taken up residence with a bevy of elderly men, all discussing the benefits of hunting for land-management purposes. He'd been forced to send a note to Dahlia explaining why they couldn't meet. He'd promised to find another meeting place, but that hadn't proven as easy of a task as he'd thought. Every time he thought he'd found a secluded corner, one or another of the duchess's guests—and oddly enough, sometimes the duchess herself—appeared as if summoned. It was frustrating, to say the least.

He and Dahlia had much to discuss, and the sooner the better. Of course, a discussion wasn't truly their purpose in meeting. They had kisses to practice, damn it! He fairly burned for her since their last meeting, but every time he'd seen her, she'd been surrounded by a bevy of other people. Thus it was that over the past two days he'd been unable to secure even a second where they could have an honest conversation, much less share an embrace.

With no other strategy left, he'd been forced to extreme measures, even rising early to intercept her before her morning walk, a stratagem that had failed when he'd found a maid lingering in the corridor through which Dahlia usually walked. He'd been reduced to wandering close to her at various gatherings hoping the crowd about her might thin—but to no avail. She was never alone.

Frustrated, he'd poured himself into his valet's proscribed therapy. Every morning since he and Mac-Creedy had agreed to it, Kirk had devoted one to two hours to the excruciating exercise required, which was much more physical and infinitely more painful than Kirk had expected. But if it helped, it would be worth every iota of pain and sweat.

This morning, returning from his exercise, drenched in sweat and gritting his teeth against the deep ache in his leg, he'd caught sight across the courtyard of Dahlia entering the castle, her face flushed from her walk, dew clinging to her cloak and glistening like diamonds. He'd called to her, but she'd been too far away to hear and had soon disappeared from sight. Bitterly disappointed, he'd limped back to his room, growling at anyone who dared hail him along the way.

He was certain Dahlia wished for them to meet as much as he did. There were times when their gazes would meet across the duchess's salon or dining table and Kirk could see something in the velvety depths of her eyes—was it desire? That's what he felt, and plenty of it, too. Since their last kiss, he'd been unable to think of anything but her soft lips and generous curves, and their unplanned separation had whetted his already significant appetite for her company.

And so, his determination to see her alone grew. Last night, he'd even sat through an impromptu dance that had sprung up after dinner in the hopes of gaining a few words with her. The dance had been organized by the duchess, who declared that seeing young people dancing was her greatest joy. Under the best of circumstances Kirk hated watching people dance, but it had been pure torture seeing Dahlia breathless and laughing as she whirled about the floor with her partners. There was nothing he could do about it except pretend he didn't give a damn, and wait. To his utter frustration, the second the music ended, admirers surrounded her and he was cut out once more. He'd toyed briefly with following his natural instincts and storming through the herd of fribbles and sweeping Dahlia away, but he knew that if he wished their time alone to last more than a few seconds, stealth would be necessary.

Today had been just as bad, although there had been a moment when he'd dared hope that his luck had turned for the better. Just ten minutes ago, Dahlia had been alone at the pianoforte that had been moved into the Blue Salon for this evening's reading and performances. Most of the other guests had already left to change for dinner, so only a few souls were about.

Kirk had hurried toward her, but just as he was within calling distance, he was waylaid by Lady Charlotte, who wished his opinion on—of all things—the order of the readings planned after tonight's dinner.

He didn't give a damn about tonight's reading, but Lady Charlotte had been insistent and by the time he'd managed to untangle himself, Dahlia had been claimed by the duchess, who had whisked her from the room.

As the duchess closed the door, she'd glanced over her shoulder and he'd caught the triumph in her eyes. And it was then that he'd realized that both Lady Charlotte and her grace were protecting Dahlia from him.

He would not tolerate it. Tonight, come hell or high water, he'd find Dahlia alone, even if he had to break every damn rule society posed, and irk his own god-mother, as well.

Still, he'd felt oddly betrayed by the duchess's interference. She was supposed to be helping him, damn it. Grumpy as hell, he was now heading to his bedchamber, alone and unsatisfied in every possible way. As he turned the corner, his leg twisted slightly. Hot, searing pain stabbed his calf and he gasped, dropping the cane to grab his leg with both hands. As MacCreedy had instructed, he kneaded the pained area, sweat breaking out on his brow. *Bloody hell. MacCreedy had better know what he's doing, for I'll be damned if I'll live with this agony for the rest of my life.*

Slowly, slowly, the agonizing sensation subsided to

a low, hot ache. Teeth gritted, he slowly straightened and tried to regain his breath. MacCreedy had assured him that these painful muscle seizures were proof that the muscle and scar tissue were being stretched back to their correct lengths, but they were so agonizing, it was damn near impossible to view them as positive.

Scowling, his breathing still labored, Kirk retrieved his cane and slowly continued down the hallway. When he came within sight of his door, a noise behind him made him look over his shoulder. The gray-snouted roly-poly pug that had interrupted his kiss with Dahlia in the library days ago trotted up the hallway, his tongue half out of his mouth.

Kirk leaned upon his cane. "What do you want?"

The dog's twirled tail wagged and he looked at Kirk's bedchamber door.

"No. How do you know that's my room?"

The dog sneezed.

He eyed the chubby dog. "Someone should put you on a reducing diet. It's unseemly."

The dog dropped heavily onto its back haunches, its tongue lolling out one side, not in the least put out by such a truthful observation. He looked at the door again, his expression hopeful.

"I said no and I meant it." Kirk shook his head at the size of the dog's stomach "There's no excuse for that. I've seen you begging for lamb at the table. Just last night the duchess gave you enough for four dogs your size, and you gobbled up every bit. I daresay you threw it all up on her carpet later in the evening."

The fat pug's graying muzzle parted in a wide, panting grin.

"Rejoin your mistress. I don't like dogs."

The pug wagged his tail harder, as if he thought Kirk a liar.

"Good God, I don't know who is sillier: you for wanting to come into my bedchamber as if an exalted guest, or me for talking to you. Off with you! Trundle back downstairs, where your cohorts and mistress await." With that, Kirk entered his bedchamber and shut the door behind him.

MacCreedy was just putting away a stack of neatly starched cravats. "Ah, me lor'. I was just getting ready to put oot yer evenin' clothes."

"Ask for a tray to be sent to my room. I have decided to join the company after dinner, after that damned reading is over." He no longer held out any hope of getting a private word with Dahlia while the duchess and Lady Charlotte were in the room.

"What reading is that, me lor'?"

"Lady Charlotte and her grace are attempting to organize guests to perform after dinner."

"Tha' sounds like a pleasant way to spend an evening."

"Not for me. In a moment of utter weakness, I foolishly agreed to read a poem. So I shall avoid the entire affair and send a note to her grace that I won't be joining them."

The valet bowed. "I shall tell her grace ye've a headache."

"Why would you tell her that?"

"Ye have to give a reason fer refusin' to go to dinner, me lor'. 'Tis only polite."

"Politeness can go to hell. It's a bother and rarely gets one what one wants." Kirk dropped into a chair and let his cane fall against the footrest.

"Och, ye seem a bit miffed, me lor'. Ye've been miffed fer two days now, and I'm beginnin' to wonder if 'tis a permanent condition."

Kirk wished his knee didn't hurt, for he'd like nothing better than to kick the footstool. He contented himself with a short "It's Miss Balfour."

"Ah, the object o' yer affections."

"Yes, or as I've come to think of her, 'the woman who should be spanked.'"

"Mind if I ask why ye've been thinkin' such a thing aboot Miss Balfour?"

Kirk scowled. "Several days ago, she challenged some of the ladies of the house party to a duel."

MacCreedy lifted his brows. "Pardon me, me lor', but did you say a *duel*?"

"Yes. Her weapon of choice was a battledore paddle." Kirk dropped his head back against the high cushions of the chair and looked at his valet. "And you can stop pretending you didn't know about the match, for I'm sure it was discussed as much belowstairs as it was abovestairs."

"I may ha' heard some'at of it earlier." When Kirk raised his brows, MacCreedy added, "But 'twas obvious ye dinna wish to talk aboot it, so I dinna bring it oop."

"I still don't. It's a colossal embarrassment. Thanks to that damned battledore duel, which every person in the castle apparently attended, I'm now treated as an object of pity."

"Sure 'tis no' so bad as tha'."

"Just this morning, two gentlemen—*gentlemen*, MacCreedy—got into a tussle over which would hold the breakfast room door for me."

The valet winced.

"Exactly. I yanked the door from their hands and ordered them in before me. And that's just one example. Everyone is suddenly anxious to accommodate me, as if I were an invalid. Except Miss Balfour. She can't seem to find ten minutes to spare for a conversation." And his godmother, who'd suddenly switched sides in this battle and was now working for the enemy.

The valet placed a dark blue silk waistcoat with the coat on the bed. "Do ye know wha' I think ye need, me lor'?"

"A battledore paddle to use on Miss Balfour's bottom?"

"I was thinkin' ye needed a wee dram." The valet nodded to where a tray sat upon a small table beside the fire, a crystal decanter catching the light of the flames. "I had it brought up, thinkin' ye may need a bit to soften oot the day."

"Good God, yes. Pour me a heavy one, please."

The valet smiled and soon brought a drink to Kirk, who was rubbing his leg. "Had another seize oop, did ye?"

"Yes, in the hallway as I was turning the corner."

"'Tis the twistin' that's causin' it. I know it hurts, me lor', but ye'll be glad ye're workin' it—ye truly will."

"I hope so." Kirk leaned back in his chair and took a generous drink. "By Zeus, that's good."

"Jus' wha' ye needed. Take another sip, and then tell ol' MacCreedy aboot Miss Balfour and why ye think she's avoidin' ye. Ye canno' keep a Scot from a spate o' gossip."

"Hell, there's not a person under this roof who hasn't involved themselves in my business, so why not you, too?" The whiskey was warming Kirk into a better mood with each swallow. "It began two days ago. As you know, I offered to teach Miss Balfour how to kiss more genteelly."

"And she agreed?"

"Yes, and we had our first encounter." The memory was so fresh that it almost stole his breath. Aware of the valet's gaze, he said quietly, "It went well."

"Tha' is good."

"Is it?" He frowned at his glass and took another drink, this one slower as he savored the whiskey. "I think it frightened her."

"Ah—and now she'll no' meet ye at all."

Kirk stared at the remaining amber liquid. "There's a bit more to it than that. After the battledore match and everyone started whispering about me, I was angry."

"Were ye now?"

"Yes, and I hauled her into the salon and demanded to know what she thought she was doing."

"And other people saw this?"

"Yes."

The valet winced.

"I know, I know, but I was vexed."

"So now she willna' speak to ye."

"I believe someone else has a hand in it. It dawned on me this evening that Lady Charlotte and the duchess have been involved in keeping Dahlia and myself apart. I don't believe it's at Dahlia's behest."

"I see." The valet shook his head. "Women do like to tie a man into knots, me lor'. There's a maid I've been wishin' to walk oot wit', and she's a cheeky lass. She's no' made it easy."

"They never do."

"Nay." MacCreedy came to stand at the end of the bed. "If Miss Balfour's been avoidin' ye, then dinna ye think tha' is all the more reason to go down to dinner and read yer poem, like ye promised to? Be visible, as it were, rather tha' givin' oop."

"I'm not giving up. I'm merely looking for a more strategic position." Kirk finished his drink. Before he'd even swallowed, the valet had scooped it up and refilled it. "You're good, MacCreedy."

His valet grinned as he handed the glass back. "I know me way aboot a whiskey bottle, me lor'." He went to the wardrobe and pulled out a pair of neatly pressed breeches and placed them on the bed with the other clothes. "If ye go to dinner and read yer poem, 'twill show Miss Balfour tha' ye are no' the sort as ye'll turn into a hermit jus' because things are no' goin' yer way."

"She already thinks me a hermit."

"She can think it all she wants, but if ye dinna go to dinner and read yer poem, then she'll know it to be true, me lor'."

He sighed.

"Or," the valet added with a shrug, "ye can jus' quit an' leave it all be."

"I'm a Kirk. Kirks never quit. I was going to go down *after* the performance."

"But ye dinna know if she'll still be aboot or no'."

Kark paused. "That's true."

"Ye've a stout heart, me lor'; I've seen it meself. But ye're missin' the strategy o' showin' yerself to advantage tonight. Ye could win a bit o' favor, which can only help ye."

"By reading a poem. What foolery." Yet the taste of Dahlia's kiss was still fresh, and he longed for another. "Miss Balfour was very taken when I repeated a few lines of Byron in the library."

"Mayhap ye could read her a poem fro' the book ye bought her. 'Tis by Byron, is it no'?"

"Yes."

"So read her a poem, and make her a gift o' the

book after. Tha' would be a pretty gesture, and 'twill make the book seem all the more special."

Kirk supposed there was no harm in trying. Anything was better than merely hoping, and that's what he'd been reduced to doing. He took another sip of whiskey, its warmth easing the pain in his leg even more.

*Perhaps I've been going about this all wrong. Perhaps I should prove myself to her, show her that I'm willing to meet her halfway.* His gaze found the books he'd had the valet purchase for him and he remembered the smile on Dahlia's lips when he'd quoted Byron in the library. *It might be just the thing.*

A scratching noise came from the door, and a low growl followed as a paw appeared under the door, reaching as if in search of a treat.

Kirk's gaze narrowed. "One of the duchess's pudgy pugs followed me here."

"Ye dislike animals, me lor'?"

"Of course not. I just don't like them in the house. They belong outside, where—"

A low, mournful howl erupted from the hall.

Kirk glared at the closed door.

MacCreedy unsuccessfully hid a smile. "He's pinin' fer ye, me lor'."

"He's pining for anyone who will give him food."

Another howl, even more mournful.

"Should I let him in? If he sees we've no food, mayhap he'll wander back oot."

Kirk muttered a curse, grabbed his cane, went to the door and yanked it open. When the pug saw Kirk, he became a wiggling, happy ball of fur.

"What in the hell are you doing, yowling like that?" Kirk demanded.

The pug plopped his haunches onto the floor and then looked pleased, as if he'd performed a mighty trick.

"I'm not impressed," Kirk told the mutt.

MacCreedy peered around Kirk. "Tha' is Randolph, the oldest pug. MacDougal says he canno' take the stairs on his own now, bein' too feeble."

"Or lazy."

"MacDougal suggested tha' as weel, me lor'. I'll ring fer someone to fetch 'im."

"Don't bother; it's not worth their time. I'll carry him back downstairs when I go." Kirk eyed the dog. "Don't get any ideas, mutt. You are only to be allowed into this bedchamber this one time."

The dog wagged his tail and peered up at Kirk in a way that made MacCreedy snicker.

Kirk snapped his fingers. "Randolph, come!" He turned and went back to his chair and whiskey.

Behind him, he could hear the tap tap tap of Randolph's nails as the dog waddled after him. MacCreedy shut the door, smiling.

Kirk drank his whiskey as Randolph toured the room, snuffling the rug, the wardrobe, and finally the legs of Kirk's breeches that hung over the side of the bed.

"Och, dinna muss his lordship's clothin'." Mac-Creedy rescued the breeches, placing them higher on the bed.

Randolph sniffed the place where the breeches had been and then sneezed.

MacCreedy tsked. "Ye're a right wisty pup, aren't ye?"

The dog wagged his tail as if to agree. Perhaps it was the generous amount of whiskey MacCreedy had poured, but Kirk found himself smiling at the cheeky dog. "He's spoiled, but he's well behaved. Except for the howling, that is." He nodded toward the clothes on the bed. "I suppose I should get dressed."

The valet brightened. "Ye're goin' to dinner and the entertainment after all, then."

"I suppose so. You'd make a masterful negotiator, MacCreedy."

"So Duke Wellington always tol' me. Do ye know which poem ye wish to read, me lor'?"

"Lud, no." Kirk rose and began dressing. "Poetry's nothing but tripe, but if it makes Dahlia smile, I'll do it."

"An' smile whilst ye do it."

"Don't ask for too much, MacCreedy. It's enough that I'm even going."

Randolph found a spot on the rug that seemed to please him, for after sniffing it thoroughly, he dug at it.

"Randolph, stop!" Kirk commanded.

The dog looked abashed, circled three times, and with a monstrous sigh, plopped down.

"Good dog."

Randolph panted, his tongue lolling out the side of his mouth.

"At least *you* do what you're told," Kirk said to the dog.

"And all he wants is a bone fer his trouble," Mac-Creedy said.

Kirk looked at the book of poetry, a thought flickering through his mind. Finally, he nodded. "Mac-Creedy, help me into this coat and then hand me that blasted book. If I'm to do this, then I'm going to do it right. I'll pick the shortest poem and memorize the blasted thing. Surely that will make Miss Balfour happy."

"Tha' is the spirit, me lor'!"

An hour later, the poem freshly committed to memory, Kirk was on his way to dinner, the book tucked in his coat pocket.

# Fourteen

**From the Diary of the Duchess of Roxburghe**

Roxburghe is fond of saying, "Never predict your fellow man, for you'll fail every time." Until Lord Kirk's performance tonight, I didn't understand the true meaning of that phrase. But now . . . oh my.

When Dahlia entered the Blue Salon she saw Miss MacLeod and Dalhousie sitting at the pianoforte, which had been moved to a prominent spot near the fireplace, rows and rows of chairs lined up before it. Now that dinner was over, the guests were wandering into the salon while Lady Charlotte fluttered here and there, handing out beautifully handwritten programs and trying to herd everyone to their seats.

As Dahlia approached, Anne pointed to the program on top of the pianoforte. "I see you're playing two songs."

"What?" Dahlia frowned. "I only offered to do one."

"That's quite all right," Dalhousie said. "Apparently I'm reading"—he squinted at the program—"'an edifying sermon.'"

Anne giggled. "You! A sermon!"

He sent her a mock-stern look before flashing a grin at Dahlia. "It wouldn't be acting if it were true to life—right, Miss Balfour?"

Dahlia had to smile back. "Very true."

"The big surprise is Lord Kirk." Anne pointed to the final name on the list. "He's reading a poem."

"Which one?"

"It doesn't say."

"A pity, for I've been wondering about that since I heard him tell Lady Charlotte days ago that he'd do so." Dahlia had to fight to keep the smile on her lips. The last few days had been difficult. After she and Kirk had had their disagreement about the battledore game, Lady Charlotte and the duchess had warned her about allowing Kirk to "set the pace" on the relationship and had opined that perhaps things were progressing "far, far too quickly."

Dahlia had been embarrassed that they were so closely monitoring her relationship with Kirk, but that wasn't why she hadn't protested when the two older women had begun chaperoning her more thoroughly.

She had no fear of Kirk. He was painfully honest, and while he was more than willing to break society's rules, she knew he would never, ever touch her in a way she didn't want. The real trouble was that she was beginning to realize how much she *did* want him to touch her. She didn't mistrust Kirk; she mistrusted herself.

Anne, who'd been arranging sheet music in a pile to match the program, glanced up at Dahlia. "Do you know both songs you're to play?"

"I know one of them very well. The other one, well enough that only the musically inclined will know when I've made a misstep."

"You're fortunate, then, for I heard Miss Dapplemeyer say that she'd never even heard of the song Lady Charlotte put her down for."

"At least she can plead off," Dalhousie said. "But those of us who've been instructed to read an improving sermon are stuck, for we can't pretend we've forgotten how to read."

Anne laughed. "Yes, but you—" Her gaze suddenly locked over Dahlia's shoulder, then she turned back to the sheet music. "*Someone* is walking this way."

*Kirk!* Dahlia held her breath and waited. But as the seconds passed and no shiver warmed her skin and no breathlessness overtook her, she realized it wasn't him. She was just turning to see whom it might be when Lady Mary's nasally voice broke into her thoughts.

"Ah, Miss MacLeod and Lord Dalhousie." There was a slight pause, then Lady Mary said, "And Miss Balfour. I'm looking forward to this evening's entertainment."

Dahlia turned to find Lady Mary and Miss Stewart standing behind her. They curtsied as she turned, so she returned the favor. "Good evening."

They smiled and murmured a return greeting. Since their battledore match Lady Mary had been polite, but no more. So Dahlia was surprised when the taller lady offered a faint but encouraging smile. "Miss Balfour, I wish to speak to you." She glanced at the others and hesitated, but then continued with a dogged air. "Miss Stewart feels that we owe you and Lord Kirk an apology. After some rather heated conversations, she has won me to her way of thinking."

Miss Stewart added in a faintly husky tone, "The whole thing grew out of proportion very quickly. We didn't mean any harm, either of us."

Dahlia blinked. "I see. I assure you that you don't need to—"

Lady Mary threw up a hand. "I do and I know it. I'm not very good at saying 'I'm sorry,' but allow me to do so now." Lady Mary's smile was stiff, but genuine regret shone clearly in her sharp gaze.

Dahlia smiled. "Of course. Allow me to say that I never intended for our little disagreement to become so public, either."

"Neither did I." Lady Mary picked up the program from the pianoforte, the candlelight catching the faint bruise that still discolored the bridge of her nose. "I see you are performing on the pianoforte. I look forward to hearing you play."

"Thank you. I'm looking forward to hearing you sing."

"I fear you'll be sadly disappointed. I have no talent, you know. I'm only singing because Alayne—Miss Stewart—had to cancel due to a sore throat, and Lady Charlotte was determined to find a replacement."

Dalhousie, who'd been idly riffling through the sheet music, drew back a little. "Miss Stewart, if you're ill, it would be best if you'd confine yourself away from the rest of the duchess's guests."

Anne sent Dahlia a mischievous look. "Dalhousie fears illness worse than death."

Miss Stewart chuckled, her voice noticeably hoarse. "Lord Dalhousie, I promise to stay far, far from you until I'm better."

"Thank you, Miss Stewart. I, and my valet, who would have had to nurse me back to health, thank you."

"You are quite welcome."

"It's a pity you won't be singing," Anne added. "I had the pleasure of hearing you sing at school, and you have a lovely voice."

Miss Stewart blushed so red that she appeared to have been slapped. "Now I'm glad I'm not singing, for all of this praise would have made it too difficult to—" She coughed. "Excuse me, but—" She pulled a kerchief from her pocket and covered her mouth, coughing heavily the entire time.

Dahlia noted Miss Stewart's flushed face and wondered if the poor woman had a fever. "Miss Stewart, perhaps you should ask the duchess to call her physician?"

"I'm fine. I shall berate my little brother when I go home, though. He was just beginning to cough and had a touch of fever when I left, and he insisted on a proper good-bye kiss." She coughed again, too hard to speak.

Lady Mary threaded her arm through her friend's. "Come, Alayne, let's get you a glass of orgeat. That will do your throat the most good." With a nod to the others, she started to lead her friend away when Dahlia stopped them.

"What! Miss Stewart dropped her handkerchief." She picked it up and pressed it into Miss Stewart's hand. "I hope you feel better soon."

"Thank you, Miss Balfour. That's very kind." With a smile, Miss Stewart went with Lady Mary to the refreshment table, which had just been set up at the other side of the room.

"Poor thing," Dahlia said. "She was quite flushed."

"And all of that coughing!" Dalhousie waved a sheet of music in the air as if to blow away Miss Stewart's illness. "I hope none of us succumbs."

Anne frowned at him. "You are such a child when it comes to illness."

"I'm cautious. There's nothing wrong with that."

Anne turned back to Dahlia. "If Miss Stewart doesn't feel better soon, then someone must put a word in the duchess's ear about fetching her physician."

"I'll be sure to—"

Lady Charlotte clapped her hands, her lace cap fluttering about her round face. "Come, everyone! Pray sit! Her grace will say a few words about our evening's entertainment, and then we will begin."

Everyone wandered toward the chairs. Dalhousie procured seats for Anne and Dahlia, who sat to either side of him. As Dahlia watched the others take their seats, she caught sight of Lord Kirk limping into the room, the last one to arrive.

His gaze swept the crowd and locked on to hers. For a long moment they gazed at each other, but then Lady Hamilton gestured for him to take the empty seat beside her. With obvious reluctance, he pulled his gaze from Dahlia and took the offered seat.

Dahlia pretended to listen to the story Dalhousie was telling Anne, but her attention was several rows back, fixed on Kirk. Was he still angry? She hoped not, but she had to admit that in the days after the match, the other guests had gone out of their way to be more solicitous. Too much so. Each time someone pulled his chair from the table or rushed to pick up something for him, she'd cringed. For a proud man, that attention must be onerous, and she reluctantly admitted it was partly her fault. The battledore match to defend his honor had painted him as incapable in some way. *Blast it, I never meant for that to happen.*

Lady Charlotte pinged a silver spoon on the side of a wineglass. "Her grace is going to welcome us."

MacDougal assisted her grace onto the raised hearth. Dressed in an evening gown of blue gauze, the bottom of her skirt finished with a triple band of mustard-colored silk that mirrored the mustard silk tabbed at her waist, she was the picture of fashion and good breeding.

She patted an errant curl that had loosened from her red wig as she smiled upon her guests. "Welcome! Tonight we celebrate the talents that are among us.

Many of you did not know this until now, but you were all carefully invited as guests based on your performance value."

Many laughed at this, which made the duchess smile more brightly. She continued to expound upon the performances she expected from her guests, but Dahlia didn't hear another word, for Dalhousie was now whispering.

"Good lord, he's sitting directly behind us."

"Who?" Dahlia asked.

"Kirk. He was sitting beside Lady Hamilton, but he just moved closer."

Anne instantly craned her neck, but Dalhousie whispered a harsh "Don't look!"

"I'm sorry," she whispered back.

"I wonder if he's actually going to perform"— Dalhousie squinted at the program—"a poem, after all."

"He must or he wouldn't be here," Anne returned. "Dahlia, you know Kirk best. Do you think he'll—"

To Dahlia's relief, their conversation was interrupted by applause as the duchess finished her welcome speech. She curtsied gracefully, took Mac-Dougal's hand, and stepped off the "stage."

With that, the performance was under way. Mrs. Selfridge opened with a sonata that was surprisingly good. That was followed by the reading of a passage by a solemn Viscount Dundee.

His chosen text was obviously a favorite of Lady Charlotte's, for as the final word faded she leapt from her chair, clapping furiously. "Excellent! Excellent! That's *exactly* how I heard it in my own mind!"

Several more guests offered renditions of various poems and readings, and then Dahlia played her two pieces. She was aware the entire time of Kirk's dark gaze upon her. Feeling flustered, and aware that she'd rushed through the last song until it sounded more like a Scottish reel than the graceful, elegant piece it should have been, Dahlia returned to her seat.

Next, Lady Mary sang her assigned song, often looking toward Miss Stewart for guidance during the more difficult portions. Though her face was damp and flushed, Miss Stewart rewarded her friend with the largest of smiles at the finish of the song.

It was really quite sweet, and put Dahlia back in charity with both of them.

Lord Dalhousie was next, reading the "improving text" selected by her grace. It was long winded, stilted, and totally without merit, especially when Dalhousie himself yawned in the midst of it. Finally finished, he took his seat to tepid applause.

Next was a reading of the balcony scene from *Romeo and Juliet*, performed by Mr. and Mrs. MacLind, who did so with such exaggerated expressions that Dalhousie and Anne convulsed with laughter. Dahlia, aware of the glances sent their way, shushed them.

Finally, they came to the last performance of the evening: Lord Kirk's. A collective rustle passed over the crowd as he went to the front of the room, and

Dahlia realized that the others were just as curious as she about his performance. It was hard to imagine such a usually taciturn and abrupt man reading a poem.

He conferred for a moment with Lady Charlotte, his dark head bent near hers. Her eyes widened as he spoke, and she looked at the duchess. At a nod from her grace, Lady Charlotte broke into a smile, and then nodded vigorously. To everyone's surprise, she ordered a footman to douse half of the lights. And as the room gradually fell into semidarkness, the crowd's murmur increased in excitement.

A footman went to stir the fire, but Kirk halted him with an upraised hand. "No. Pray leave it." At the surprised look from the footman, Kirk added, "For ambience."

"Ah, setting the stage, are you?" Lady Hamilton called out, looking amused.

"Indeed, madam." He blew out a candle on a table near Miss Stewart. As he did so, their eyes met and she flushed an instant and deep red, and looked away, coughing into her kerchief.

Beside her, Lady Mary tsked, though she seemed amused. "Lud, Alayne, it's just a poem."

"But which poem?" Kirk asked. He held a candle before him and moved to the hearth as a hush fell over the crowd.

Dahlia found herself leaning forward, waiting for his first word.

He put his hand upon the mantel and turned slightly, his eyes meeting hers.

Instantly, her heart pounded against her throat.

"'Sonnet to Genevra.'"

"Byron," Anne said breathlessly.

"'*Thy cheek is pale with thought, but not from woe.*'" His deep voice was hushed, barely loud enough to be heard, yet it rolled as rich and deep as the ocean. "'*And yet so lovely, that if Mirth could flush its rose of whiteness with the brightest blush, My heart would wish away that ruder glow.*'" His soft, deep voice seemed to stroke each word. "'*And dazzle not thy gray-blue eyes—but oh! While gazing on them, sterner eyes will gush, And into mine my mother's weakness rush, Soft as the last drops round Heaven's airy bow.*'"

"Oh my," Anne breathed.

Dahlia was not only leaning forward to catch each word, but also holding her breath, as if afraid to break the spell being woven around her. And a spell it was, for she could no more look away than she could stop living.

Kirk kept her gaze locked with his, as if each word were for her alone. "'*For, though thy long, dark lashes low depending, The soul of melancholy gentleness gleams like a seraph from the sky descending.*'"

The fire flickered over his face while the shadow hid his scars, and for a moment every person in the room was treated to how Kirk must have looked before the accident; a raw and pure masculine beauty. His eye and cheek unblemished, his mouth so sensual, so powerful, so—

"'*Above all pain, yet pitying all distress; at once such*

*majesty with sweetness blending.'"* He stepped forward away from the firelight, his lone candle's light racing over his scar, a strike of lightning over his perfect face.

And his gaze never wavered from Dahlia's as he finished, *"'I worship more, but cannot love thee less.'"*

As the last word faded into the silent room, only the hiss of the fire could be heard.

Dahlia couldn't think, couldn't speak. Never had she heard a poem so beautifully read. Had there been no one else here, she would have thrown herself into his arms, demanding the kiss she'd been yearning for during the last few days with such desperate anticipation. Her body ached with desire.

The spell was broken as someone stood and clapped, and like a wave, it spread over the audience. Soon everyone was on their feet, clapping and calling, "Hear, hear!" "Bravo!" and "More! Read more!"

And still, Kirk stared into Dahlia's eyes.

She could almost feel him tugging her closer with each word, each—

Lady Charlotte suddenly stood before Kirk, her hands held up to ask for quiet as the footmen began to relight the lamps and candles. "I'm certain Lord Kirk will read us another poem." She looked over her shoulder at him hopefully.

"No. I cannot." He walked from the stage and was instantly swarmed.

Dahlia noted the expressions of those all around him, how they now saw Kirk differently. *They see him now as I've always seen him: capable, strong, and beautiful.*

An odd light entered her heart and she smiled, proud of him, though as enthralled and surprised as the others. He'd quoted a few lines of Byron the other day, but she'd never imagined he could recite with such deep understanding and emotion. Her mind buzzed with the words, the emotion, and the feelings he'd caused.

And during the reading, he'd looked directly at her as if he'd been talking to her alone. Over and over, she heard his voice caress the phrase, *I worship thee more, but cannot love thee less.* She pressed a hand to her thudding heart. *He loves me.* Her soul leapt with blinding joy, shocking her so much that she sat back down.

"Dahlia?"

She looked up to find Anne watching her with concern. Dahlia forced her trembling lips to smile. "I'm sorry, I was just lost in that poem. I love Byron."

Anna sighed. "So do I."

Dalhousie, who'd been talking to Mr. Ballanoch in the row in front of them about hunting tomorrow, made a face. "All women love Byron, but for the life of me, I don't know why."

"That's because men have no soul," Anne told him in a sprightly manner.

He looked injured. "I have plenty of soul. I'm just not a maudlin sort."

"Ha! You are a fribble, and care only for the polish of your boots. You told me so the other day."

"I didn't say 'only,'" he protested. "I said boot

blacking was important, but not *the* most important thing in a person's life."

"Oh? What else is there?"

He grinned. "There's also the starch of one's cravat."

"Ha! Fribble. I knew it."

As they continued to banter, Dahlia lost herself in wonder. *I'm happy. My entire body feels as light as a feather, my soul is singing, my heart tripping—* She suddenly stood, too happy to sit still.

Anne and Dalhousie looked at her with surprise.

She didn't know what her feelings meant, but she had to speak to Kirk. "If you'll excuse me, I need to—" *Fly to Kirk's side.* But a quick glance in his direction told her how impossible that was. Even more people surrounded him, and he was beginning to look irritated. This wasn't the best time to speak to him. But she couldn't wait until tomorrow—she simply couldn't.

She smiled at her friends. "I was going to retire, but there are too many people crowding the door. I'll just wait."

It took almost thirty minutes before Kirk broke away from those around him. Looking grim, he limped toward her, his cane loosely held in his hand. "Miss Balfour?"

She'd been rehearsing her greeting in case he managed to approach her, but now that he was here, she could only stare up at him.

He held out his hand.

It was a preemptory gesture, but Dahlia didn't care.

She placed her hand in his, a shiver traveling through her as his fingers closed over hers.

"Kirk! Just the man I wanted to see," Dalhousie said. "I believe you made an error in your recitation."

Anne murmured her disapproval, but Kirk merely raised a brow.

Undeterred, Dalhousie continued. "It's not 'gray-blue' eyes, but deep blue. The Earl of Perth read it at his wedding two months ago, and went on and on about how his wife's eyes were exactly like the ones in the poem—deep blue."

"Did I say gray-blue?" Kirk's gaze flickered to Dahlia. "I wonder how I came to make such a mistake."

Her cheeks warmed.

Kirk continued, "Pardon us, but I'm parched and must find the refreshment table."

"Of course." The viscount turned to Anne. "Next time, I shall memorize a poem. It's much better received than a sermon."

"As if you've ever memorized a poem in your life."

Kirk pulled Dahlia away from the arguing couple, murmuring in her ear, "I believe we're no longer needed here."

He walked down the length of the room, bowing to this person, nodding to that. Dahlia was intensely aware of the warmth of his hand over hers, and found herself reliving his kiss. And caress. And each tantalizing touch.

He paused by the double doors leading to the foyer and then glanced about. Everyone was crowding toward the refreshment table. "No one is looking. Come." He pulled her through the double doors and soon they were alone in the foyer.

"Where are we going?" she asked.

"We can't talk in there."

The noisy salon behind them, Kirk led her through the foyer and down a long hallway, and soon the soft thump of his cane was the only sound.

Dahlia's mind was too full of thoughts to converse. She didn't know where they were going, or why, but she didn't care. His words still warmed her, his gaze still held her in its spell. It was as if she were wrapped in his performance, mesmerized still.

Halfway down the hallway, Kirk stopped by a pair of ornate doors.

Dahlia glanced around curiously. "I've never been here before."

"This set of rooms is only in use when the duke is in residence."

"Would Roxburghe mind we are here?"

"I don't plan on informing him. Do you?"

She had to smile in spite of herself. "No."

"Good." Kirk flashed her a smile that made her feel both naughty and desirable, then opened the door. "After you."

Dahlia looked at his hand where it rested on the brass knob, and instantly a hard knot of desire tightened in her stomach. With hands that trembled ever so slightly, she gathered her skirts and walked through the doorway.

## Fifteen

**From the Diary of the Duchess of Roxburghe**

All of the women are thoroughly agog over Lord Kirk. I never thought I'd see a man so transformed by a poem, but then again, I never heard a man read a poem with such feeling. Even I felt a bit flushed afterward.

There is something to be said for a man's voice when it caresses a word. Nothing is as pleasurable.

Dahlia's eyes slowly adjusted to the dim light of the fire, which had been reduced to embers. At one end of the room she saw a cluster of leather chairs near an overstuffed settee, and at the other end a billiards table.

Kirk crossed the room to light a lamp that stood on a side table. The warm glow turned the heavy velvet and fringed curtains to waterfalls of molten gold, adding a luxurious air to the room. He then went to the fireplace to stir the embers back to life, adding several pieces of wood from the brass holder beside the hearth.

Dahlia watched him from under her lashes, noting the strong masculine beauty of his hands as he stacked the wood over the embers. She regarded him from head to toe, marveling at the breadth of his shoulders, the narrowness of his hips, and the powerful ripple of his thighs as he hefted more wood onto the fire.

When she'd known him before, she'd thought him attractive, but not as deliciously so as she did now. It was as if she'd suddenly seen another side of him, another facet that made him gleam more. And as he'd recited the lovely poem directly to her tonight, saying all of the things she'd always wanted him to say, he'd become the personification of everything romantic. Her heart swelled with happiness.

There was something different about Kirk since he'd come under the duchess's care, something beyond his clothes and improved manner. It was something more . . . physical. For one thing, he was moving more easily. Just now, on entering the room, he'd set aside the cane without any thought. Although he still limped, he didn't seem to need it as much.

Unaware of her regard, he stirred the fire into flames, his handsome profile outlined as he returned the poker to its stand.

She'd always felt an affinity for this man, as if they were part of the same book. But that hadn't been enough. She needed to feel as if they were on the same page, too—as if their connection was due to more than common interests, or coming from the same village. She'd wanted to feel connected to his *soul*. And tonight, when he'd recited the poem to her, she'd felt exactly that.

"There." He dusted his hands. "It will be warmer in a moment."

She tugged her shawl up over her shoulders. "Thank you. It is a bit cold." The cool air raised goose bumps, yet in spite of the chill she felt flushed, her heart thudding with anticipation.

They were alone, and the memory of their previous kiss warmed her thoughts. Now, stirred by his words, she wanted more. *I want him.* The thought sent a shiver through her, powerful and pleasurable in its own right.

He frowned. "There's a lap blanket on the back of the settee. I'll—"

"No. I'm fine."

"Good." He turned to light a lamp near the billiards table.

She bit her lip and waited, sighing a little when he seemed to take an inordinate amount of time to adjust the wick. Perhaps *she* should proceed.

The thought tantalized her and she found herself smiling. *How does one begin a seduction? Hmmm . . . I think we need to be closer.*

She crossed to the billiards table, which was closer to him. "Do you play?"

Done adjusting the lamp, Kirk turned in time to see Dahlia's slender fingers slide along the polished wood rail. His mouth went dry. "Ah, yes. I play." Mac-Creedy thought it a good way to develop flexibility, as one had to twist oneself into a variety of positions.

"Ah." She traced the curve around one of the netted pockets.

He cleared his throat. "It's an excellent table. Apparently Roxburghe had it sent from Italy."

"Only the best for the duke." She reached into one of the webbed pockets and pulled out a ball. "Ivory. They are quite lovely."

He found himself watching breathlessly as she cupped the ball in her palm. He couldn't help imagining what that would feel like, to have her warm fingers cupped about him. His body stiffened at the thought, and he fought back a groan.

He had to clear this throat before he could ask, "Do you play?"

"Oh yes. Father has a table, although it's not as large as this." She shot him a look from under her lashes. "Would you care to play a game?"

"Perhaps." What he wanted was to kiss her until she couldn't breathe, slide his hands over her full breasts and hips, mold her soft body to his, and take her— *Stop that. You won't be able to talk at all, and this battle is far from won.*

He turned to the side table, where a decanter glistened. He poured some into a glass and then slanted her a glance. "I wish there was some sherry for you, but there's only whiskey."

"I like whiskey."

His surprise must have shown, for she smiled and added, "My father has a glass after dinner each night, and sometimes I join him. I actually prefer it to sherry." She pulled more balls from the pockets and placed them on the table.

"Then by all means, have some whiskey." He poured a small amount into a glass for her, and then carried it to her.

She took the glass, her eyes twinkling as she compared it to his. "Kirk, please, I'm a Scot."

She was more than a Scot. She was a bold and lovely woman with gray-blue eyes that mirrored every thought, and he wanted her so badly that his body ached.

Her gaze locked with his and slowly, she tipped the glass up and drank the mouthful of liquid. She smiled as she swallowed and handed him the empty glass. "At least a finger pour this time, please."

He smiled and returned to the sideboard to pour her a finger's width of whiskey, then brought it to her.

She cupped it in both hands. "Thank you." She took an appreciative sip. "This is excellent."

She tilted her head to one side and regarded him, a thoughtful smile on her lips. "The poem tonight was lovely. You've always had a talent for reading aloud."

*It was worth it, to see that smile.* He placed his glass on the edge of the table and captured her hand. It was so small, fitting inside his own perfectly, the fingers long and tapered. He turned it over and pressed a kiss to the palm.

Her fingers trembled as she closed her hand over the kiss, as if to hold it there. "Kirk, do you . . . do you enjoy being here, at the castle?"

"I suppose so. Why?"

"I don't know. I had such high hopes for coming here. I thought I'd find romance and excitement and—" She uncurled her fingers and looked at her palm as if she thought she'd find an answer there. "Sometimes it can be a bit lonely. Even with all of these people about, I feel alone in some way. But then I see you, and things seem better."

"I suppose I remind you of home." He hesitated and then said, "Life was simpler there, wasn't it?"

"We were, at least." Her gaze dropped to the amber liquid in her glass as she swirled it slowly.

He watched her face, noting the thoughts flitting over it. "You're not happy."

She shot him a surprised look and then shrugged. "I should be. Life here is everything I'd imagined it would be: sumptuous, lavish, beautiful, and—"

"Dull."

She hesitated. "Not dull, but . . ." She frowned. "Do you ever feel out of place?"

"Every moment of every day. But I've never been comfortable around people."

"Even before the accident?"

"Society was never my preferred way of life." He cocked a brow at her. "But you enjoy it."

"I do, and I've met some lovely people, but . . ."

She smiled and shook her head. "I'd dreamed for so long of having a season, of attending balls and having lovely gowns. And now here I am, the guest of a duchess determined to provide us with the best of every amusement. I should be grateful—I *am* grateful—for it's been a lovely experience. But . . . I miss home." Her gray-blue gaze turned to him. "I didn't expect that."

"Perhaps you'll get used to it. You haven't traveled much."

"That's another difference. These people have all done so much more than I have—they've been more places, seen more things, know more—"

"Pah! They may have traveled more physically, but I doubt any of them know the value of where they've been. Lord Dunsteed had the temerity to complain that the ruins he visited in Greece were in such sad shape, the walls tumbling down and columns upon the ground, that it was hard to envision what they should look like, and that the government should come in and 'redo them all.'"

She blinked. "But they're *ruins*."

"Exactly what I told him. That's how we found them, and that's how they should be preserved. But he maintained that we should rebuild them and even add to them, to bring them 'up to level.'"

"What a fool!"

"Exactly what I thought. He even suggested that with the right seating and the leveling of the dirt, the Coliseum might make a fine cricket stadium—"

She burst out laughing.

Kirk had to grin. "I'd better not mention what he thought should be done with the Temple of Venus."

"I can't even imagine."

"I should hope not. So don't sell yourself short, thinking that just because these ninnies have traveled more, that they're any better than you."

"They're not all ninnies." But she had to admit, at least to herself, that he was right. She took a sip of the whiskey, listening to the fire crackle as she savored the warm liquid. The fire illuminated the amber liquid in Kirk's glass and cast intriguing shadows over his face. Her gaze flickered lower, and she wondered how he'd look without the pressed cravat and fancy coat. Was he as muscular as he felt when she'd kissed him?

He looked down at his shirt. "Is something wrong with my waistcoat?"

*Yes, you're wearing one.* Not giving herself time to think, she set down her glass, stepped forward, and placed her hand on his chest.

His dark gaze raked over her, brushing her like a touch and making her stomach quiver as he set his glass beside hers and then captured her hand, his warm fingers closing over hers.

Dahlia's heart thudded harder. "Kirk, I—" Words fled. "I want—" She wanted *him*, but more than that, she wanted him to touch her, to tease her to life, to show her how—

He kissed her, and all thoughts disappeared under a thunderous wave of passion.

Kirk felt her soften instantly against him and he slipped his arm about her waist, holding her against him as he deepened the kiss. She instantly responded, her hips moving wantonly against his as she urged, invited, begged.

And he was all too willing to oblige. He traced her curves, sliding his hands from her waist to her hips and onto her rounded bottom. He held her to him, reveling in her full curves. She grasped his arms, his shoulders, and then slid her hands to his chest, fumbling with the buttons of his waistcoat.

Passion burned through him unchecked. God, he wanted this woman! His body demanded it, demanded her. But he couldn't, wouldn't, harm the delicate accord they'd finally reached. With the greatest reluctance, he broke the kiss and, panting heavily, rested his forehead against hers.

She scowled up at him, almost causing him to laugh. "What are you doing?" she demanded.

"I must hear you say this is what you want." He cupped her face, marveling at the silk of her skin. "We've made so many errors, and I don't want this to be one of them."

"I'm certain. What you said earlier tonight . . . *Yes, Kirk. Yes, yes, yes!*"

*What I said earlier? What was that?* "Dahlia, I—"

She raised up on her tiptoes and pulled his mouth to hers, pressing her soft body against him. All thoughts disappeared, burned away by a hot sear of passion. He slipped his hand up from her waist, and cupped her breast. She gasped, then pressed into his hand. Her gown was as thin as a wisp and he could feel the lace of her chemise beneath the material as he found her peaked nipple and teased it with a gentle brush.

She moaned and rubbed her hips to his, inviting and pleading without words.

He lifted her to the billiards table and pressed between her legs. She opened for him, her legs parting, her skirts lifting to her calves.

She clutched at his waistcoat, pulling him closer, rocking against him suggestively as her kisses grew more desperate.

He slid his hand from her ankle to her bared calf, where he cupped the glorious fullness. Her skin was so warm, so wonderfully silken. He followed the line of her calf to her knee, and then onto her thigh, sliding her skirts up as he went.

Dahlia gasped at his boldness. The warmth of his hand on her bare leg, combined with the cooler air in the room, made her shiver with delight. She felt free and unfettered as his hand roamed higher. When his fingers brushed her most intimate folds, she went rigid with shock. He stroked again, raining kisses over her face and neck, distracting her with his murmurs and caresses.

Each time he stroked her it stirred something deep inside, making her writhe in pleasure, awash in a desire for something she couldn't name. "More," she whispered against his lips.

He obliged her, stroking her more firmly as she

pressed into his hand, her thighs damp with passion. Then, as suddenly as a star streaking across the sky, sweet release slammed into her and she grasped his wrist and jerked forward, wave after wave of passion tumbling through her.

He held her tight, burying his face in her neck as she clutched him, his cock aching as he felt her wetness. "I want you," he growled. He wanted her, needed her, *had* to have her. He kissed her with every bit of passion he felt and she returned it, her body still shaking with tiny tremors, easy to re-arouse.

Suddenly there were too many clothes between them and they were both tugging, pulling, trying to get closer. She fumbled with his waistcoat and he pulled back.

"No. We don't need—" He undid his breeches and pushed them down, his cock springing forward.

Dahlia's eyes widened but she didn't hesitate, her warm hand encircling him firmly. Gritting his teeth against the onslaught of sensual waves, he gently grasped her wrist and freed himself, her arms going around his neck as he tugged her forward on the table. And then he was pressing against her, the tip of his manhood searching for her slick heat.

Dahlia had never felt anything so exquisite. She grasped his shoulders and arched against him, pressing into him, onto him as he slipped inside her. The size of him surprised her and she gasped and froze in place. He lifted her thighs and tugged them about his hips. Instinctively, she locked her legs about his waist and surged forward. There was a moment of resistance and then he was moving, sending waves of heat and delicious fullness through her, so overwhelming that she could only close her eyes and gasp with the wonder of it.

As Kirk thrust firmly, again and again, the heat began to rise inside her. She writhed in an attempt to pull him closer, to capture this moment, and all of him, shivers of wildness racing through her.

Through her lashes she caught a glimpse of his face, his eyes closed tight, his thick lashes upon his cheeks, an expression of pained pleasure on his face as he took and gave, all in the same stroke.

Had she known how blissful this was, she never would have hesitated. Wanting more, she tightened her legs and pulled him closer, opening for him.

He groaned, his brow damp as he rocked against her, pressing kisses to her shoulder, her neck, his warm breath making her moan in return. Her breasts felt heavy and full and she ran her hands over his arms, his powerful shoulders, the heat between her legs turning molten. The fire deep inside her began to rage, pushing her into mad desperation. She clutched him as wave after wave of passion raced through her, deeper and more fully, each stroke increasing her madness.

Her pleasure seemed to inflame his, for he was suddenly moving faster and faster. Then he arched against her, pulsing deep within her as he held her tight—and as he buried his face in her hair, he cried out her name.

# Sixteen

**From the Diary of the Duchess of Roxburghe**
One moment they were there, and then they weren't. I don't think anyone noticed, either. Later on, someone was looking for Lord Kirk to congratulate him on his reading, but I told them he'd asked to be excused with a headache.

I told him she would respond to a poem. I do hope he remembers to thank me when he sees me tomorrow.

For long moments afterward neither said a word, their harsh breathing and the crackle of the fire the only sounds in the otherwise silent room. Dahlia slowly became aware of the hardness of the table under her hips, of the chill of her side turned away from the fire, of the awkward splay of her legs where Kirk leaned between them. Yet still she clung to him, her face pressed into his neck, refusing to let the moment go.

He laid his forehead against her temple as his

breathing slowly returned to normal. The warmth of his breath made her snuggle closer.

Finally, he lifted his head and looked into her eyes. She offered a tentative smile.

"That was—" He shook his head. "There are no words."

Her face was already as heated as it could get, but she managed a nod.

He pushed away from the table and pulled her skirts back into place, his hands lingering in a way that made her smile. "Here." He reached into his pocket and pulled out his handkerchief and pressed it into her hands. As he did so, he kissed her forehead.

His warm breath sent a delicious aftershock shiver racing through her. Smiling, he turned to the fire and made a show of banking the blaze.

She cleaned herself, pulled down her skirts, and then crossed to the fire to toss the handkerchief into the flames. As she did so, she caught sight of herself in the mirror that hung over the mantel. Her hair was falling down, her face was flushed a soft pink, and her lips were swollen and red. She looked . . . fulfilled.

She smiled, and began fixing her hair as best she could.

Kirk came behind her, slipped an arm around her waist, and kissed her ear. "Mmmm."

Her lashes lowered and she leaned into him, turning her head to offer him better access to her neck. She met his gaze in the mirror and smiled. "I can't seem to get enough of your touch."

"A perfect match." Kirk bent to gently nip her shoulder. He couldn't seem to stop touching her, tasting her. *Each touch makes me crave another.* "We're compatible in so many ways."

"Oh no. You're not going to reduce this down to something as mundane as compatibility."

He chuckled and pulled her back so that she was tucked against him. "Compatibility is a good thing. It's real, unlike that ridiculous poem."

She stiffened in his arms. "Ridiculous?"

"Thoroughly." He captured a strand of silken hair and twined it about his fingers. "I don't know how anyone could like Byron, for his style could only be called exaggerated sappiness, but—" He shrugged. "I knew you like his work, so I read it for you."

She pulled away and turned to look up at him, a question in her eyes. "So the poem . . . it wasn't about me?"

He laughed. "You'll have to ask Byron who it's about, but I doubt it's you since you have the wrong color eyes."

"You changed the color to mine."

"Oh, that. Lady Charlotte suggested it before the reading."

"Then you . . . you never said those words from the poem to me."

His smile faded. "I read it to you, of course, and everyone else in the room. Why—"

"*Oh!*" She pulled away and pressed her fingers to her temple, and he noted that her hands were shaking.

"Good God. I thought—" She couldn't seem to get the words out.

"You thought what?"

"I— Kirk, you didn't choose that poem because it reminded you of me."

He could see the answer she wanted, but honesty made him say, "I picked it because it was short, and I had very little time to memorize it."

"But . . . you looked at me through the entire recitation."

"I didn't dare look at anyone else." At her blank stare, he added, "I was nervous. I know you. I trust you. I thought . . . Yes, I looked at you."

She said bleakly, "I thought you meant that poem was about me. About us."

Her pale face alarmed him. "Dahlia, I am very serious about us, and about our future."

"Our future?"

"Of course. Once we marry."

"*Marry?* But you haven't even— *No*, Kirk!" She threw up her hands and moved away from him. "You still don't understand. Not even after—" She clamped her lips together. "I'm not marrying you."

"Of course you will," he said impatiently. "You must."

"There's no must in this."

"Don't be foolish. After what we just did, how could we not marry?"

"Easily." She locked gazes with him. "People do

what we just did all the time, and not all of them marry."

He started to argue, but her paleness gave him pause. Something was wrong—very wrong. But what? "Dahlia, what's wrong? You were happy until just now."

"The emotions in that poem—they weren't yours. I thought they were." The bleakness in her voice chilled his soul.

"I never claimed that. Besides, how could they be, when I didn't write them?" He raked a hand through his hair, feeling as if he were standing upon very, very thin ice in the center of a huge, frozen pond. "Dahlia, if you want me to write you some damned poetry, I will, but I'm not good at that sort of thing. It would be wretched."

"'Damned poetry.' Lovely. That's exactly what I'd like—damned poetry. Pray do not put yourself through such torture on my behalf."

"It would be unpleasant, I admit it, but I wouldn't call it torture," he said generously.

Her expression hardened and she turned away and picked up her shawl from the edge of the billiards table. "I am such a fool. I thought you wished to marry me because you cared for me."

"Of course I care for you."

"How much?"

Good God, how did one answer a question like that? "Plenty."

"'Plenty.'" Her flat tone told him what she thought of his answer. "You 'care' for me 'plenty.'"

He hurried to add, "Marriage isn't always based on some sort of soon-forgotten love. We're fond of one another, and that's worth so much. We're compatible in so many—"

She threw up a hand. "I don't ever want to hear that word again—'compatible.' I *hate* that word."

"But we *are*. We both love to read and we enjoy quiet evenings and history, and— We just found out that we're also compatible in bed."

"And?"

He rubbed his cheek. "And what? Isn't that enough?"

"No. I want love. Kirk, do you *love* me? Really, *really* love me?"

He sighed. "Dahlia, look. We both came here to find a mate, and we found the perfect candidate in each other. Why must you cloud the issue with talk of love and—"

"First of all, we *didn't* both come here to find a mate. *I* came to find love, and then hopefully marriage. Marrying for love is *not* the same as marrying for convenience, and because you find the other person 'compatible.'"

"Those are just words. You're making a big to-do about nothing," he said impatiently.

Her eyes flashed dangerously. "Nothing? Is that how you see it?"

He raked a hand through his hair. "I don't know what you want from me, Dahlia."

"I want love, Kirk. And I deserve that."

"I read you a damned poem. Doesn't that count?" he asked, raking his hands through his hair again in frustration.

"You picked that poem because it was easy to memorize, not because it reminded you of me. So reading it wasn't romantic at all. It was just a task to you. I want to be told that I'm loved, Kirk, and that you find me attractive, and that you like my laugh and think my eyes are pretty. I want to be worth some *effort*."

"Oh," he said, relieved. "I can do that. I *do* find you attractive—surely you can tell that. Your eyes are quite nice and you're a pretty woman—"

"Stop! Just *stop!*" She pressed her hands to her cheeks. "This is impossible. I refuse to give up all hope of romance merely because you refuse to acknowledge it—or worse, you don't feel it."

"Dahlia, I care for you. You know that. I always have."

"Yes, well, I care for my sister, and her grace cares for her dogs, and the butler cares for the pocket watch his grandfather gave him when he was a child—but 'care' is not what I want. I want someone to love me so much that losing me would make him mad with it. I want him to adore me and think I'm beautiful beyond compare, and to write sonnets to my eyes and . . . well, it would be nice if you at least *wanted* to write sonnets. I would be happy with that."

His jaw tightened. "I'm not the sort of man who can string words together like paper snowflakes. That's for men like Dalhousie, who spout drivel that would make a healthy man's stomach turn. But I do care for you."

"*Do* you? So much so that you can talk about marriage without so much as a by-your-leave?"

He opened his mouth and then closed it. "You want to be asked. I should have known that, after the last time."

"Of course I want to be asked! What woman doesn't?"

"I asked you once, and you said no."

"You didn't ask me to marry you. You suggested that we'd make a 'tolerable rub' of it 'despite' my father's sad monetary habits."

It did sound horrible when she put it like that. Still, he refused to be cowed. By God, he wanted her, so he'd be damned if he'd quit now. "We enjoy the same pursuits—books, the outdoors, history, music. Most couples don't have the luxury of compatibility when they wed—"

"Damn it, I don't want compatibility. I want *love*, Kirk. Love. Do you love me?" she demanded.

"Of course."

She looked at him expectantly.

He frowned. "I said, 'Of course.'"

"Oh! You won't even—" She threw up her hands. "That's it."

"That's what?"

"There is nothing more to say. I will not marry you."

His jaw tightened and he found his hands in fists. "You must. We just—"

"Nothing happened. And if you try to say it did, I shall tell her grace that you are spreading horrid rumors about me, and I'll ask her to send you packing."

"You can't deny us."

"I can, and I shall."

He crossed the icy space that threatened them and yanked her forward, her body pressed to his. "Do you feel that? That's *passion*, Dahlia—not this milksop love you think you want. I admire you and respect you. I think you're the most intelligent, attractive woman of my acquaintance."

"But do you *love* me? I won't accept anything less." Her eyes sparkled with anger and hurt.

He sighed. "'Love' is such a fickle word, Dahlia. Isn't it enough that I want you and—"

She spun away and, with a sob that tore his heart, she fled.

# *Seventeen*

**From the Diary of the Duchess of Roxburghe**

Was a house party ever so cursed as this one? While I do not blame Miss Stewart for her illness, my physician thinks it might be Spanish influenza, which is a wretched business indeed. Although Miss Stewart has been confined to her chambers for the three days since the very first signs of her illness at the poetry reading, the news has sent terror rippling through my guests. Eleven fled this morning, and I suspect that several more might do so before nightfall.

Charlotte and I must make a decision today about whether or not to have the Christmas Ball, which is a great pity as the footmen just put up a huge tree in the ballroom and spent hours hanging it with silver ropes and stars. Still, reality must be answered, and if more guests leave, we'll have no choice but to cancel the thing.

Another disappointment is that, since Dahlia has been assisting in the nursing of Miss Stewart, she has barely spoken two words to Lord Kirk, which has made him as growly as a bear with a sore paw. And here I thought they were making progress!

La, so many problems. If I must cancel the ball, so be it. But I will not give up on our star-crossed lovers.

Dahlia looked at the tea tray Freya had placed on the small table in the hallway outside Miss Stewart's bedchamber and smiled before whispering, "Scones and weak tea. Just the thing for our patient."

Freya glanced at the half-open door behind Dahlia. "Is she any better?"

"Some. Lady Mary managed to get Miss Stewart to take some tea and dry toast late last night. We think she's turned a corner." Which had been a sweet moment indeed. The last few days had been filled with such uncertainty that as soon as Miss Stewart asked for another bite of toast, both Lady Mary's and Dahlia's eyes had filled with tears.

She brushed at her eyes impatiently, surprised they were once again brimming with tears. *Goodness, what's wrong with me?* But she knew. The long, silent hours by Miss Stewart's bedside had left Dahlia with too much time to think. She caught Freya's worried frown and shook her head. "I'm sorry. I'm just tired." Because of her unsettled thoughts, she'd slept only two hours last night before it was her turn to assist with Miss Stewart.

She pressed a hand to her aching head. It had been a long three days. After leaving Kirk in the billiards room, Dahlia had been hurrying to her own room, wanting nothing more than to be alone, when she'd caught Lady Mary on the staircase. The poor woman had been frantic, wringing her hands and looking as if she might burst into tears. Although Dahlia felt much the same way, she'd put her own feelings aside and had asked if she could help.

Dahlia had quickly discovered that Miss Stewart's condition had worsened and Lady Mary, realizing that her friend's fever was rising, was concerned. Dahlia had asked MacDougal to send for the duchess's physician and then she'd followed Lady Mary to Miss Stewart's bedside. Since then, she and Lady Mary had shared in nursing their patient back to health.

Dahlia had managed to take her morning walks between her shifts at Miss Stewart's side, but sleep was another thing altogether. Once she was alone, Dahlia's thoughts had roiled in turmoil over her last encounter with Kirk. She wasn't sorry for sharing her passion with him, but oh how she wished she'd realized the truth about his feelings before she'd so plainly shown her own. She was now torn between embarrassment and anger.

Fortunately, her duties in nursing Miss Stewart had kept her from any awkward confrontation with Lord Kirk. She now knew the truth—as much as she hated to admit it, he wasn't able to feel for her the way she wished him to. The sooner she accepted that cold fact, the better off she'd be. Yet that did nothing to help the deep ache that filled her.

"Miss?"

Dahlia realized she hadn't heard a word her maid had just said. "I'm sorry, I was thinking about something else."

"Och, ye're exhausted, ye are. Come back to the room and take a wee nap."

"I shall, but I think I'll take a walk first. I need to clear the cobwebs from my head." And if she were good and tired she might actually sleep, not just stare at the ceiling trying not to think about Lord Kirk and failing miserably. She felt as if she were in a fog, wrapped in wool and unable to think clearly except where Kirk was concerned. In that one area, her unwanted thoughts were painfully clear.

Freya's brows lowered in concern. "Ye should let me ha' a turn takin' care o' Miss Stewart."

"I would, but she gets very agitated when she wakes up and someone she doesn't know is there."

"Then thank God she's some'at better. Ye and Lady Mary canno' keep up such a schedule."

"We're coming to an end of it, I'm sure. She's better every day." Dahlia rubbed her shoulder.

"Ha' ye hurt yerself, miss?"

"I've been sleeping in a chair, so I'm a bit sore." Which explained why her head was starting to ache, too.

Freya scanned Dahlia's face. "Pardon me, miss, bu' are ye sure ye feel well? Ye look pale, ye do."

"I'm healthy as a horse. I've played nursemaid for everyone at Caith Manor, so this is quite natural to me. Besides—" She glanced at the half-opened door and lowered her voice. "Someone must assist Lady Mary and she won't accept help from anyone else."

"She do seem fond o' Miss Stewart."

"She is. Far more than I'd realized." And perhaps more than Lady Mary had realized, too. Over the last three days, Dahlia had gotten to know Lady Mary and had discovered a softer, gentler side to the woman who'd always been so unfriendly.

"I must return to Miss Stewart; she's due her medicine." Dahlia lifted the tea tray from the side table. "If you'll get the door, I'll see if I can cajole our patient into eating some of this scone."

"Verrah weel, miss. Dinna hesitate to ring if ye need me."

"Thank you, Freya." With a reassuring smile at the worried maid, Dahlia went into the darkened room. She made her way to the table she and Mary had moved from under the window to a more useful location near the bed, and placed the tray upon it, sighing as she straightened.

At the rattle of china, Miss Stewart opened her eyes and then squenched them closed. "Ohhhhhh."

"Headache?" Dahlia asked quietly.

Miss Stewart tried to swallow and then nodded, only to wince again. She covered her eyes with hands that shook.

As pale and weak as she looked, she was much better than the first night Dahlia had visited. The poor woman had been out of her mind with fever, talking with people no one else could see, and refusing the medicine Lady Mary had tried to press upon her.

Dahlia went to the washbowl and found a fresh cloth, dipped it in the cold water, then pressed it into Miss Stewart's hand. "For your eyes."

Miss Stewart gratefully placed the cool cloth over her eyes. "Thank you." Her voice was as rusty as a churchyard gate, but it was steady now.

Heartened, Dahlia glanced at the clock on the side table. "You are due another dose of medicine. I thought we might put it in a cup of tea with some sugar, since you don't care for the taste."

Miss Stewart managed a faint smile. "I complained quite a bit last time, didn't I?"

"No more than I would have had someone tried to get me to take such a bitter draught when I didn't feel well." Dahlia put three lumps of sugar into a cup and then poured tea over them. Stirring quickly, she added a dose of medicine. As she returned the small brown bottle to the table, the door opened and Lady Mary came in.

She brightened when she saw Miss Stewart holding a cloth over her eyes. "I see our patient is awake."

Dahlia smiled. "I was just going to give her some tea. Her medicine is mixed in."

"Ah yes. Or, as she called it yesterday, 'pig swill.'"

Miss Stewart peeped from beneath the cloth. "Did I say that?"

"You were complaining horribly, which is always a good sign," Dahlia teased.

Lady Mary smiled gratefully. She was dressed as fashionably as ever in a morning gown of fine cambric with full sleeves caught at her wrists with gold bands. She took the cup from Dahlia and sat on the edge of the bed. "Alayne, take your medicine."

Miss Stewart removed the cloth from her eyes and reached for the cup.

"Let me, dearest. Your hands are shaking."

Miss Stewart didn't argue, and was soon sipping the tea.

When she finished it, Lady Mary couldn't have appeared happier. "You're much improved."

"I feel wretched and my hands won't stop shaking."

"You're still weak." Dahlia pointed to the scone. "Eat when you can, as it will give you strength."

Miss Stewart smiled weakly and leaned back against her pillows.

Dahlia bent to retrieve her shawl where it had fallen to the floor, wincing as she did so. She rubbed her lower back. "If we're to sleep in this room any longer, we need to request a settee."

Lady Mary looked surprised. "You said you'd slept comfortably when I asked about it yesterday."

"That was before I awoke today feeling as if someone had beaten me." She smiled. "It's nothing that a good walk won't fix."

Lady Mary looked concerned. "Before you go, you

should talk to her grace's butler. Dalhousie and Miss MacLeod were thinking of going for a ride, but I overheard MacDougal telling them there's a bitter cold wind from the north and it always brings rain."

"Dalhousie and Anne?"

Lady Mary sent her an arch look. "Oh yes. While we've been confined to the sickroom, life has been marching on. I believe they've been keeping each other company."

"Good for them!" Dahlia glanced at the shuttered windows and wondered if she should wear her cloak over her pelisse.

"You're determined to walk, aren't you?"

"It clears my thoughts. And you need have no fear that I'll be caught out in the weather, for I plan on a very short walk."

Lady Mary returned the empty teacup to the tray and adjusted Miss Stewart's bed linens. "Miss Balfour—Dahlia, before you go—" She straightened and faced Dahlia. "I don't know what Alayne and I would have done without you. Thank you so much for your assistance."

Miss Stewart, already struggling to stay awake, managed a faint smile. "Yes, thank you."

Dahlia waved her hand. "Think nothing of it. I'm sure you both would have done the same for me."

"We would have, indeed. Especially now." Mary walked with Dahlia to the door. "Don't worry," she said in a low voice. "I shall get Alayne to eat, even if I have to drop crumbs of the scone into her mouth."

"See that you do. She's better, but needs her strength."

"And you need your rest, so make it a very short walk." Mary gave Dahlia a quick hug.

Surprised, Dahlia barely had time to return the gesture when Mary released her.

Mary's face was flushed, although she looked pleased. "You've been an angel. When we first met I was rude, and I shouldn't have been. I've always had an unruly tongue."

"I wasn't any better." Dahlia grinned. "We deserved each other."

Mary smiled. "Perhaps, but this situation has made me consider Alayne. Sometimes she's been held to the brutal edge of my tongue, for no more reason other than she's much kinder than she should be." Mary pursed her lips. "I will never treat her so again."

"You're being too hard on yourself."

"Now who is being too kind?" Mary regarded Dahlia for a long moment. "You've given up a lot to help Alayne."

"A few evenings of whist, " Dahlia said dismissively.

Mary's expression grew arch. "Oh, I think you gave up much more. It was obvious the night of the poetry reading that Lord Kirk has a decided interest in you. And since then, you've spent almost every waking hour assisting poor Alayne."

Dahlia felt her smile tighten, but she managed to say in an even tone, "Lord Kirk is not interested in me."

"Are you certain?"

"Very."

Mary's eyes narrowed. "Ah. You've had a tiff."

Dahlia started to deny it, but the knowing look in Mary's eyes made her sigh instead. "We didn't disagree so much as we realized we have different ideas of how a relationship should progress."

"Oh?"

"I've known Lord Kirk for some time, and words are not his strong point."

"But the poem—"

"Was recited—nothing more. He doesn't understand the beauty of it or what it means or—" She clamped her lips closed as she heard the pained tone in her voice. "To quote him, he thinks we're 'compatible,' but that's all."

"Oh dear. That's too bad, for he seemed quite taken with you during the reading."

"Merely because he feared that if he looked about, he might forget the lines."

"It seemed as if there was more than that. I wonder . . ." Mary cast a quick glance back at the bed where Miss Stewart now slept. "I daresay you haven't met Miss Stewart's parents, because they rarely travel."

Surprised by the change in subject, Dahlia shook her head. "No, I haven't. Someone said Mr. Stewart was once a groom."

"He was one of the best, but opened his own stables and does quite well for himself. I've spent many Christmases with them. My own parents are quite busy and—" She shrugged, some of her smile disappearing. "Fortunately, Miss Stewart and her parents have always welcomed me. Mrs. Stewart is a lovely woman, warm and engaging, but Mr. Stewart is more difficult to get to know. He's not given to speaking much."

"That must make things awkward."

"At times, yes. But over the years, I've come to understand him. Now I can think of no man I admire more. Mr. Stewart and Lord Kirk seem very similar to me. Neither likes nor appreciates fashion, neither enjoys the niceties of a waltz nor a well-executed bow, and neither has the least desire to become a romantic ideal."

"Kirk would rather have his hand cut off."

"Mr. Stewart is much the same. I once asked Alayne if she'd ever heard her father declare himself to her mother, and she admitted that she hadn't. Not once."

"How sad for Mrs. Stewart."

A look of wonder warmed Mary's face. "I don't think she cares. In all of the holidays and summers I've spent with the Stewarts, I never once saw Mrs. Stewart get even one drop of rain on her, nor one gust of wind disorder her hair. If it was windy, Mr. Stewart made certain his wife traveled in a closed carriage with the curtains fastened. If it was raining, he held an umbrella over her head, refusing to allow the footman to do it. If the sun shone, he carried her parasol. If she was hungry, he immediately set about organizing dinner. If she was ill, he called the doctor and then sat beside her until she was better. Everywhere they go, everything they do, he makes certain she's safe, warm, and well." Mary's face held a touch of amazement. "If that's not love, then what is?"

Dahlia blinked. Up until now, she'd thought all of the shortcomings in her failed relationship with Kirk came from his lack of romantic appreciation. But was Mary right? Was some of the fault hers? Were her expectations unrealistic? At any time, had she taken into account Kirk's other attributes? Or was she too focused on one thing only: her own desire for romance?

The entire situation was too complicated for her fuzzy mind to understand. Despite her bone-deep weariness, a brisk walk seemed even more appealing. Perhaps she would recover her clarity of thought then.

She smiled at Mary. "Thank you. You've given me a lot to think about."

Mary's return smile was wistful. "One day, I would like to meet a man who wants to hold my umbrella."

Miss Stewart stirred and then plucked at the blankets. "Is there another pillow? I'd like to sit up."

Mary hurried to see to the patient's comfort, and Dahlia took the opportunity to slip away. Back in her own familiar bedchamber, she fetched her pelisse and—after a quick glance outside at the windy, gray day—her cloak, refusing to even look at the inviting bed. With a scone tucked into her pocket from a tray Freya had left for her, Dahlia hurried down to the foyer.

She walked past the ballroom where the great tree sat alone. Draped in silver, it reminded her that her time at the duchess's was growing shorter. In just a few days, with the remaining guests in attendance, the great Christmas Ball would be held, and then . . . that was it. She would be returning home, older but not any closer to finding what she'd been wanting.

She reached the foyer and smiled at the footman who jumped forward to open the door. Instantly, the bitter wind grabbed her cloak and swirled it about her ankles. She shivered and pulled the hood over her head as she stepped outside, then glanced up at the gray, swirling clouds. She'd definitely make it a quick walk.

Shivering, she tucked her gloved hands into her pockets and, head bent against the wind, she continued on. She'd just turned onto the gravel path that skirted the formal gardens when the creak of a gate caught her attention. She looked up as a man dressed in the black broadcloth suit of a gentleman's gentleman came out, something hanging over his arm. Dahlia recognized him, as Freya had pointed him out to her once. *Kirk's valet. I wonder where he's going?*

As she watched, the man hurried down the path to the stable and then entered, a golden spill of light briefly illuminating the cobblestone yard before the door closed. *A valet in the stable. That is odd.*

Dahlia found herself walking in that direction, and she soon heard a cacophony of voices raised in excitement. Were the servants having a dance, perhaps? She tilted her head to one side and listened, but she could hear no music.

As she neared the doorway she could make out a chorus of male voices raised in calls, along with— She frowned. Was that the thump of a fist? Goodness, but it sounded like a prizefight!

Her curiosity as hot as the air was cold, she tiptoed toward the wide doors that were partially ajar. Reaching the doors, she gave a quick glance around, then peeked inside.

A group of men—stable hands and grooms, judging by their clothing—stood in a half circle. In the center a sack of grain hung from the rafter on a thick rope. The valet stood to one side, a robe hung over his arm as he watched a man who was stripped to the waist pummel the hanging bag like a prizefighter, his cloth-wrapped fists slamming into the bag over and over, puffs of wheat dust filtering through the air with each hit. The valet watched intently, occasionally giving curt instructions, as the other men yelled at every especially brutal hit.

Whose groom could he be? His bare back glistened with sweat as he attacked the sack again and again, pummeling it with a fury that made her gasp. He was very fit, his muscles gleaming in the glow of the lamps. Though it was quite unladylike, she admired his physique as he cocked back his muscled arm and threw a hard punch that sent the grain sack reeling away, only to swing back as if in retaliation.

The man pivoted out of the way awkwardly, moving as if his leg were stiff—

Dahlia blinked. *Kirk?*

As if he could hear her, he turned to say something to the valet, and his profile confirmed her suspicions.

What was Kirk doing in a stable, feinting and pounding the bag of grain as if his life depended on it? Dahlia could only look . . . and look again, held in place with amazement.

He lifted his fists and a burly man set the bag in motion. Kirk threw another punch at the swinging bag, catching it on one side, which sent it spinning away and then back. Each hit set the bag in motion, which required him to dodge and duck. Then he'd hit it again.

He'd successfully landed dozens of hits when, after a particularly punishing thump, the sack of grain spun wildly about and then hit him in the shoulder.

Dahlia gasped as Kirk went reeling. He staggered to one side, landing on his weak leg. It was all Dahlia could do not to yell for someone to help him. *Can't they see he is in pain?*

A groom started to move toward him, but Kirk's valet grabbed the man's arm and refused to allow any assistance. *What is that man doing?*

Kirk wobbled a moment more, and then fell heavily to the ground. The other men fell quiet as he rolled to his side, straw and dirt stuck to his damp skin. But then, as if he'd done it a thousand times before, he grabbed a nearby stall door and levered himself to his feet, saying something to the men that made them all laugh heartily.

Her heart ached. The grooms didn't understand how much this cost him, but she did. *He has so much pride. Why is he doing this? What does he have to gain?*

Apparently Kirk was done for the day. Leg held stiffly to one side, Kirk found a small stool and limped to it, and then sat down. He rubbed his leg with both hands, his face damp with sweat and pain. The grooms, seeing their entertainment was over, called out a few congratulations and then wandered off to attend to their duties, leaving the two men alone near the door.

Dahlia wished she could hear them, but she was too far away. She stepped back from the stable doors and looked around. A large shuttered window was latched a bit farther down; perhaps she could hear better there. Holding her cape about her, the wind whipping her skirts around her legs, she made her way to the window and peered through the wide cracks between the shutters.

"Ye did verrah weel, me lor'." The valet lifted a bucket of water that sat nearby and handed it to Kirk.

"Thanks. As you warned, it hurts like hell, but it's getting more flexible." Kirk lifted the bucket and poured the water over his head.

Dahlia's mouth went dry as the water flowed over Kirk's head to his muscled shoulders and back. She remembered the feel of those muscles under her fingers, the warmth of that skin— She shivered with something other than cold and leaned closer to the window.

"Och, ye did verrah, verrah weel today, me lor'. Ye should be proud."

"I'll be prouder when I can move quickly enough to keep from getting knocked down." He accepted a small hand towel from the valet and wiped his face. As he did so, the valet moved and the lantern bathed Kirk's body in gold light.

Dahlia found herself leaning forward, her face almost pressed to the shutters. Her gaze traveled over Kirk's broad back to where his water-soaked britches clung so lovingly to his muscular bottom and thighs, an odd breathlessness holding her in its thrall. Suddenly, it seemed very unfortunate that their encounter in the billiards room hadn't been long enough for more exploring.

The valet pulled a larger towel from where it had been hanging over the edge of a stable door and handed it to his master. "How's the pain, me lor'? Less than yesterday?"

"Some. The hot wraps you put on it last night helped." Kirk dried his hair, shoulders, and arms. "Although it still feels as if someone stuck it with a hot knife."

"Aye, but look at how ye were dodgin' and divin'. Ye couldna do neither two weeks ago."

"True. My leg is much more limber. Though the work is painful, it'll be worth it. '*Optimum quad premium*: That is best, which is first.'"

"An' ye wish t' be first?"

"I already was. Now I just have to stay there."

*What does that mean?* Dahlia pressed closer to the shuttered window. *Why is he putting himself through this?*

A stable boy led a large bay right in front of the window, blocking Dahlia's view, so she moved two windows down. She could still see, but she couldn't hear a word now.

*Perhaps Kirk wishes to ride again.*

Dahlia watched as the valet placed the robe over Kirk's shoulders and they began to talk earnestly, looking at the swinging bag of wheat. The entire time, Kirk continued to rub his knee.

She frowned. What was he thinking, engaging in an activity that put so much pressure upon his leg? But Kirk's expression held her. Though he winced when he stood and put weight on his leg, he also had a pleased glow to his face.

Kirk pulled on his robe, the silk clinging to his damp skin. When he tied the belt around his narrow waist, the robe outlined every delectable muscle. Dahlia's heart thudded an extra beat, her breasts tingling as she imagined peeling Kirk's silk robe from his shoulders, of kissing his broad chest, of stroking every bit of his muscled frame and—

She caught her unruly imagination, her blood heated nigh until boiling even though her teeth were nearly chattering. *For all of his flaws, he's a magnificent-looking man. But it's more than that. He's intelligent,* quick-witted, painfully honest, and sensual in ways I've never imagined. It's no wonder I care for him. He's— She blinked. *I do care for him. And . . . even more than care. I think I love him.*

She pressed her hands to her suddenly pounding head. *But I can't love him—not when he merely thinks of me as compatible. I can't be the only one who loves.*

Her thoughts jumbled, she blindly turned from the window. *I need to think, to understand how this happened.* Her throat tight, she strode up the path toward the moors.

# Eighteen

**From the Diary of the Duchess of Roxburghe**
And now the weather has turned. What else can possibly go wrong? Oh, wretched Christmas Ball! I had such hopes . . .

Cane in hand, Kirk strode from the stables, the icy wind stealing his breath. His progress should have cheered him, but since his argument with Dahlia he'd been miserable. And not just a little, but thoroughly, deeply, troublingly so.

Everything he ate tasted like sawdust, every joke he heard was unfunny, every activity proposed for the guests' amusement sounded dull and repulsive. Never in all of his life had he ever felt so low. All he could do was think about his last conversation with Dahlia and suffer his own regrets in silence.

It might have helped if he'd been able to speak to her, but since their disastrous argument, she'd been locked away helping with Miss Stewart.

He'd heard this morning that Miss Stewart was

much improved, and for the first time in three days, his heart had lightened. He and Dahlia had to talk, and they couldn't do it if they never saw each other. He wasn't certain they could find a solution, but he couldn't bear for things to stay the way they were now. He couldn't bear the thought of her being unhappy, of her gray-blue eyes filled with tears, as they'd been the last time he'd seen her. That image tormented him, disturbed his sleep and thoughts until he felt he might go mad with it.

A coach rolled past and he watched it. Yet another fleeing guest, he supposed. There were few enough of them left. He made his way into the castle, where he was greeted by four footmen and a herd of yapping pugs.

He glared at the dogs. "You are a pack of wild ones."

Gray-haired Randolph, calmer than the rest, sat off to one side, though his tail waggled crazily.

Kirk nodded his approval. "You know how to behave, don't you? But the rest of you are disgraces."

One of the footmen offered, "They're hopin' to get to the tree, m'lord. Her grace just closed the doors to the ballroom and refuses to allow them to enter."

"Why would dogs care about a Christmas tree?"

"They love to grab the silver strings and run off with them. Her grace dinna like tha', as she worries they might eat them and get sick, so she sets us to watch the beasties." He suddenly straightened and stared ahead as the butler sailed out of a side hallway.

"Och, me lor', allow me to take yer coat," Mac-Dougal said.

"No, thank you. I'd like to keep it on, for I'm not appropriately dressed to meet another guest." It was almost laughable that he heard himself say such a thing. Good God, he was becoming a dandy.

A burst of wind hit the front of the castle, banging the shutters and sending an icy wisp under the doors. The dogs barked and ran in circles.

"Silence, ye wild beasties!" MacDougal shook his head. "'Tis a north wind, me lor'. When they come, they bring us icy rain or snow."

"Lord Kirk, there you are." Her grace sailed out of the Blue Salon, dressed in a green gown adorned with a multitude of furbelows. "Just the man I wished to see."

He bowed. "Your grace. May I help you?"

"Yes. Lady Charlotte and I wish to speak to you."

"I need to bathe and change my clothes first."

"Nonsense. Roxburghe rides from dawn until dark and reeks of the stables from the day he arrives until he leaves for London, so I'm quite used to such things. Come. It won't take a moment." Without giving him time to speak, she turned and disappeared back into the salon, the pugs falling in behind her.

MacDougal gave Kirk an apologetic look. "She's been oop since dawn, worryin' aboot the guests as are leaving. I canno' blame them, fer the Spanish influenza is naught to treat lightly."

Kirk nodded. "I'm not leaving. Not unless Miss Balfour does."

The butler smiled fondly. "Och, she's no' goin' anywhere, is Miss Balfour. She's a heart as stout as her head."

"I know. Sadly, she's set them both against me."

"Ye think so, me lor'? I was well on me way to thinkin' she was showin' herself to be fond o' ye."

"If only I were so lucky." Sending the butler a wry look, Kirk went into the Blue Salon.

At the opposite end of the room, her grace and Lady Charlotte sat at either side of the fire. Her grace was on a settee, one of the pugs in her lap, while Lady Charlotte occupied a plump chair. She was knitting while also trying to read a book that lay open upon her knee, and doing neither particularly well. With every few rows of knitting, her yarn would catch the edge of the book and slide it off her knee.

He bowed. "Your grace. Lady Charlotte."

Her grace patted the settee beside her. "Come. Sit." It wasn't a question.

"I would rather stand, if you don't mind."

"I mind. Now come and sit."

He reluctantly did so. Randolph rose from his place in front of the fire and shuffled to Kirk's feet, snuffed his boots, and then dropped into a ball across the toes.

"Well?" Lady Charlotte said.

"Well what?"

Her grace sighed. "I don't have time for nonsense,

Kirk. There's Spanish flu on the loose and my guests are leaving in droves, so pray cut to the chase and don't pretend everything is fine between you and Miss Balfour. We know something is wrong."

He blinked. "Has she said something?"

"Lud, no. Every time we say your name, she just gets quiet, which is quite annoying." Her grace looked at Charlotte. "I do wish women were more outspoken."

"Me, too." Charlotte knitted on.

Kirk sighed. "Dahlia's been attending Miss Stewart. That's all."

"I don't believe you."

"Why not?"

"We've eyes in our heads," her grace said sharply.

"Oh yes," Lady Charlotte said, her book starting to slip. "It's obvious to everyone that you're not speaking to each other."

Randolph looked up as if to agree.

Kirk patted the dog. Should he tell Lady Charlotte and her grace about his mistake? If he was careful, he could explain a portion of the issue. Perhaps they could advise him in how to proceed. God knew, he could use the help. "You're right; Miss Balfour and I had an argument. She seems to think that something I said was a grievous mistake."

"A mistake?" Lady Charlotte's hands couldn't knit faster. "Another one?"

He almost winced. "I feel maligned."

Her grace patted his hand where it rested on his

knee. "There, there. No need to look so upset. Tell us what happened."

He sighed and leaned back. "It's about the poetry reading."

"Which was lovely," Lady Charlotte said.

"Very," her grace agreed. "I thought Dahlia very touched by it."

"She was," he agreed. "I did as Lady Charlotte suggested, and changed the eye color mentioned in the poem to match Dahlia's."

Her grace beamed at Lady Charlotte. "So that your doing."

Lady Charlotte blushed. "I thought it would make the reading more personal."

"Sadly, it did." He gave a short laugh and raked a hand through his hair. "Dahlia thought the words of the poem were about her, and she responded very warmly." If he closed his eyes right this second, he could still feel her warmth about him. "*Very* warmly."

"Oh my." Lady Charlotte leaned forward.

The duchess did the same. "And?"

"And so I proposed to her again."

"Good for you!" her grace said.

"No, not good for me, because once again, she refused me." He threw up his hands. "And damned if I know why! When she told me she wished I would ask, and not just order her to marry me, I asked her right away."

The duchess's brilliant blue eyes narrowed. "Hold

a moment, Lord Kirk. How, exactly, did you ask her to marry you?"

"I said nothing about her family."

"But?" she prompted.

"I merely pointed out that she needed to marry me."

"Needed to? Why?"

*Because I compromised her.* But he couldn't say that, so instead, he said, "Because that's the way it is—she must marry me." That wasn't a lie, either. She had to marry him. She must. He didn't know how or why, but it had to happen or the rest of his life would be the way it was this instant, colorless and cold.

"'That's the way it is'?" The duchess pressed a hand over her eyes. "Lord Kirk, pray tell me you didn't use quite those words."

"Actually, I believe I used exactly those words."

Lady Charlotte groaned. "Lord Kirk, after all of the work we've been doing!"

Her grace dropped her hand from her eyes. "We don't need to ask Miss Balfour's reaction, as we can already guess."

"She was angry," Lady Charlotte said.

"And perhaps sad," her grace added.

"And hurt," Lady Charlotte added.

"And definitely disappointed."

Kirk grimaced. "That's exactly what she was. She thought the poem I read was about her, but of course it wasn't, and that started things off poorly."

Lady Charlotte stopped knitting. "Wait, it *wasn't*

about her? You didn't select it because it reminded you of her?"

He shrugged. "It was short."

Her grace and Lady Charlotte exchanged glances before her grace said, "And you admitted that."

"I'm not going to lie to her."

Her grace sighed. "No, of course you aren't. Though there are times I wish you would."

"Surely you can't mean that."

"Perhaps. So you told Dahlia the poem wasn't about her, that you only selected it because it was short, and that you only changed the eye color because Lady Charlotte thought it might strengthen your suit."

"Yes."

"Oh dear. Lord Kirk, let me explain something to you about women: we like to be asked for things."

"I *did* ask."

Her grace lifted her brows.

His face heated. "Fine. I could have asked first, and not demanded, but my intent was the same. I wished to be with her for the rest of my life. Besides, she doesn't really have a choice, not after——" He caught Lady Charlotte's surprised expression and hurried to add, "That is, she needs to be reasonable. We would suit better than anyone else; she must be aware of that. The problem is that she has this idealized concept of what a marriage proposal should be, like something from a novel."

Lady Charlotte patted the book on her knee. "Novels are lovely."

"They're not realistic."

"Not every scene, no—it would be boring to read about what someone wants for breakfast or whose shoelaces were broken. Books focus on special moments, which we all have. And a marriage proposal should be special enough for a book."

Her grace nodded. "We're not talking about Dahlia's expectations for everyday life, but there's nothing wrong with wanting an occasional romantic moment. Why not?"

Kirk considered this. Perhaps that was the difference right there—he didn't differentiate one moment from the next. With Dahlia, they all seemed to be special. *With her, life would be.* He sighed. "Why do those moments matter so damn much to women?"

"They just do—and that's all you need to know about it." There was a note of finality in the duchess's voice. "Lord Kirk, what would you think about being married to someone who didn't regard your opinion as important?"

"Or didn't laugh at your jokes?" Lady Charlotte added.

"Or disliked your taste in drink so much as to disallow it in the house?"

"I wouldn't like it at all. But those are items of comfort."

"They're also items of respect. When you dismiss Miss Dahlia's wishes as if they aren't important, you're in essence telling her that *she* isn't important."

Lady Charlotte nodded, her lace cap fluttering. "That's how I'd see it."

"Damn it, she's not so foolish as to believe that," Kirk said heatedly. "I've proposed to her twice now. She *has* to know I respect her and—and care for her, and all of that."

"She doesn't 'have' to know anything—unless you tell her." The duchess reached out and placed her hand over his. "Tell her, Kirk. And for the love of God, stop being so selfish and this time, use some pretty words."

She noticed how his gaze narrowed as he considered what she said.

"You're right." He stood, grasping his cane lightly, a look of determination blazing across his face. "As soon as I'm able, I'll fix things with Miss Balfour. Thank you for your advice."

"It's our pleasure." Margaret waved a hand. "Now, off to your bath. We're so low on company that I've planned a very light lunch, and we're serving dinner at the ungodly early hour of six. To make up for it, there will be whist afterward if we still have enough guests to make up some rubbers."

"Thank you, but I don't think I'll play."

"Oh, but you will. And I shall make certain you are very, *very* happy with your partner. That will give you time to talk to Miss Balfour."

He grinned, his face transforming so that Margaret almost gasped. "Thank you, your grace. I appreciate your assistance."

"It's the least I can do. Now off with you. Lady Charlotte and I have much to discuss about the Spanish flu and whatnot."

He bowed and, with one last pat on Randolph's gray head, he left.

As soon as the door closed behind him, Charlotte picked up her knitting. "He can't seem to stop proposing."

"It's impulsive. The second she signals in any way that she finds him less than repulsive, he blurts out a command that she marry him."

"Love is a difficult beast to tame."

"I'm not convinced he even knows he *is* in love. Yet when he looks at her, it's as if he could devour her whole and still not be satisfied." Margaret had to smile. "It's actually quite adorable."

"If only we could get him to translate that look into words." Charlotte's book slipped off her lap, but she caught it and returned it to her knee. "Sadly, Dahlia is much younger in spirit than Lord Kirk, and she possesses a strong romantic streak. Perhaps too strong."

Margaret nodded thoughtfully. "Heavens, what a mull. I fear we'll have to allow fate to have its way, at least for now. Meanwhile, you and I must discuss our ball." She scooped up Meenie, who was staring at her with sad eyes, and settled the pug in her lap. "So. Shall we have the ball? Or shall we not?"

"There. Ye're as fine as five pence, me lor'."

Kirk glanced at himself in the mirror, dressed in the requisite black and white required of dinner at the duchess's, and grimaced. "I don't see why her grace insists on such formality. We're in the country, for God's sake. She should think of her guests' comfort."

"Indeed, me lor'. I'm surprised the weight o' yer clothes hasna broken yer broad shoulders and crumbled yer guid leg, too."

Kirk sent a hard look at MacCreedy, who grinned unrepentantly.

Randolph, who'd been snoozing on the bed, twitched in his dreams and whimpered, his paws flailing about.

Kirk placed his hand over the dog's head, instantly calming the sleeping mutt. "Leave the rabbits alone."

The dog's eyes opened and he wagged his tail, then sleepily rolled to his tummy.

"Och, dinna be spoilin' him, me lor'. Her grace's staff is all too willin' to do tha' now. Not only are they carryin' him oop and down the stairs, but he's started pretendin' he canna eat his food, so now they're givin' him the choicest meat fro' the table."

"He's not a dog, but an actor."

MacCreedy agreed. "A shameless one, me lor'. As we all are upon occasion."

"I shall pretend I don't think you are speaking about me." Kirk scratched the dog's gray chin. "Randolph, do you see what impertinence I am subjected to? My motives questioned without remorse."

The valet grinned. "Och, Randolph, dinna ye believe a word his lor'ship be sayin'. 'Tis a faraddiddle when he says he dinna like to wear fine clothin', fer he enjoys lookin' so elegant fer his miss."

"I don't have a miss. Yet."

"Ye will, me lor'. Ye will." MacCreedy took the clothes brush to Kirk's shoulders. "Tonight ye'll play her at whist and whisper into her ear, and all will be right."

A boom of thunder made Randolph jump to his feet and bark. Rain suddenly pelted the glass. Mac-Creedy shivered. "It do sound horrid outside, me lor'. 'Tis glad I am no' to be travelin' today."

A knock sounded on the door.

"Pardon me, me lor'." MacCreedy opened the door and stepped outside. Low voices could be heard for several moments before he returned and closed the door behind him, a worried look upon his broad face.

Kirk frowned. "What is it?"

"Tha' was MacDougal, me lor'. Miss Balfour's maid is frantic wit' worry. Apparently the young miss ne'er returned from her mornin' walk."

"Bloody hell! And no one noticed it until now?"

"Miss Balfour has been helpin' nurse Miss Stewart.

Ever'one thought she was there, but she'd left mid-mornin'. MacDougal just requested tha' grooms be sent out to look fer her."

Kirk cursed and tugged at his cravat, yanking it free before he threw it on the bed. "Get my buff breeches and blue coat. Fetch my overcoat, too."

"The grooms will find her, me lor'."

"I doubt it." Kirk dropped his coat and evening breeches onto the bed. "They have no idea where to look, but I do, for I've seen which path she takes." Kirk swiftly changed his clothes, stomped his feet into his boots, and then knotted a tie about his neck. "Chances are, she stopped to read and didn't notice the weather changing. She gets lost in a book the way some people get lost in a forest." He took the overcoat MacCreedy held out.

"Be careful ridin', me lor'. Yer leg is much improved, but an active horse could undo all your work."

"I don't give a damn about that. I have to find Miss Balfour." He picked up his hat and cane and limped out the door. "With any luck, I'll have her back before dinner."

Kirk made his way downstairs as quickly as he could. "MacDougal, I'm off to the stables to procure a mount. I'm going to find Miss Balfour."

"Me lord, there's no need fer ye to go out in this weather. We've sent twenty men ridin' oot to find her."

A sharp crack of lightning boomed through the sky and made the floor tremble.

"I'm going," Kirk repeated. "Have Miss Balfour's

maid prepare a hot bath. She'll be frozen through if she's gotten caught in this downpour."

With that, he limped toward the doorway. Two footmen sprang forward to throw the huge oak panels wide, and rain and wind swirled into the foyer.

Kirk fixed his hat more firmly on his head, tugged his collar higher around his neck, and strode outside.

# Nineteen

**From the Diary of the Duchess of Roxburghe**
Since our talk with Lord Kirk, I've been remembering the various proposals I've received over the years. Some were romantic, some not. Some were honest, some not. But oddly enough, I can remember each and every one, ending with the proposal from Roxburghe, who lightened the moment with a bottle of rare champagne and a ring that still feels too heavy upon my hand. But it was his smile that made me say yes.

If there's one thing you can trust, it's a man's smile.

Lightning flashed across the sky in a jagged race with the howling wind. The rock ledge where Dahlia had taken shelter didn't provide much protection, for it sloped the wrong way, welcoming the water in long puddles, but it kept the worst of the wind and rain off her.

As the rain increased, so did the flow of water,

threatening the meager fire she'd built close to the wall. The flames, weak as they were, offered far more comfort than she'd expected, for the wall of rain kept in the heat. Sadly, it also kept in a good bit of smoke, making her cough every few moments.

She'd coughed so much that her chest ached. Her shoulders and back also protested as she huddled against the wall in the one place where the puddles couldn't reach. All in all, she was thoroughly miserable, but dry. So far.

A gust swirled through the rain, making the small fire sputter. Dahlia drew her arm over her face and coughed hard, wincing as her chest protested yet again.

Finally able to catch her breath, she slumped against the wall, tugging her cloak closer. She must have been more tired than she realized for she'd actually dozed most of the afternoon, waking now and then to stir the fire and add from her dwindling stack of damp sticks.

She wasn't certain what time it was now, though the sky was getting dimmer. She coughed at the smoky air, rested her head against the rock wall, and closed her aching eyes. She'd been a fool to go for a walk this morning, but her mind had been so full of thoughts of Kirk, her heart so pained with her unhappiness, that she'd forgotten the cold, forgotten the impending bad weather, forgotten everything except how she could resolve the hollowness that had taken the place of her heart. She'd felt that, by walking, she might find the answer somehow, somewhere. An answer that eluded her still.

A shiver wracked her, and she tucked her gloved hands under her arms and wondered if there was any way she could be more miserable. *I doubt it. I've reached a new level of miserableness. One only found in certain fables and legends.*

Lightning flashed, the brightness making her peek through her lashes. Through the unremitting gray, she saw something moving through the pouring rain—a huge horse, by the shape of it. On its back was Kirk.

For a second, she didn't believe her eyes, but then he climbed off the horse and dashed through the rain. "Dahlia! Are you injured?"

She wondered vaguely why he was yelling. *Oh yes. The rain is loud.* She wondered why she hadn't noticed it before.

"Are you injured?"

She shook her head, or thought she did.

His face showed concern. "Come with me!"

She should get up and run into his arms, but her legs were heavy, and her head hurt an amazing amount. "It's raining too hard. We should wait until it lets up," she said faintly.

He crouched before her, water dripping on the cave floor as his gaze flickered over her face. "I see you've made a fire."

"Of course." Dahlia gestured to the dry spot beside her. "Sit down. We'll leave once this passes."

He crouched beside her, his broad form dwarfing

her little cave. "It's dry in here." He sounded surprised. "I was picturing you alone and cold and frightened."

"I *am* cold." So cold that her shivers were growing, and she couldn't stop them. *I've never been this cold.*

He brushed a curl from her cheek with his gloved hand. "I should have known you'd take care of things."

"I don't need a keeper." Or a "compatible companion," either. The thought almost brought tears, so she added instead, "I used to light all of the fires each morning at Caith Manor."

He smiled approvingly. "It's a bit smoky, but it's much warmer."

She thought to nod, but her aching head protested, so she pressed a hand to her forehead and rested it there. As she did so, the horse stuck his head inside their cave and sniffed, as if looking for a carrot. She eyed the huge animal. "Surely you didn't get that horse out of the duke's stable."

"Where else would I have gotten it?"

"A tanner's yard."

He laughed. "It's the oldest nag there. Neither of us is a rider, and I didn't want a horse that might bolt at thunder." He removed his gloves and then reached out and patted the horse's nose. "I was told that even were I to scream in its ears, it wouldn't startle. He's the perfect horse for us."

Dahlia supposed she should feel offended by that, but she was caught in the grip of a lethargy so deep that her shoulders were weary from it. *What's wrong with me? I can't seem to think well, and my head aches so.* She closed her eyes, willing the pain away.

She wasn't certain if she fell asleep or if time simply stopped, but suddenly, long cool fingers grasped her chin as Kirk tilted her face toward his. She found herself looking into his eyes. He had the most beautiful eyes. She could drown in those eyes. Lose herself completely to—

He pressed a hand to her forehead, his brows snapping down. "Damn it, you're burning up."

She struggled to follow his words. Burning? No, the fire was burning. She was just cold. It was cold outside, for she could see her breath. Or was that the smoke? She wasn't certain anymore.

"Damn it, I have to get you home. We're leaving right now."

But she was so, so tired. *What's the hurry?* she wanted to ask, but he had already kicked out the fire, the smoke carrying the scent of damp peat.

A cough caught her by surprise, shaking her until she thought she couldn't breathe. When she opened her eyes, Kirk was back out in the rain, untying something from the horse's saddle. She thought it was his cane until he unfurled an umbrella and brought it to the ledge. "Come."

She looked up at the umbrella. In the back of her mind, she heard Lady Mary say, *One day, I would like to meet a man who wants to hold my umbrella.*

Well, Dahlia knew one man who would bring her

an umbrella, and here he was, holding it for her now. It was too bad he didn't know what it meant.

Her eyes welled with tears and she desperately blinked them back. To cover her embarrassment, she put a hand on the damp ground and pushed herself upright. But as she struggled up, her knees gave way and, with a mumbled cry, she fell forward, straight into blackness.

# *Twenty*

**From the Diary of the Duchess of Roxburghe**

I aged nearly twenty years when Lord Kirk carried Miss Balfour through the front door. She was so pale, and burning with fever. We put her to bed and sent for the doctor, who pronounced that she, too, had Spanish influenza. Thank goodness he had medicine for her, or things could have gone much, much worse.

I'm sure no one is more relieved than I am. Well, perhaps one person . . .

Dahlia slowly opened her eyes until shards of light pierced her. "Ow!" she tried to say, although nothing but a croak slipped from her lips.

"Ah, you are awake!"

She forced her lids up and slowly focused on Lady Mary's smiling face.

"You gave us quite a scare."

How had she done that? She struggled to remember where she was, and how she'd gotten here. There were cool sheets against her skin, but the room looked unfamiliar . . . Where was she? *Oh yes.*

*The duchess's house party.*

*Kirk.*

*The cave.*

"Here." Mary held a rag soaked with water and dribbled some water on Dahlia's lips.

Grateful, she swallowed, the moisture easing her painful throat. "Thank you." Her voice sounded old and creaky, as if it belonged to someone else.

"You're quite welcome."

"What day . . ." She couldn't finish.

Mary gave her some more water. "Only two days. You've been even sicker than Alayne, but it passed quicker, which is good."

Dahlia looked at Mary with a frown.

"She's fine now. Her parents have arrived and they're with her. The poor duchess is quite sad, for she's had to cancel her ball, something she'd never before done. But she's relieved you're better."

"Have . . . have you been here the entire time?"

Mary gave her a curious look. "You don't remember?"

"Remember what?"

"That—"

The door opened and Lady Charlotte looked in. "Oh! You're awake!" She hurried forward, all soft lace and plumpness. "We've been so worried about you. But I told her grace you would be just fine."

"Thank you for nursing me."

"Oh lud, it wasn't me, although I would have been glad to do it. Lord Kirk was here and he refused to leave your side. Grew quite nasty about it when MacDougal tried to get him to leave for a nap one day—" Lady Charlotte went on and on, but Dahlia had already closed her eyes, her mind whirling slowly through a sudden spate of fogged memories.

She remembered a deep voice whispering in her ear, reading poetry and telling her to hang on, to never give up, to stay with him forever . . . *That was Kirk.*

Dahlia smiled and, with a great sense of peace, she drifted back asleep.

Two days later, ensconced upon a settee by the fire in her bedchamber, Dahlia took the teacup Freya held for her.

The maid smiled. "Ye've no tremble in yer hands today."

"I'm almost better. Just a little tired is all." Dahlia smiled. "Thank you for suggesting the bath. I thought it would be too much, but it's made me feel more like myself."

"It took a while to dry yer hair. Shall I pin it oop?"

"No, let's just leave it down." It felt so soft and silky, cascading over her shoulders in lavender-scented curls. "I'm too comfortable to move."

"Her grace says yer da will be here tomorrow."

"He needn't come."

"Och, I think she's glad to have some company. She's no' used to havin' under a dozen guests at Christmas."

"I'm so sorry she had to cancel her ball."

Freya brought a blanket to Dahlia and then lit a lamp at her elbow, the soft glow warming the room. "Aye, it was to ha' been tonight, but she dinna care, miss, no' since his grace returned."

"Roxburghe is here?"

Freya beamed. "Aye. We think Lady Charlotte wrote to him and tol' him how her grace was mopin' aboot."

"That's—" She tilted her head to one side, the swell of music lifting in the room. "I hear music."

"Aye. Her grace ha' already paid the orchestra, so she's havin' them play, anyway."

Dahlia smiled. "Good for her."

Freya agreed and picked up Dahlia's supper tray. "I'll take this to the kitchen now, miss. I'll be back soon to see if ye need anythin' else."

"Thank you, Freya."

The maid smiled and left.

Dahlia leaned against the high back of the settee, closing her eyes to rest them. Lord Dalhousie and Anne had departed yesterday, although both had left her kind letters. This morning Lady Mary had left with Miss Stewart and her family, along with the final few guests who'd lingered.

She would miss them all, but the person she missed the most was Kirk. Since she'd awakened, she'd neither seen nor heard from him. *What if he's left, too?* She frowned. *If he has, I know where to find him.* She did, too, but what would she say when they met? How could she describe her change of heart? Although it wasn't really a change, but an awakening.

Her heart pressed against her chest as the music ebbed and flowed. Trying to distract herself, she imagined how the ballroom would have looked, filled with women in ball gowns and men in formal finery. It would have been a beautiful sight.

The door opened.

She didn't bother to open her tired eyes, but said to the maid, "I love this music."

"I'm not Freya, nor do I love this music," came a deep voice.

Her gaze flew open. "Kirk!"

He was walking toward her, smiling faintly, and looking as dark and dangerous as ever.

But it was his clothing that caught her attention. She blinked once, and then twice. "You're dressed as if you're going to the ball."

He shrugged. "Can't a man dress once in a while without raising suspicions?"

"Not you." She smiled and patted the seat beside her on the settee.

He took the seat she offered, his thigh only inches from hers. He took her hand in his and looked at it, rubbing his thumb gently over the back of it. "Thank you," he said gravely.

"For what?"

"For being alive."

Something in his voice made her eyes fill with tears and she had to fight the odd desire to throw herself in his arms. *I am so weepy tonight.* She blinked back her tears and gently removed her hand from his. "I'm the one who should be thanking you. Lady Charlotte told me how you searched for me, then carried me all the way here and then cared for me after."

"And I would do it again if I needed to." He looked at her searchingly. "Are you well? Really well?"

"I'm fine. I even took a bath today. I can't take a long walk yet, but I thought I might go downstairs tomorrow for breakfast."

"That's good." He opened and then closed his mouth. Finally, he said, "Dahlia, I—" He rubbed his chin, looking so perplexed that she almost smiled.

"Yes?" she asked gently.

After a long, agonizing moment, he said, "I don't know what to say."

She had to swallow a sudden lump in her throat before she could reply. "Neither do I."

"I don't know where to start, but we're going to talk, we two. And we're not going to stop talking until this is done."

She found herself leaning toward him, holding her breath. "I'm listening."

"I'm torn." The words burst from him as if dragged out.

That wasn't what she expected to hear. She pulled back a little. "About what?"

"Us. Dahlia, I've been thinking about us. I've made such a mull of things and—"

"You stayed with me while I was sick," she interrupted.

He frowned. "Yes, but—"

"And you came for me when I was out in the storm."

"You were ill, but you'd made a fire. The footmen would have found you when they'd come looking."

"I was ill and didn't realize it, but—" She shook her head. "It doesn't matter. Kirk, I've been thinking, too." She raised her gaze to his. "I was wrong. We are very compatible. Perhaps I shouldn't expect more."

"No."

She blinked.

"You were right to expect more. I was being selfish, seeing things only from my own perspective and not from yours." He gave a short laugh. "I came to the duchess's with the purest of intentions, but once you arrived and didn't seem to appreciate all I'd done to change myself, I couldn't seem to keep from acting in ways that—" He rubbed at his scar. "I don't even recognize myself at times."

"I did appreciate your changes, but . . . they were just your clothes. I wanted you to be different on the inside. Which wasn't fair of me. I was wrong to want that."

"Were you? I'm not certain." His gaze grew steady, warm. "Dahlia, whatever we—you—decide, I'm not going to quit. I've invested too much in you—too much in us." He spread his hands. "I know I've said some things I shouldn't have. And I know that's pushed you away." He gave a short laugh. "And I thought I had everything so well planned out. Bloody hell, there's not even a dance tonight for me to claim, and I wanted one. And now there's not—"

"A dance?"

He nodded.

"But you can't dance."

His eyes lit with humor. "Who says?"

"You do."

A pleased smile touched his mouth. He tilted his head and listened to the faint strains of a waltz that drifted up from the ballroom. "That will do nicely. Come, Dahlia. Dance with me." He leaned his cane against a chair and held out his hand.

"Are you serious?"

He grinned.

She placed her hand in his. "I don't understand. What are you doing?"

He pulled her to her feet. "Are you strong enough to dance, if just a little?"

"Yes, but—"

He bowed. "Miss Balfour, may I have this dance?"

Her gaze dropped to his leg. "But you'll hurt yourself. I can't—"

"Yes, you can." He took her shawl from the settee and tucked it about her shoulders, and then—with the most graceful of movements, he pulled her close and swept her into a slow waltz.

A real waltz, though. Perfectly performed, each movement executed to the final degree. They were dancing, and though he was moving stiffly, there was no flicker of pain on his face. Dahlia held her breath, waiting, but Kirk moved steadily, if the tiniest bit awkwardly.

"You said you couldn't dance."

"I've been working on strengthening my leg since I arrived."

She had an instant image of him in the barn, his body glistening with sweat. So that's what he'd been doing. "It must have been difficult."

"It wasn't easy," he admitted. "But it was all worth it for this single moment."

She closed her eyes, surrounded by him, his arm warm about her waist, his hand clasping hers as they moved almost effortlessly. A deep rumble in his chest made her smile as she realized he was humming the song as they moved.

When the song ended he drifted to a stop, pulling her gently into his arms, his chin against her hair. He sighed, a deep, satisfied sigh. "I've wished to dance with you like that since the first day you told me how much you enjoyed it."

Her smile trembled and she looked up at him. "You did that—strengthened your leg, learned the steps—just so you could dance with me?"

He looked surprised that she found it amazing. "Why else would I wish to dance, if not because you wished it?"

Dahlia's heart swelled. He'd never talk about the hours he'd spent working in the stable or the pain he'd endured because of it, but she knew. She knew and she was humbled by his efforts.

Kirk was a man of few words. He might never think to tell her he liked her gown or thought her hair looked pretty curled, but he would always hold her umbrella.

And that was love. True love. The kind that carried on and lasted through the good days and the difficult days. The kind of love that always gave, and never hurt. It might not be the kind of mad love poets wrote about, but it was the kind of love strong enough to build a home upon, secure in the knowledge that this man would be there when things went wrong, and would do everything in his considerable power to make things right again.

She turned her face against his coat and pressed against him.

Instantly, his arms tightened about her, warm and strong, as his chin came to rest on her head.

They stayed there for a long, long time, and then Kirk gave her a final squeeze and then stepped away. "Thank you for the dance. I'd better leave, for Freya will have my head on a platter if I overtire you."

"No, no. I'm fine."

He looked as if he might say something more, but instead, he pressed a kiss to her fingers. "I must go." Kirk knew that if he stayed a second longer, he would sweep her into his arms and never let her go. And that was not how he—how she—needed him to proceed. He'd promised himself that he'd go slowly, show her how he felt, and win her back one day at a time, even if it took forever. It was the hardest thing he'd ever done, but he slowly released her.

"Kirk, don't." She placed her hand on his chest and looked up at him, her gray-blue eyes silver with tears. "You love me."

She didn't ask, but said the words as if she knew.

His heart lurched against his chest as he nodded. "I've never thought that word had any meaning, but—" His throat tightened. "When you were ill, I promised you I'd never leave you. The truth is, I can't leave you. You are a part of me, Dahlia. A part of who I am."

Her eyes shimmered. "And here I was making peace with the idea that you would never be a man of tender words."

"I'm going to do better."

"And so will I. Kirk, I love you, too. So much. But we both had things to learn. And now it appears that we did just that—learned to value each other as we should have been doing since the day we first met." She looked up at him and smiled. "You know what this means, don't you?"

"What?"

"It's my turn now." She took his hand and pressed a kiss to his fingers before she looked up at him and said with the most deliciously saucy smile he'd ever seen, "Lord Kirk, would you do me the honor of marrying me?"

"Dahlia, are you certain?"

She laughed. "I've never been more certain of anything. I love you, Kirk. I think I have for a long time, but I was too silly to know it. I—"

She might have been ready to say more, but he couldn't wait. He kissed her, possessing her with a heated passion that set her own afire.

When he broke off the kiss, she sighed in disappointment. "Why did you stop?"

"For this." He picked her up and carried her to the settee, where he settled her in his lap. "And this." He cupped her face in his hand, his fingers warm on her skin. "Dahlia Balfour, I accept your offer of marriage." Then he tenderly pressed a kiss to her forehead, her nose, and then her lips.

She snuggled against him, soaking in his strength. "Forever."

He tucked her closer. "Forever, Dahlia, my dear. Forever and ever."

*Epilogue*

**From the Diary of the Duchess of Roxburghe**

Ah, I have surprised myself yet again. Another match made in heaven . . . It wasn't easy this time, for fate seemed set against our lovers. There was wind, rain, illness, and tribulations. But as with all true love, they have found their way.

I, along with Lady Charlotte and the Roxburghe pugs, have performed our magics. We can rest in peace now that the Balfour sisters are all happily wed, their husbands beaming with pride, their hearts full.

After such triumphs, I thought to retire, but then a thought crept in . . . a small one, mind you . . . a thought about my companion, lovely and generous Lady Charlotte.

Her? a novice might wonder. Can she find true love at her age? I laugh at such silly questions. I've been married many times, and can promise you that love does not end with youth.

Neither does matchmaking. Trust me on this . . . if it has to do with love and matchmaking, I shall never quit.

Never.

Turn the page to meet Dahlia's sister Lily
and the handsome Russian prince
she falls in love with in

*How to Pursue
a Princess!*

**From the Diary of the Duchess of Roxburghe**

Huntley arrived early and I spoke to him at length, delicately suggesting that it was time for him to wed again. He nodded thoughtfully, and I believe he has already come to this conclusion himself. I'm sure that all it will take is one look, and the deal will be done. All I have to do is find Lily.

We seem to have somehow misplaced her.

Lily slowly awoke, her mind creeping back to consciousness. She shifted and then moaned as every bone in her body groaned in protest.

A warm hand cupped her face. "Easy" came a deep, heavily accented voice.

Lily opened her eyes to find herself staring into the deep green eyes of the most handsome man she'd ever seen.

The man was huge, with broad shoulders that blocked the light and hands so large that the one cupping her face practically covered one side of it.

His face was perfectly formed, his cheekbones high above a scruff of a beard that her fingers itched to touch.

"The brush broke your fall, but you will still be bruised."

He looked almost too perfect to be real. She placed her hand on his where it rested on her cheek, his warmth stealing into her cold fingers. *He's not a dream.*

She gulped a bit and tried to sit up, but was instantly pressed back to the ground.

"*Nyet,*" the giant said, his voice rumbling over her like waves over a rocky beach. "You will not rise."

She blinked. "*Nyet?*"

He grimaced. "I should not say '*nyet*' but 'no.'"

"I understood you perfectly. I am just astonished that you are telling me what to do." His expression darkened and she had the distinct impression that he wasn't used to being told no. "Who are you?"

"It matters not. What matters is that you are injured and wish to stand. That is foolish."

She pushed herself up on one elbow. As she did so, her hat, which had been pinned upon her neatly braided hair, came loose and fell to the ground.

The man's gaze locked on her hair, his eyes widening as he muttered something under his breath in a foreign tongue.

"What's wrong?"

"Your hair. It is red and gold."

"My hair's not red. It's blond and when the sun—" She frowned. "Why am I even talking to you about this? I don't even know your name."

"You haven't told me yours, either," he said in a reasonable tone.

She hadn't, and for some reason she was loath to do so. She reached for her hat, wincing as she moved.

Instantly he pressed her back to the ground. "Do not move. I shall call for my men and—"

"No, I don't need any help."

"You should have had a groom with you," he said, disapproval in his rich voice. "Beautiful women should not wander the woods alone."

*Beautiful? Me?* She flushed. It was odd, but the thought pleased her far more than it should have. Perhaps because she thought he was beautiful as well.

"In my country you would not be riding about the woods without protection."

"A groom wouldn't have kept my horse from becoming startled."

"No, but it would have kept you from being importuned by a stranger."

She had to smile at the irony of his words. "A stranger like you?"

The stranger's brows rose. "Ah. You think I am being—what is the word? Forward?"

"Yes."

"But you are injured—"

"No, I'm not."

"You were thrown from a horse and are upon the ground. I call that 'injured.'" His brows locked together. "Am I using the word 'injured' correctly?"

"Yes, but—"

"Then do not argue. You are injured and I will help you."

*Do not argue?* Goodness, he was high-handed. She sat upright, even though it brought her closer to this huge boulder of a man. "I don't suppose you have a name?"

"I am Piotr Romanovin of Oxenburg. It is a small country beside Prussia."

The country's name seemed familiar. "There was a mention of Oxenburg in *The Morning Post* just a few days ago."

"My cousin Nikki, he is in London. Perhaps he is in the papers." The stranger rubbed a hand over his bearded chin, the golden light filtering from the trees dancing over his black hair. "You can sit up, but not stand. Not until we know you are not broken."

"I'm not broken," she said sharply. "I'm just embarrassed that I fell off my horse."

A glimmer of humor shone in the green eyes. "You fell asleep, eh?"

She fought the urge to return the smile. "No, I did not fall asleep. A fox frightened my horse, which caused it to rear. And then it ran off."

His gaze flickered to her boots and he frowned. "No wonder you fell. Those are not good riding boots."

"These? They're perfectly good boots."

"Not if a horse bolts. Then you need some like these." He slapped the side of his own boots, which had a thicker and taller heel.

"I've never seen boots like those."

"That is because you English do not really ride,

you with your small boots. You just perch on top of the horse like a sack of grain and—"

"I'm not English; I'm a Scot," she said sharply. "Can't you tell from my accent?"

"English or Scot." He shrugged. "Is there so much difference?"

"Oh! Of course there's a difference! I—"

He threw up a hand. "I don't know if it's because you are a woman or because you are a Scot, but thus far, you've argued with everything I've said. This, I do not like."

She frowned. "As a Scot, I dislike being ordered about, and as a woman, I can't imagine that you know more about my state of well-being than I do."

His eyes lit with humor. "Fair enough. You cannot be much injured, to argue with such vigor." He stood and held out his hand. "Come. Let us see if you can stand."

She placed her hand in his. As her rescuer pulled her to her feet, one of her curls came free from her braid and fell to her shoulder.

She started to tuck it away, but his hand closed over the curl first. Slowly, he threaded her hair through his fingers, his gaze locking with hers. "Your hair is like the sunrise."

And his eyes were like the green found at the heart of the forest, among the tallest trees.

He brushed her curl behind her ear, his fingers grazing her cheek. Her heart thudded as if she'd just run up a flight of stairs.

Cheeks hot, she repinned her hair with hands that

seemed oddly unwieldy. "That's— You shouldn't touch my hair."

"Why not?"

He looked so astounded that she explained. "I don't know the rules of your country, but here men do not touch a woman's hair merely because they can."

"It is not permitted?"

"No."

He sighed regretfully. "It should be."

She didn't know what to say. A part of her—obviously still shaken from her fall—wanted to tell him that he could touch her hair if he wished. Her hair, her cheek, or any other part of her that he wished to. *Good God, what's come over me?*

"Come. I will take you to your home."

She brushed the leaves from her skirts and then stepped forward. "Ow!" She jerked her foot up from the ground.

He grasped her elbow and steadied her. "Your ankle?"

"Yes." She gingerly wiggled it, grimacing a little. "I must have sprained it, though it's only a slight sprain, for I can move it fairly well."

"I shall carry you."

"*What?* Oh no, no, no. I'm sure walking will relieve the stiffness—"

He bent, slipped her arm about his neck, and scooped her up as if she were a blade of grass.

"Mr. Roma—Romi— Oh, whatever your name is, please don't—"

He turned and strode down the path.

"Put me down!"

"*Nyet*." He continued on his way, his long legs eating up the distance.

Lily had little choice but to hang on, uncomfortably aware of the deliciously spicy cologne that tickled her nose and made her wonder what it would be like to burrow her face against him. It was the oddest thing, to wish to be set free and—at the same time—enjoy the strength of his arms. To her surprise, she liked how he held her so securely, which was ridiculous. She didn't even know this man. "You can't just carry me off like this."

"But I have." His voice held no rancor, no sense of correcting her. Instead his tone was that of someone patiently trying to explain something. "I have carried you off, and carried off you will be."

She scowled up at him. "Look here, Mr. Romanoffski--"

"Call me Wulf. It is what I am called." He said the word with a faint "v" instead of a "w."

"Wulf is hardly a reassuring name."

He grinned, his teeth white in the black beard. "It is my name, reassuring or not." He shot her a glance. "What is your name, little one?"

"Lily Balfour." She hardly knew this man at all, yet she'd just blurted out her name and was allowing him to carry her through the woods. She should be screaming for help, but instead she found herself resting her head against his shoulder as, for the first time in two days, she found herself feeling something other than sheer loneliness.

"Lily. That's a beautiful name. It suits you."

Lily's face heated and she stole a look at him from under her lashes. He was exotic, overbearing, and strong, but somehow she knew that he wouldn't harm her. Her instincts and common sense both agreed on that. "Where are you taking me?"

"To safety."

"That's a rather vague location."

He chuckled, the sound reverberating in his chest where it pressed against her side. "If you must know, I'm taking you to my new home. From there, my men and my—how do you say *babushka*?" His brow furrowed a moment before it cleared. "Ah yes, grandmother."

"Your grandmother? She's here, in the woods?"

"I brought her to see the new house I just purchased. You and I will go there and meet with my men and my grandmother. I have a carriage, so we can ride the rest of the way to your home."

*I was right to trust him. No man would involve his grandmother in a ravishment.*

He slanted a look her way. "You will like my grandmother."

It sounded like an order. She managed a faint smile. "I'm sure we'll adore one another. However, you and your grandmother won't be escorting me home, but to Floors Castle. I am a guest of the Duchess of Roxburghe."

His amazing eyes locked on her, and she noted that his thick, black lashes gave him a faintly sleepy air. "I met the duchess last week and she invited us to her house party. I was not going to attend, but now I will go." His gaze flicked over her, leaving a heated path.

Her breath caught in her throat. *If the duchess has invited Wulf to the castle, then perhaps he is an eligible parti.* Suddenly, the day didn't seem so dreary. "I beg your pardon, Mr. Wulf—or whatever your name is—but who are you, exactly?"

He shrugged, his chest rubbing her side in a pleasant way. "Does it matter?"

"Yes. You mentioned your men. Are you a military leader of some sort?" That would explain his boldness and overassuredness.

"You could say that."

"Ah. Are you a corporal, then? A sergeant?"

"I am in charge." A faint note of surprise colored his voice, as if he couldn't believe that she would think anything else.

"You're in charge of what? A battalion?"

He definitely looked insulted now. "I am in charge of it all."

She blinked. "Of an entire army?"

"Yes." He hesitated, then said in a firm voice, "I shall tell you because you will know eventually since I plan on joining the duchess's party. I am not a general. I am a prince."

"A pr—" She couldn't even say the word.

"I am a prince," he repeated firmly, though he looked far from happy about it. "That is why her grace finds it acceptable that my grandmother and I attend her events. I had not thought to accept her invitation, for I do not like dances and such, and you English—"

She raised her brows.

"I'm sorry, you *Scots* are much too formal for me."

"Wait. I'm still trying to grasp that you're a prince. A real prince?"

He shrugged, his broad shoulders making his cape swing. "We have many princes in Oxenburg, for I have three brothers."

She couldn't wrap her mind around the thought of a roomful of princes who looked like the one carrying her: huge, broad shouldered, bulging with muscles and grinning lopsided smiles, their dark hair falling over their brows and into their green eyes . . . *I fell off my horse and into a fairy tale.*

Hope washed over her and she found herself saying in a breathless tone, "If you're a prince, then you must be fabulously wealthy."

He looked down at her, a question in his eyes. "Not every prince has money."

"Some do."

"And some do not. Sadly, I am the poorest of all my brothers."

Her disappointment must have shown on her face, for he regarded her with a narrow gaze. "You do not like this, Miss Lily Balfour?"

She sighed. "No, no, I don't."

One dark brow arched. "Why not?"

"Sadly, some of us must marry for money." Whether it was because she was being held in his arms or because she was struggling to deal with a surprising flood of regret, it felt right to tell him the truth.

"I see." He continued to carry her, his brow lowered. "And this is you, then? You must marry for money?"

"Yes."

He was silent a moment more. "But what if you fall in love?"

"I have no choice." She heard the sadness in her voice and resolutely forced herself to say in a light tone, "It's the way of the world, isn't it? But to be honest, I wouldn't be looking for a wealthy husband except that I must. Our house is entailed, and my father hasn't been very good about— Oh, it's complicated."

He didn't reply, but she could tell from his grim expression that he disliked her answer. She didn't like it much herself, for it made her sound like the veriest moneygrubbing society miss, but that's what she'd become.

She sighed and rested her cheek against his shoulder.

He looked down at her, and to her surprise, his chin came to rest on her head.

They continued on thus for a few moments, comfort seeping through her, the first since she'd left her home.

"Moya, I must tell you—"

She looked up. "My name is not Moya, but Lily."

His eyes glinted with humor. "I like Moya better."

"What does it mean?"

His gaze flickered to her hair and she grimaced. "It means 'red,' doesn't it? I hate that!"

He chuckled, the sound warm in his chest. "You

dislike being called Red? Why? It is what you are. Just as what I am is a prince with no fortune." His gaze met hers. "We must accept who we are."

She was silent a moment. "You're dreadfully poor? You said you'd just bought a house."

"A cottage. It has a thatched roof and one large room, but with a good fireplace. I will make stew for you. I make good stew."

It sounded delightful; far more fun than the rides, picnics, dinner parties, and other activities the duchess had promised. "I like stew, but I'm afraid that I can't visit your cottage. It would be improper." Furthermore, she didn't dare prolong her time with such a devastatingly handsome, but poor, prince. She had to save all of her feelings so that she could fall in love with the man who would save Papa.

Wulf's brows had lowered. "But you would come to my cottage if I had a fortune, *nyet*?"

Regret flooded her and she tightened her hold about his neck. "I have no choice; I *must* marry for money. I don't know why I admitted that to you, but it is a sad fact of my life and I cannot pretend otherwise. My family is depending on me."

He seemed to consider this, some of the sternness leaving his gaze. After a moment he nodded. "It is noble that you are willing to sacrifice yourself for your family."

"Sacrifice? I was hoping it wouldn't feel so . . . oh, I don't know. It's possible that I might find someone I could care for."

"You wish to fall in love with a rich man. As my

*babushka* likes to tell me, life is not always so accom-
modating."

"Yes, but it's possible. I've never been in love before,
so I'm a blank slate. The duchess is helping me, too,
and she's excellent at making just such matches. She's
invited several gentlemen for me to meet—"

"All wealthy."

"Of course. She is especially hopeful of the Earl of
Huntley, and so am I." Lily looked away, not wishing
to see the disappointment in his gaze yet again.

Silence reigned and she savored the warmth of his
arms about her. At one time, a wealthy gentleman had
seemed enough. Now, she wished she could ask for a
not-wealthy prince. One like this, who carried her so
gently and whose eyes gleamed with humor beneath
the fall of his black hair. But it was not to be.

She bit back a strong desire to explain things to
him, to tell him exactly why she needed to marry a
wealthy man, but she knew it wouldn't make any difference. As he'd said, he was who he was, and she was
who she was. There was no way for either of them to
change things, even if they wished to, so it would be
better for them both if they accepted those facts and
continued on.

For now, though, she had these few moments.
With that thought in mind, she sighed and rested her
head against his broad shoulder. *This will have to be
enough.*